JAMI

DEADLY DOG DAYS

A DOG DAYS MYSTERY

Cover Design by Lou Harper at Cover Affairs

❀ Created with Vellum

1

Old Dan started dowsing again the day I found the body. I sat beside the canal, tossing bits of wheat bread from my sandwich to Metamora Mike and his flapping, quacking raft of followers, and I didn't notice anything strange at first. If Dan hadn't strolled by holding his divining rods, I never would've diverted my attention from the town's fat, feathered mascot to the opposite bank, where a slender hand lay splayed in the mud.

The rest of her was underwater, so I didn't know who it was. It looked like she'd slipped and fallen in. Maybe she hit her head on a rock? I stood up too fast, making my left knee gripe and complain, reminding me I was two days from forty and could stand to skip a few lunches.

The fleeting thought crossed my mind that maybe she wasn't dead, but it was pushed aside by the fact that she hadn't moved since I sat down in the grass about thirty minutes ago. Nobody could hold her breath that long without gills. But then I guess she wouldn't need to hold her breath if she had gills.

Mike let out a sharp quack meant to admonish me for standing there like a stump. "Right," I said. "I'm coming."

I hustled across the wooden bridge and down the opposite bank to where the hand lay, pressed in the mud. Kneeling in the damp grass, I stretched and grasped for the closest finger.

"Don't touch," Old Dan said, startling me so badly that I slipped and landed on my rear in the mud. "She's gone," he said. "It's a crime scene now. Better call Ben."

The last thing I wanted to do was call Ben, my husband from whom I was separated, and the only police officer in historic Metamora, Indiana. Metamora was an unincorporated canal town, so the official authorities that responded to emergencies came from the neighboring town of Brookville. Since there were barely enough full-time residents in our little tourist trap to fill a hat, Ben, having been a "big-city" cop in Columbus, Ohio, for seventeen years before moving back, was hired privately and stationed in town to be our first responder until the Brookville PD arrived.

After righting myself and getting on my feet, I crossed back over to the far side of the canal and scooped up my bag. I shoved my hand inside, digging around in the many pockets and pulling out every item *but* my cell phone. I kept telling myself I didn't need to carry such huge handbags, but I always found ways to stuff them full.

Finally, I tugged my phone out and dialed Ben's number. He answered on the first ring. "Cam, I told you I'd talk to her. I haven't had time. If she calls again—"

"It's not about your mother," I said, watching Mike swim lazy circles right about where the dead woman's head would be under the water. "I found a body in the canal."

"You what?"

"I found a body. Looks like she drowned. I was sitting on the opposite bank eating lunch and—"

"Who is it?"

"I don't know. I can't see anything but her hand."

"Did you call 911?"

"No. I called you."

He let out the deep, annoyed sigh that I'd grown familiar with over the course of our four years of marriage. Funny how six months of separation couldn't erase the tension that sigh always shot through me. I wondered if Ben's first wife still felt it sometimes, like a phantom limb.

"Cameron," he said, in his best authority figure voice, "in a life threatening situation, you dial 911."

"Well, *Ben*, the life-threatening part of this situation appears to have been over a while ago, and since the body isn't going anywhere, it's not exactly an emergency, either."

"I'll call it in to Sheriff Reins. Do not move until he gets there. I don't want anyone coming along and contaminating the scene."

I wondered if he thought duck poop was contamination. "I'll wait for him," I said. "When will you get here?"

"Not for a while. I'm about an hour and a half away."

"An hour and a half away?" It was a Tuesday, just before one in the afternoon. "Aren't you at work?"

"No. I'm over in Nashville," he said.

Nashville, Ohio, was a little village filled with shops and bed -and -breakfasts and ... and ... A female laugh on Ben's end of the line told me all I needed to know. "Thanks for calling Reins," I said, and hung up, chest swelling and eyes burning. When would I get past the pain and ache? I didn't want to be married to him, so why did it hurt to know he was with someone else? Wasn't it reasonable to think he'd wait more than six months?

I plopped back down on the grassy bank and studied the hand in the mud across from me. There were no age spots or bulging veins. My guess was that she was young. It was the right hand, so I couldn't tell if she was married. The fingernails were unpainted and the middle nail was broken off short.

Mike swam by her again, flapping his wings and splashing. The water rippled against the bank, and something red could be seen wrapped around the woman's wrist.

What if I knew her? I probably did. There were only a couple hundred people in Metamora. Chances were good I knew Ben's lady friend, too.

I shook my head. A woman had died. The last thing I should've been worried about was with whom my soon-to-be ex-husband was waltzing around Nashville.

He never took me to Nashville. He said we lived in a town made up of shops and inns, and the last place he wanted to go was another one.

Sirens wailed. Police cars streaked down the road. Mike and his flock flew off, shaking water in my direction as they passed over. Big, dumb ducks.

Sheriff Reins pulled down the road that ran between the shops and the opposite side of the canal from where I sat. He parked in front of Odd and Strange Metamora, the paranormal freak -show shop claiming Metamora was a hotbed of all sorts of phenomenon that were impossible to prove but completely fascinating. His siren blared as he sat in the car talking into his radio. Probably calling for backup.

I made my way over to the bridge again, ignoring the pang in my left knee, which was a sure sign rain was on the way. Reins saw me coming toward his cruiser and blessedly silenced the screaming siren.

By this time Old Dan, dowsing rods erect and grizzled beard hanging down his chest, had been joined by his son, Frank Gardner, who operated the oldest running grist mill in the state. Sue Nelson was beating feet across the road from the Soda Pop Shop, and it would only take another ten minutes for the whole of Metamora to be gathered around the canal waiting for the body to be dragged out.

"Mrs. Hayman," Sheriff Reins called to me, tipping his hat. "Your husband tells me you've found a ... um ... well, I mean to say—"

"She's there." I pointed to the body, putting the sheriff out of his misery. For a man in blue, he had a delicate disposition when it came to situations beyond speeding tickets and loitering. When one of the horses that pull the canal boat accidentally trampled over a man's foot last month, Reins fainted at the sight of it. To give him credit, it was a rather gory compound break.

"And you know it's a woman, how?" he asked, stopping short of the bank and eyeing me, quizzically.

"Narrow fingers," I said. "The hand looks female to me. I could be wrong."

More sirens called in the distance, nearing with every second that passed. A brick red SUV pulled down the lane with Fire and Rescue printed on its side, followed by an ambulance.

"Stand back," Reins shouted to the gathering crowd. Fortunately it was a weekday, so the shops were closed and most of the shopkeepers were at their full -time jobs out of town. Only a few remained during the week, running online retail sites and stocking inventory. Still, there were a good dozen milling about. Old Dan, Frank, and Sue were joined by Fiona and Jim Stein, who ran the train depot, and Jefferson Briggs of Court House Antiques.

To complete the circus-like atmosphere as Sheriff Reins and the rescue crew traipsed down the bank of the canal to recover the body, the Whitewater Valley train chugged into the station, blowing its whistle.

"What happened?" Sue Nelson yelled over the riot, edging up beside me. "Who is it?" Despite the eighty-degree heat of late June, she wrapped her arms around herself like she was freezing.

"I don't know. Only a hand was visible. I found her." For some reason, I was beginning to feel guilty for spotting that hand and reporting it.

The paramedics took hold of the body, and I could no longer watch. Something made me turn around and close my eyes. It was one thing to know she was dead, but quite another to see it firsthand.

The last of the steam left the train's engine on a sigh. The crowd was gravely silent, making it easy to hear the sound of a waterlogged body being lifted out of the canal, and then—

Sue screamed. A gut -wrenching, grief -stricken cry.

Murmurs broke out bringing the name of the victim to my ears. "It's Jenn Berg." "Jenn Berg's dead." "Poor Sue!"

The air rushed from my lungs. Jenn Berg was Sue Nelson's daughter. Sue Nelson, who was standing there beside me with her arms wrapped tight around her middle.

2

Don't worry, Cam, not everyone thinks you did it," Brenda Lefferts said, taking a sip of her hot tea like she didn't just strike me a deathblow. "At least, I don't."

"Why would anyone think I had anything to do with it? I only found her. And I'm beginning to regret not leaving her there for someone else to stumble on."

"Don't say that," she said, shushing me and looking around Soapy Savant's to see who might have overheard me. Most of Soapy and his wife Theresa's products ran along the lines of scented lotions, soaps of course, and candles, but they also had a little coffee shop and café. Brenda was the proprietor of Read and ReRead, a used bookstore, located next door to The Soapy Savant.

"You know why," she said, "and it's terrible this had to happen at all, but especially now with her dating Ben."

I gulped my mouthful of coffee and scorched my throat. "*What?*" I said, wheezing.

"Oh. You didn't know? I figured you just didn't want to talk about it. I mean, she is—was—so much younger and ... " Brenda lifted her cup to her mouth and stifled her babbling with another sip of tea.

"I had no idea. I suspected he was seeing someone, but I never imagined—she was in her twenties! That's closer to his daughter's age than his." Ben's daughter Mia, my stepdaughter, was sixteen. "Wait. Then he's not with her in Nashville?"

"No, I suppose not," she said. "Clearly, she's here."

"Clearly."

Brenda patted the bun on the back of her head and checked to make sure the bobby pins securing the oval lace doily were in place. She was around my age, slim as a pole, smart as a whip, and although she didn't gossip herself, she always knew what was being spread around town.

Sheriff Reins pushed through the door and ordered a cup of coffee at the counter before heading my way. "Mrs. Hayman, ready to make your statement?"

It was Cripps-Hayman, actually, but I didn't feel it was the appropriate time to correct him, even if answering to Mrs. Hayman made me feel like my mother-in-law, which might be worse than being suspected of murder.

"I'm ready," I said, wondering if he too was harboring a hunch that I had something to do with Jenn ending up in the canal.

"I'll see you later," Brenda said, clearing out at the speed of light, but leaving me with a battered paperback before disappearing. *The Clock Struck Midnight*, was the title. I adored old mysteries, and she never left me without a good book to read.

Reins took her seat and settled in, creaking like an old tree as he stretched his long limbs. "Quite a day," he said, stirring a spoon around in his caramel-colored coffee.

"Yes," I said, wishing Ben would show up and navigate this unfamiliar territory for me.

"So, walk me through finding Miss Berg." He tapped his teaspoon on the side of his cup before setting it aside and catching my eyes with his. I felt held hostage, locked in his steely stare.

"Well," I said, and coughed, the word coming out hoarse. "I was on my lunch break, sitting by the canal." I relayed the short story of Old Dan walking by and me spotting the hand in the mud. "That's when I called Ben. And he called you."

Reins tapped his index finger on the table. “Did you know Miss Berg?”

“Did I know her? No.” A sour feeling crept around in my stomach. “I mean, I met her before. She’s Sue’s daughter, so I met her, of course, but I didn’t *know* her.”

“Where were you last night, Mrs. Hayman?”

My burned throat started to ache. “At home.”

“Was anyone there with you?”

“No. I live alone since Ben ... since he moved out.”

Reins pushed his coffee away, like the sight of it disgusted him all of a sudden. “Were you aware of your husband’s relationship with Miss Berg?”

“Relationship?” I was starting to sweat. How could I feel guilty for something I didn’t have any part of? “No, I wasn’t aware of any ... ” Dizziness swept through me, and I swayed in my chair. My stomach roiled. I jumped up, jarring my knee. “I think I’m going to be sick,” I said, before dashing away from the table and into the ladies’ room.

When I exited the bathroom, Sheriff Reins told me we’d talk again some other time when I was less worked up. I wondered when that would be. Hearing about your husband dating the much younger woman you just found dead in the canal and learning the whole town was pointing fingers at you for having killed her didn’t seem like something I’d become less worked up about any time soon.

Outside, the flashing lights and sirens were gone, and the train had left. Two of Brookville’s finest had the bank of the canal roped off with yellow crime scene tape and were doing whatever it was that police officers did to investigate a scene.

I didn’t watch too closely, only noticing Old Dan had joined them, staying outside the taped off area, walking back and forth with his dowsing rods. The officers humored him, like we all did. At ninety-six, he was the oldest Metamoran, and if not altogether of sound mind, he was respected as patriarch of one of the town’s founding families. Over my four years here, dementia had taken a firmer hold on Old Dan and we all watched out for him, taking him in and welcoming him at our dinner tables when Frank Gardner was busy at the grist mill, working long hours trying to keep the family tradition of milling flour and grits alive.

The bottom fell out of the tourism economy a few years back, and the Metamorans who remained in town with their shop doors open were suffering. The amateur actors and musicians among us were trying to drum up the town's performing arts reputation by putting on a play. To help sell tickets, I set up a makeshift phone bank in the basement of Metamora Faith and Friends Church. (In Columbus I ran a call center, an automated one where you didn't have to dial manually and hope a passing thunderstorm didn't take out the phone lines.) I was overdue back at the phone bank, so I turned in that direction.

Not to be a pessimist, but I couldn't help but think it was going to take more than an amateur play in a converted barn to bring people to The Middle of Nowhere Metamora to shop, dine, and stay at the inns. But, for the time being, my phone bank of five volunteers was busy contacting past patrons of the town to invite them back for the big show. *Oh Horrors! It's Murder!*—a musical mystery comedy—was being performed live on stage in the Metamora Playhouse (a grand name for a converted barn). We were two weeks to curtain and tickets weren't exactly sold out.

Given the dead body found in the canal, I suddenly realized the title of the play might seem a tad insensitive, but possibly this would all blow over before opening night.

Who was I kidding? Nothing ever happened in this town. A dead body turning up was as rare as winning the lottery and getting struck by lightning on the same day.

My mind kept pinging back to Ben as I walked over the bridge and the three blocks to the church. What on earth could he possibly have in common with a woman as young as Jenn Berg? She waitressed at the Cornerstone restaurant/bar and lived in the gatekeeper's cottage at Hilltop Castle, where the owner of the Cornerstone, Carl

Finch, lived. Carl, in addition to being the man who hired and paid Ben, was a business-minded eccentric who was very religious. He built a real modern-day castle on the top of the highest hill in Metamora and raised an enormous cross next to it, where everyone driving down Route 52 could admire it. He claimed Metamora was the location of the Ark of the Covenant, the gold chest said to hold the tablets the Commandments were engraved on, among other religious relics.

If you ask me, his castle looked like an homage to the Knights Templar, but that was probably just me watching too many conspiracy shows on the History Channel.

Word was, years before Ben and I moved to town, some vandals decided to pay Hilltop Castle a visit and ever since, the gate at the bottom of the hill has been shut tight and the gatekeeper's cottage occupied by a guard; most recently, Jenn Berg and her five big dogs.

From what I knew of Jenn and her busy work schedule at the Cornerstone, it was the dogs that did most of the gatekeeping. Sue Nelson was always complaining about how if she wanted to see her oldest daughter, she had to pop into the bar and have a drink. It wasn't really a complaint though. Sue spent most of her time finding ways to run into Carl Finch. She said a man's eccentricities were a lot less quirky when they came with a bank account the size of Finch's. I supposed she might be on to something.

Workers were busy scraping the old, peeling paint from the florist next to the church when I meandered by, reminding me that my own house needed painting. I'd have to ask Andy about it. Ever since I hired him to plow the snow from my driveway over the winter, the twenty-one-year-old amateur filmmaker had become my unofficial handyman, always hanging around doing yard work and fixing shutters or nailing on shingles.

Like me, Andy Beaumont was not actually from Metamora. Unlike me, he chose to be here. At his age, that showed a heck of a lot of dedication to his work, which at present was documenting Carl Finch's search for the Ark of the Covenant on film. Which meant he spent a lot of time at Hilltop Castle and most likely knew about Ben and Jenn, too. The little weasel hadn't said a word to me about it.

Inside the small church, the familiar smell of damp assaulted my nose as I took the rickety stairs down to the basement. One of the hazards of a building in a canal town was flooding, and there was no doubt that this basement had been filled with water on more than one occasion.

Pastor Stroup preached at the newer, larger church up a ways on Route 52, but this smaller building was still where he kept his office and hosted the ladies' quilting circle. The older Metamorans preferred to think of this ramshackle building near the canal as their church instead of the bigger one filled with families and crying babies from neighboring towns.

My phone bank was tucked into a back corner in the basement. Old black -and -white linoleum tiles were peeling from the floor, and dark spots of mold shadowed through the white paint on the stone block walls, but we used our second-hand school desks and donated office phones from the eighties and did what we could.

Once in passing I'd mentioned the idea of marketing for the town by phone to Irene, my mother-in-law, and it was all downhill from there. She had me assigned to the task and set up in the church basement two days later.

I reached the phone bank and took stock of the scene.

None of the five volunteers who worked for me wanted to be working for me; they were only doing it for the community service hours. Three of them court -ordered. Nick Valentine: Assault, Roy Lancaster: DUI, and Johnna Fitzgerald: Theft. Johnna was a chronic kleptomaniac who ran Canal Town Treasures. Most of those treasures weren't hers to sell. Anna Carmichael and Logan Foust were going to be seniors at Metamora High School in the fall and were getting a jump-start on the volunteer hours needed to graduate.

"How are ticket sales?" I asked, seeing only one of them actually on the phone. Logan. He wouldn't be able to slack off if his life depended on it. He'd feel too guilty and confess if he did.

"You really want us hawking tickets for *Oh Horrors! It's Murder!* when one of our own was just found dead?" Roy asked, rubbing his stubbly chin. He had the perpetually red nose of an alcoholic and droopy eyes of someone who never slept. "Wasn't Jenn in the musical? How will the show be put on with a cast member killed?"

"Better yet," Johnna said, looping her yarn around a knitting needle, not even pretending to be making calls, "who's going to take her dogs? She has five, I believe, or is it six now with the pup? I think I'll head on over there and see what needs taking care of."

"No, no. I'll look after the dogs," I said quickly. "I'm certain Sue will want to have a chance to go through her daughter's belongings before anyone else. The police will most likely have her cottage secured anyway." The last person who needed to get her sticky fingers on Jenn's belongings was Johnna. They'd never be seen again, and I'd have her in my phone bank doing community service until the devil opened a snow cone stand right here in Metamora.

Roy leaned back in his chair. "You'll look after her dogs, eh? Got something on your conscience then, Cameron Cripps-Hayman?" Roy always called me by my full name. He thought keeping my maiden name was an abomination, but after years and years of making professional contacts, it was easier to add Ben's name on than to subtract mine altogether.

"She's only doing her part for the town," snapped Anna, who was fiery in her feminist spirit and hair color. "Just because a woman's husband is dating a girl who ends up in the canal doesn't mean that woman had anything to do with it."

Did *everyone* but me know about Ben and Jenn?

"It was probably an accident," Logan said, coming in on the conversation after hanging up his phone receiver. "Two more tickets sold."

"Overachiever." Roy scowled. "You're ruining it for the rest of us."

Nick ignored them. He never said much. I placed him around twenty, so he was like my middle child in the group with Roy and Johnna firmly in their sixties. He rode in on the scenic Whitewater Valley train from Connersville every day and boarded it in the afternoon to go back home. With his dirty blond hair sticking out all over his head, his nails painted black, and the way he always wore a band t-shirt, he reminded me of a misplaced rock star. I imagined he played the guitar, or maybe the drums, and sang songs that would make my head pound and my ears bleed. Songs I never would've listened to, even as a teenager. When I was in high school, I loathed hard rock hair bands and was all about the New Kids on the Block. Alas, my dream of becoming Mrs. Jordan Knight never came true.

"Hey Cam," Ben's voice boomed down the stairs and across the basement. "You down there?"

My mind flashed to Jenn Berg and Ben. Together. Kissing. Did he know his girlfriend was dead? He had to. Reins would've talked to him by now, or someone in town would've gotten to him. "I'm here," I said, heading back across the basement to the stairs. Ben had a serious aversion to dark, damp basements. My evil mother-in-law probably locked him in theirs when he was little.

Who was I kidding? Ben was the biggest mama's boy on the planet. She'd never do that to him. Certainly, with gun drawn, he'd face the boogieman in the basement if he had to. He was a police officer after all, and had faced much worse than black mold.

At the bottom of the steps, I looked up and saw him standing on the landing. He wore his faded jeans and work boots, like always, but had on a navy blue shirt I'd never seen before. A baseball cap covered his wavy brown hair, perpetually in need of a trim. The words Metamora Law Enforcement Officer were printed over the hat's bill. It was strange, but ever since we separated, whenever I saw him, I sometimes couldn't remember what was so terrible about being married. "Your knee's bothering you," he said. "It's supposed to rain tonight."

"You were dating Jenn Berg," I said. "She's dead." No one could accuse me of having tact, but Ben knew that about me, along with most everything else.

"Calling it dating is pushing it, but I heard she was the woman you found in the canal."

Should I feel bad for him, or want to strangle him? I'd never been in this position before, so I wasn't sure. All I really felt was sad and a little anxious that he might have come to arrest me. "I'm sorry for your loss, I guess," I said, hoping to smooth things over, but managing to make them more awkward.

He gripped the railing and stepped down to the first stair off the landing. "She was a nice girl, Cam, but when I count my losses, she's not one of them." His dark eyes held mine. Maybe I only wanted to see regret there, or maybe it was real. Either way, it was like a giant hand grabbed me by the chest and squeezed. Maybe we could work things out. Maybe—

"Dad, is she down there or what? I'm bored." Mia's head peered around the corner of the landing. "Oh. Hey," she said by way of greeting me. "Dad says I have to stay with you since you kicked him out."

The giant hand released its grip on my heart and flicked me in the forehead.

3

I didn't kick your father out," I said, walking side-by-side with Mia along the canal, toward home. Since it was near four o'clock anyway, I told my phone crew to call it a day. We'd regroup tomorrow when I would hopefully have an idea what direction the town players were going to take with *Oh Horrors! It's Murder!* "How was the end of your sophomore year?" I asked her, hoping to change the subject. We hadn't seen Mia since Christmas break, just before Ben had moved out. She was staying only for the week, and then her mom was taking her on a Caribbean cruise. So the appeal of Metamora was lost on Mia, or maybe it would be more accurate to say it was buried under white sand and crystal blue seas. Ben was lucky to get a week out of her.

She let out a deep sigh. "Why does everyone want to ask me about school? School's school, okay?"

"Okay," I said, taken aback, watching her flip her dark hair over one shoulder. "Are you going to see your Grandma Irene while you're here?"

"Do I have a choice?" she asked, sneering. Disdain for Irene was something the two of us had in common. I knew what my problems were with my mother-in-law (and there were several), but I had no idea what Mia had against her. Being the only grandchild, and a girl, Mia wasn't only doted upon, but she was a Daughter of Metamora. To Irene, that meant royalty.

Two weeks after we were married, Ben's mother, Irene Hayman—aka President of the Daughters of Historical Metamora—summoned us here with the gift of her family's ancestral estate. Ellsworth House, a large Greek revival on the far end of the canal, had been passed from generation to generation since the early 1800s. All of the other homes around it had sold out long ago to commercialism and boasted signs like Grandma's Cookie Cutter and Canal Town Treasures. The Haymans were the last of the holdouts. Except Irene and my father-in-law, Stewart, were holding out just fine over in Brookville, where they bought their gas and eggs in separate locations, and their new house didn't creek and shed shingles when the wind blew.

Ben was an only child, and his mother couldn't wait to lure him back to town. Heidi, his first wife, outright refused to move here and inherit the family home. Seeing as how my romance with Ben was a whirlwind affair, spanning two months from the time we met until we were married, I was still in the new -relationship daze—which is similar to the new car smell, only it wears off quicker—when Irene handed Ben the keys and put the house in his name. I gave up a good paying job that, if I didn't love, I could put up with, and an apartment close to my sister to move with my new husband.

"I'm surprised Irene's letting you stay with me," I said, "and not insisting on you staying with her and Grandpa Stewart."

"She doesn't know I'm here yet, and *you're* not going to tell her. I'll have to deal with her soon enough."

"Deal with her, Mia? Really? She loves you. She bought you your car!"

"And I should kiss her feet every time I see her. I know."

My patience was just about depleted. I'd never had an overabundance where Mia was concerned, but now that Ben and I weren't even together, I didn't feel like holding my tongue.

I stopped dead in my tracks and planted both hands on my hips.

Mia took two more steps before realizing and turning around. She took one look at me and knew she was about to get an earful. “I don’t have to listen—” she started, but I held up my hand.

“You *will* listen. For a girl who has everything she could want—a smart, pretty girl—you have the *worst* attitude I’ve ever come across. Your mother and father and grandparents spoiled you rotten. Now, I’m not your grandma’s biggest proponent, but she does deserve to be treated with respect from her sixteen-year-old granddaughter. When we get home, you’re calling her and telling her you’re here, and you will spend time with her. Do you understand me?”

Mia crossed her arms and rolled her eyes. “Fine,” she said. “I’ll call her. But just so you know, she’s not going to be happy to see me, because I totaled my car.”

“You totaled your car? The one you just got on your birthday last month?” This girl never ceased to amaze me. “How? Were you hurt?” She didn’t look hurt. Ben would’ve told me if she’d been hurt.

“It was just a stupid accident.” She pivoted on her heel and began walking away from me.

I’d never had someone blatantly turn her back on me during a conversation before. If she were an employee, I’d write her up for insubordination, but I’d never had kids, so what was I supposed to do with her?

Good gravy, this was going to be the longest week of my life.

I let Mia walk on ahead of me, past Grandma’s Cookie Cutter with a new *I Love Lucy* cookie jar among the hundreds in the front windows, then past Schoolhouse Antiques with all the bric-a-brac out on the front lawn that looked like junk to me, before getting to Ellsworth House. Andy was outside pressure washing some of the peeling paint off the front of the house.

“It’s like you read my mind,” I called to him over the noise of the sprayer.

He lowered the nozzle and flipped the machine off. “The house needs painting. I thought I’d get you an estimate.” Andy’s eyes wandered over to Mia. She was five years younger than him, and light years of maturity apart.

"Andy Beaumont," I said, "this is Ben's daughter, Mia. Mia, this is Andy. He helps out around here."

"Hi," she said, throwing Andy a cool, yet oddly seductive smile for a sixteen-year-old girl. "I thought you didn't have a job," she said to me. "Does my dad pay him to keep up the house since you kicked him out?"

"I *told* you, I didn't kick your dad out." I'd been with Mia less than an hour and had never been so exasperated by someone in my life. "Let's go inside and call your grandma. I'm sure she's dying to spend time with you." If there were any fairness in the universe, Irene would rush right over and pick Mia up.

Mia marched up the porch steps and opened the door—nobody in Metamora locked their doors—and Andy shot me the wide-eyed, brow raised, incredulous expression of someone who couldn't believe what they just witnessed. "Good luck with that," he said before flipping his pressure washer back on.

"Yeah. Thanks," I said—to myself, because he couldn't hear me.

I stepped up the two cement stairs onto the square porch flanked by white columns harboring carpenter ants and boring bees and went inside, shooing a few of the buzzing pests out before closing the door. The house carried the warm-earth smell that old houses have and made creaking sounds of settling in. It had bothered me at first, and I bought plug-in scented oils for each outlet and jumped at every tap and groan from the windows and floorboards. Living without Ben now, the scents and sounds were more like characteristics of another person living with me than the house itself, and kept me from feeling alone.

Spook, the black cat that appeared out of thin air one day in my attic, helped too. I didn't know where he came from, but I figured he found a way in up under the eaves of the roof. He really was quite the phantom, disappearing sometimes for days only to curl up on my lap unexpectedly as I watched TV. I always left food and water out for him and wondered if he had another home somewhere that he visited when he left. Spook was a drifter who couldn't be tied down.

He was in the midst of a disappearing act at the moment, but I expected him back any day now.

Down the hall, past the living room on the right, and into the kitchen in the back of the house, I took note of all the clutter and cleaning I'd let slide since nobody else lived with me. Mia would be sure to blab about it to Irene and Ben and Heidi, aka Wife Number One. Sometimes I wondered how Ben could've ever gone on one single date with me, let alone married me. I was so different from blonde, tall, professional Heidi. She was a prosecutor and Ben was a cop, that's how they met. They had so much in common.

"You have no food in this house," Mia said, standing at the open refrigerator.

"It's only me here. I eat out a lot." I tugged open the pantry door. "Want a cookie?" Living two doors down from Grandma's Cookie Cutter was convenient. Not for my waistline, but for my sweet tooth.

"*Oh. My,*" Mia said, staring at my stacked boxes and tins of cookies. "There's like, a million calories in your cupboard. I can *feel* myself getting fat just standing here."

I shrugged as she spun away, horrified. More for me. I took a chocolate chip one out and shoved it in my mouth. I bet Wife Number One never had cookies in the house. Jenn Berg probably didn't, either. Another blonde. Being with me must've been a momentary lapse of sanity on Ben's part. The only cookie-loving brunette in his life.

"We'll go out to dinner," I said. "Call your grandma first."

Ben would be working on Jenn's case most of the night and had told Mia he'd see her in the morning. I had a feeling with this investigation taking him by surprise, Mia would be spending most of her week with me.

While she called Irene, I made my way upstairs to my bedroom to hide. The last thing this day needed was a dose of Irene Hayman. I left the light off and lay in the center of the rickety antique sleigh bed, staring up at the ceiling that countless Ellsworth descendants and spouses had stared at before me. I was neither anymore. Well, I wouldn't be for much longer if Ben and I went through with our divorce. Then someone else would be sacked with the responsibility of the ramshackle old Greek revival on a canal that floods twice a year and needs painting and new windows. A new roof wouldn't hurt, either. Central air would be nice. The furnace usually needed a good kick to get going in the winter.

Yes, I'd leave, and if Ben didn't move back in, Irene would need to sucker another member of her family into taking over this headache of a house.

I ran my eyes along the crown molding and over the crystal light fixture, and couldn't help thinking this house was a little bit like me and my bad knee and extra pounds: not too shabby if you can see under all the layers of dust and years of neglect. Nothing some fresh paint and a little exercise couldn't cure for the both of us.

"Cameron!" Mia yelled up to me. "Grandma Irene wants to talk to you!"

I closed my eyes and stuck my lip out in a pout. "Tell her I moved."

"What?"

"I'm coming!" I shouted, pushing myself up and throwing a pillow across the room. What did that old bat want from me now?

Mia met me at the bottom of the stairs with her hand held out, offering me her cell phone. "Here," she said, thrusting it at me like it was about to blow up.

I took a deep breath and put the phone to my ear. "Hello, Irene," I said, in my best fake chipper voice.

"Why didn't you people tell me my grandbaby was coming for a visit?"

"Us people weren't informed, either."

"I would've insisted she stay with me. Ben can't keep her at FiddleDeeDoo Inn, there's not room. She shouldn't have to stay with you, even if it is her house, or will be soon enough."

"I know you're itching to kick me out, Irene, but can you at least pretend to hold back the excitement until the ink is dry on the divorce papers?" And people thought I was tactless.

"Divorce papers? I didn't ... I mean, did Ben ... ?"

"No, he didn't. It was a figure of speech. Would you like to take Mia to dinner tonight, Irene? Maybe keep her overnight at your house?" I crossed my fingers hoping for a yes.

"Oh. Well. Tonight's no good for me. I'm hosting dessert for the Daughter's of Metamora's progressive dinner. If I'd known ahead of time ... well, but I didn't, so there's nothing to be done, is there?" She made a clucking sound with her tongue. "Shame about Jenn Berg. So many members have had to cancel tonight because of it."

For a second there I thought she was actually being sympathetic. Of course Irene would only be concerned about having too much leftover cake.

"Which brings me to the point of our conversation," she said. "I've heard rumors that you're going to be taking those five smelly mutts from Carl Finch's gatehouse and keeping them under my roof!"

Just a moment ago it was Mia's roof, or almost Mia's. "I did say something about taking care of them," I said, my memory of keeping Johnna from pilfering the gatehouse rushing back to me. Apparently that news had spread and become fact. I'd better get over there and pick them up.

"I don't want those dogs in that house! Do you understand me, Cameron? Not one paw!"

Irene was heading toward full -on freak -out mode. "I'm sorry, Irene. Somebody has to take them in."

"They can go to the pound for all I care!"

"Take it up with Ben. I've got to go now. Mia's starving. Nice chatting with you. Bye, bye."

I jabbed at the phone, ending the call, and blew out a breath. I didn't exactly dodge any bullets, but I didn't take one, either. We'd call that a draw.

Mia took her phone back and laughed. Actually, it was more like a mean girl cackle.

I narrowed my eyes at her. "If you want to eat, you'll stop laughing at me," I said. "Call your dad and tell him to bring pizza over since he surprised me with your presence and didn't give me time to go grocery shopping."

"Why don't I take your car and go pick one up?" she asked, smiling sweetly.

"You totaled your car and now you want to borrow mine? I don't think so. Call your dad, please."

"You just want a reason to get him over here," she said. "You're using me to lure him back home."

Now it was my turn to laugh. "Never mind. I'll send Andy." The last thing I needed was to be out -maneuvered by a teenage girl. "You and I are going to pick up a few dogs."

"I THOUGHT YOU SAID A FEW DOGS!" Mia shouted, being pulled across the driveway by a giant black Newfoundland with a nametag that read Gus.

"Just don't let go of that leash!" I had my own problems with a graying geriatric German Shepherd named Isobel who kept snapping her jaws at me and growling.

"How are we getting five dogs in your car?"

My ancient Subaru hatchback was like my own personal sidekick. It wouldn't let me down. "They'll fit."

The dogs were kept in separate chain-link kennels outside the gatehouse. I wasn't sure how much good they did as guard dogs being penned up, but what did I know about being a gatekeeper? At least their kennels weren't locked. Unfortunately, the door to the house was, so I couldn't get to their food. I'd have to stop and buy one of those big bulk bags of kibble. I never had a dog before, but how hard could it be? These guys didn't seem too bad.

Gus was a bit on the large side, but overly friendly. How could this guy ever be a guard dog? I patted his back, sinking my fingers into soft fur. He nuzzled his head against my leg, almost knocking me down. His tongue lolled from his mouth, and I swore he was smiling. He was like a big, fuzzy bear you just wanted to cuddle.

Isobel just wanted to be left alone, so once she found a nice corner of the house to claim, she'd be all set. I just hoped she didn't bite my hand off first.

Then there were two medium-sized dogs shaped like tanks. They didn't resemble any dog I'd ever seen before, other than one another. They had short ears, long tails and square heads, with blotchy fur that stuck out all over and came off on your fingers when you petted them. Neither one seemed nice as much as dumb and eager to entertain by jumping all over you and slobbering down your pant leg. They didn't have collars on, so I'd have to make up something to call them.

The fifth dog was downright mean. It growled and barked and had a holy fit whenever Mia or I got within a yard of its kennel, which bore a sign that read: Beware of Dog. *Oh really?* There was no way I was getting the beast home short of knocking it on the head with a board and tying it to the roof of my car, but I didn't go in for animal cruelty. Anyway, there wasn't a board on earth big enough to do damage to that thick skull.

I'd send Andy back to deal with him.

For the ride home, big Gus and cranky Isobel parked it in the backseat, while Tweedle Dee and Tweedle Dum shared the hatchback. Mia sat in the passenger seat grumbling about how bad they all smelled and how she was never going to get the dog spit out of her hair from where Gus kept licking the back of her head over the top of the seat.

I felt like a fat kid at the candy counter, having always wanted a pet and never being allowed to have anything other than a fish because of my little sister's allergies to every animal in existence with fur.

Oh good gravy. My sister. She was coming for a visit, and I totally forgot. Guess she'd need to bring allergy medication. Or with five dogs and a cat that could pop in at any time, a plastic bubble to stay in.

4

Andy picked up pizza, dog food and the canine version of Satan, whose real name turned out to be Brutus, and who was a mix between a Rottweiler and a Doberman. Fortunately Jenn had introduced Andy to Brutus, and anyone who had been cleared by her was okay by Brutus. I, however, was a different story. Brutus was in my fenced backyard howling at the moon and the neighbor's cat. He and I would find a way to come to terms tomorrow when the sun was up, and I was armed with a steak bone.

Mia had picked at a piece of pizza and proclaimed herself stuffed before bounding up the stairs to her room with her phone glued to her ear. I had given her food and shelter; as far as I was concerned, my duty was fulfilled for the night. Ben could take her to Irene's tomorrow, and all would be well enough with my life again. Except for the pesky rumor about being a murderess.

"Well, I know you didn't do it," Andy said, sitting beside me on the couch scarfing his fifth piece of pizza and fending off Gus, which was no easy task. "You didn't even know Ben was going out with her, so what would your motive be?"

"Right. I didn't know, and you sure didn't tell me." I gave him the evil eye but had to look away to grab a paper plate from Dingle and

Dangle that they were playing tug-of-war with. "Anyway, Ben says they weren't dating."

That made Andy look a little nervous. He almost choked on his pizza. "Oh. Well then, you're definitely in the clear."

There was something more he wasn't telling me. Something he knew. "Out with it, Beaumont. What do you know?"

He shook his head, making his shoulder-length auburn curls sway. "Nothing. There's nothing."

The phone rang, saving him from further interrogation. I got up and went into the kitchen to answer it. In the corner, Isobel lifted her head and growled at me, harmonizing with the hum of the fridge. Crabby old lady. Speaking of crabby old ladies, Irene's name and number flashed on the caller ID, making me want to bash my head against the counter. "Hello, Irene," I said, answering.

"I forgot to tell you something earlier," she said. "I'm sending some men over to collect the weathervane tomorrow, so don't be alarmed if you hear them on your roof."

For the past six months, ever since Ben moved out, my mother-in-law had been trying to take her house back one piece at a time. A vintage chandelier, a pair of antique andirons shaped like owls—which I had particularly liked—a gilded mirror from the foyer wall that was hung the day the first Ellsworths moved in ... and now the weathervane.

I glanced out the window to where Brutus was barking his brains out, muzzle thrown back and eyes blazing up into a tall chestnut tree in the middle of the yard. Whoever she dispatched to do her dirty work would have to make it past a solid mass of teeth, muscle, and claw to get that weathervane. "That's fine, Irene. Send them over." I clicked off with a giddiness bubbling in my stomach. Serves her right.

Back in the family room, Andy had his video camera hooked up to the TV. "I want to show you the latest shoot from the castle," he said. "Finch knows a religious antiquities dealer from Indianapolis. He's authenticated a lot of Finch's collection. He had him come in and comment on some of his pieces on film today. It's pretty interesting."

"I'm eager to have my mind occupied by anything at all other than Ben, Jenn, Irene, or Mia." I curled my feet up under me on the couch for the show. "The weathervane goes tomorrow."

Andy shook with laughter. "Poor Stewart's going to be up on their roof in the storm that's on its way, screwing that thing down while she yells at him from under her umbrella that it's crooked."

It was a pretty accurate visual that he conjured in my mind, and I couldn't help but chuckle picturing it. "The poor man. She's a menace. I feel sorry for him for marrying her." Of course, if he hadn't, Ben wouldn't exist. I wasn't sure how I felt about Ben's nonexistence at this point, other than preferring not to think about it at all.

The clip was unedited and jumpy, with Andy making Carl and the antiquities dealer, Dennis Stoddard, stop and repeat things every now and then. Carl seemed like he was acting, and not in a good way, and Stoddard was all too enthusiastic about repeating his appraisal of a South American Virgin Mary statue over and over as many times as it took. I yawned, hugely, not able to hold it back.

"You know," Andy said, "I bet Dennis Stoddard could tell you what some of the things around here are worth before you go and let Irene take them out of the house."

"I'm sure Irene knows exactly what each nook and cranny in this house is worth, but you might be on to something. She's had her eye on that Saint Francis birdbath beside the shed. Maybe I can sweet-talk this antiques guy into giving me a value for it before she gets her greedy hands on it. Will Atkins thinks it's worth about a grand, but he doesn't specialize in religious antiques, so it might even be more." Will Atkins, from Schoolhouse Antiques, specialized in old records, anything Native American, and whatever else struck his fancy, by the looks of his antique shop. It was like living next door to a perpetual garage sale.

The phone rang again. "What does she want this time?" I said, pushing myself up off the couch.

"Blood would be my guess," Andy said, laughing.

But it wasn't Irene this time. It was Johnna. "I talked to Soapy," she said. "The play is on hold for now. They're having a meeting tomorrow night to decide what to do."

"Well, I guess we'll stop reserving tickets. Don't worry though, I'll figure out something for you guys to get your service hours in."

She let out a groan. "Of course you will."

"See you tomorrow, Johnna." I hung up feeling like I'd been standing on a breaking point all day and couldn't get my feet to move. If I wasn't careful, I'd fall right down into the earth and get swallowed alive. Somehow finding a dead body led to me being a suspect (although not an official one until I could talk to Reins without throwing up), finding out about Ben seeing another woman (even if he didn't call it dating), getting Mia overnight (fingers crossed it was only one night), adopting five crazy (one of them very dangerous) dogs, and the play being put on hold, which meant I had to figure out something for my phone crew to do before tomorrow.

What I needed was a way of finding out what really happened to Jenn. Was she killed, pushed, or did she simply slip into the canal and hit her head?

That was when the best idea of all time struck.

I'd use my phone crew to make calls to everyone in town, questioning them on what they might have seen or heard that could help with the case. They'd get their hours in, and I might get myself off the hook as a possible suspect. Two birds, one stone.

Ben would hate it. He'd forbid me to do it.

I grabbed another cookie from the pantry and munched resolutely. Ben would have to get over it. I had my good name to clear and the town had a show to put on if it wanted to salvage its own good reputation.

Mia refused to get up the next morning. Chances were, she'd been up all night texting friends. When Ben arrived at nine-thirty, he looked like he woke up in a nightmare. I guess he kind of had.

"I'm glad Mia's still asleep," he said, taking my arm and leading me into the kitchen. "I need to talk to you."

Oh God. Something bad had happened—other than Jenn Berg's possible murder—I could feel it in my bones. "Coffee first," I said, unable to deal with life before two cups.

He ambled over to the French door that led out to the back patio. "Why is there a dog in the backyard?"

I opened the cupboard, disturbing the old crab, Isobel, who bared her teeth at me. I needed to let her and the other three outside, but I was afraid I'd lose a leg if I opened the door. "There are five," I said. "I took Jenn's dogs."

"You did? Why?"

"Someone had to."

Ben slumped against the door, scowling at me and keeping a watchful eye on Isobel. "This is your way of showing you're innocent. Am I right?"

"They think I'm a murderer, Ben. Because you were ... They think I have a motive." I poured a generous amount of coffee into the biggest mug I could find and stared out the window over the sink. Brutus was digging to China via the backyard. "I'm not good at having people hate me for something I had no part in."

"I'm sorry." He walked around the counter, grasped me by my upper arms and stared down into my eyes with the most concerned, sincere gaze I'd ever seen on Ben. "Whatever you hear today, I had nothing to do with it. You have to believe that."

My stomach fell to my feet. "What am I going to hear today?"

He dropped my arms and turned from me. "They ruled Jenn's death a murder. I'm a suspect."

"You? Why would you be a suspect? Everyone in town thinks the two of you were going out."

Ben spun back around and banged his hand down on the counter. "Because I'm still married. Because she was pregnant."

My ears rang with the word. Pregnant. *Pregnant.*

"It wasn't mine, Cam. That's what you have to believe."

During the whirlwind time before we were married, Ben told me he didn't want another child, that Mia was enough, and he was too old to be the father of an infant. At thirty-six, I'd come to believe I'd never get married or have kids. Having already resigned myself to that fact, it wasn't difficult to accept. But Jenn Berg had been pregnant when she died. Jenn Berg, who had been doing *something* with Ben even if he didn't call it dating.

"If it wasn't yours, then whose? Everyone knows you and Jenn were—doing whatever together. How can I believe—"

"Because it's the truth!" he said, shoving his fingers through his hair. "I drove her home from the Cornerstone one night when her car wouldn't start. After that, she cooked me dinner as a thank -you. We became friends. We went to a movie. We had drinks. That's all. Friends. Making a baby takes a lot more than that."

"You never did that with her?" My head spun, and I sat down at the kitchen table.

"I never even kissed her, Cam. I swear to you. The only thing I ever talked to her about was *you* and how I screwed up and had to find a way back."

I looked up at him, trying to see the man I knew. The police officer. The workaholic. The father who wanted Mia to come stay more often. The man who was married to me, not taking other women to dinner and movies. My view of him split in two, like twin Bens stood in front of me. Mine and some other person I didn't know anymore. "How were you going to find your way back to me through her? That doesn't make sense, Ben."

He shook his head. "I wanted her perspective."

"A twenty-five -year -old woman who was never married? Her perspective?"

"She was a good listener and—" Footsteps jogged down the stairs. Mia was up. She dashed into the kitchen in a t-shirt with a cartoon pony on the front and rainbow striped pajama pants with her long, dark hair tousled from sleep—the picture of innocence—and dove into Ben's arms. "Daddy!"

Jenn Berg had been just one more young woman who had Ben totally bamboozled.

5

My crew was at their stations, or rather, wedged into their old grade school desks, when I got to the church around ten. Johnna, as expected, was knitting. Roy was sneaking a drink from a flask, Nick was typing out a message on his cell phone, and Anna and Logan were organizing our calling cards.

"Sorry I'm late," I said, lowering my handbag onto my desk with a thunk. "I had to wait for Ben to come get Mia this morning."

"I knew you'd be talking to Ben soon," Johnna said, not looking up from her needles.

"Yes, Cameron Cripps-Hayman," Roy said, eyeing me like he could see straight to my soul. "We knew."

It was obvious they'd all gotten word about the pregnancy, and now I was even more guilty in their eyes. "Well, I've got an idea for how we can help Sheriff Reins and Ben solve the case."

"The murder, you mean," Roy said, pronouncing each word more accusatory than the last.

"Yes." I deflected any bad feeling he was trying to give me. I wasn't guilty after all. "We have the distinct advantage of being able to reach out to every person living in town to question them, see what they might know about Miss Berg's ... untimely demise." I hoped I sounded tactful. The last thing I needed was for my blunt approach to make me an even bigger target.

"To clarify," Logan said, "we should call only Metamora residents and interrogate them about the murder?" Sometimes I thought Logan might have been part robot. He wanted the facts, plain and simple, with limited details. He never needed to know the why, only the what and how mattered.

"Exactly," I said. "But we need to do it carefully. Everyone knew Jenn. She was a young, pretty woman who worked at the Cornerstone and lived in the Hilltop Castle gatehouse. Her mother, Sue Nelson, and her great-grandmother, Elaina Nelson, are business owners in town, proprietors of the Soda Pop Shop and Nelson's Knitting Needles. They're neighbors and friends, and they're grieving. We need to be very clear that we're trying to help, not stir up trouble."

Anna sat up straighter, and her hand shot into the air. "I think we should call ourselves the Metamora Action Agency. It'll help if we say we're calling with a professional -sounding organization to collect information that could help Sheriff Reins and Officer Hayman. I can write a script to use if you want."

Pride surged through me. If I had a daughter, I'd want her to be just like Anna Carmichael—bright, willing, and eager. "That's a perfect idea. Thank you."

"Why don't we just go ask people?" Johnna said, wrapping her yarn into a big ball. "I can tell more from a person when I'm face-to-face with them."

"Yeah," Roy said. "I can get more from drunk folk than sober ones on the telephone. Why don't you drive me on down to the Cornerstone bar, Cameron Cripps-Hayman? I do my best work there."

"You can't get official community service hours while drinking in a bar. To make sure we're all questioning people the same way, I'd like us to work here. Maybe we can take the Action Agency into town and talk to people face-to-face when we've got our methods down."

The last thing I needed was Johnna and Roy on the loose in town. Logan and Anna would be probing and wheedling like relentless junior detectives, and who knows how Nick Valentine would work out even over the phone. This was a tricky situation, and one we needed to wade into delicately.

"Let's work on the script," I said. "Anna gave us a nice introduction. Does anyone have a suggestion for how to approach questioning?"

"Yeah," said Roy. "I'll say, 'This is Roy. Did you see who killed Jenn Berg?'" He sniffed and fiddled with his flask, itching to take it back out. "Then if they say no, I'll ask 'em what they've heard and who they think done it."

"Sounds good to me," Johnna said, tucking her knitting back into her bag. "I already talked to Soapy and Theresa last night, and Fiona, Cass, and Betty. They all think—"

"Why don't you write down everyone you've spoken too, Johnna," I said, knowing she'd already grilled half, if not all, of the town. "Then we'll have someone else talk to them, too. See if their story matches."

Her eyes lit up. "Catch them in a lie. Good idea." She picked up a pen and started jotting down names.

"Roy," I said, in my butteriest voice, "why don't you call the men you've known for years, like Frank Gardner, Jim Stein, Carl Finch—"

"Stew Hayman," he said, like it was a threat.

I maintained my cheery facade. "Yes! My father-in-law lives in Brookville now, but he might know something. And Johnna, why don't you put Irene on your list to call?"

She made a face, but nodded. I almost told her that with Irene stealing from me, maybe they could partner up and double their efforts.

"I've met Carl Finch before," Nick said from behind his phone. "Mind if I put him on my list? I don't know many people from this town."

"He's all yours," Roy said.

"I'll give you a few more names, too, Nick. Off the top of my head, Steve Longo, the owner of Odd and Strange Metamora, would be a good one, along with Jefferson Briggs."

Before I gave them the go -ahead, Roy and Johnna were dialing away. Anna slid the script she'd been working on over to Johnna, but she pushed it right back. "Elaina, it's Johnna. Dear, I'm so sorry for your loss."

Elaina Nelson was only a bit more lucid than Old Dan and a couple years younger. They'd gone to school together in the one-room school house that was now Will Atkins's antique shop. Her hair was bright red like her lipstick, and I'd never seen her wearing anything other than polka dots with a matching patent leather purse and shoes. I wouldn't have been shocked to find out she didn't even know or remember her great-granddaughter was dead.

"Hello, Mr. Longo," Nick said, drawing my attention. My crew was fullsteam ahead, not waiting for further instruction. So much for thinking I was in charge. "This is Nick Valentine with the Metamora Action Agency." He blinked a few times, listening. "The Metamora Action Agency. Yes. Well, I was going to tell you, I'm calling from—what?" This wasn't going well. Nick held out a hand to Anna and she passed over her hodgepodge of a script. "We're a group of volunteers calling residents of Metamora to aid Sheriff Reins and Officer Hayman in finding out what happened to Jenn Berg, who was found in the canal yesterday afternoon."

Nick put his hand over the receiver and let out a long, relieved breath. Then he put his hand to his forehead and winced. "Aliens? I'm not sure that's—lights over the canal three days ago? Okay."

Listening beside Nick, Roy turned his finger in loops beside his ear and mouthed crazy as his phone apparently rang.

"I'd love to knit a rose for the burial blanket," Johnna was saying. "I picked up a soft pink cashmere blend a few weeks ago that will be perfect." Her cashmere blend yarn was probably one of the many balls she had tucked under her shirt when the police picked her up in the Connersville Wal-Mart. She paid for them so she could keep them, but they pressed charges about the items in her car and here she was in the church basement. "I baked a pie for Sue. My apple's her favorite. Do you remember when she was about ten—"

We were veering off course faster than a kite caught in a hurricane.

"Sasquatch tracks by the canal, huh?" Nick said, rubbing his temple. "We'll have to pass that along."

Roy leaned back in his chair howling with laughter at something that was said on the other end of his phone conversation. "You're on! I'll bet you three bottles of Frank Gardner's finest moonshine she had something to do with it." Something told me he was betting against me.

Anna patted me on the shoulder. "Maybe it would be better if we went out and talked with people as a group? You might be able to guide us better if you were part of the same conversation."

"I think you might be right," I said, just then noticing the nickel-sized welts on Logan's neck.

"Logan! Are you okay? You have hives."

He slapped a hand over the back of his neck where I was staring. "I'm fine. A little nervous. I've never questioned anyone about a murder before."

I was in way over my head and my teenage boy-bot was ten seconds from a full-blown anxiety attack. "New plan!" I yelled, signaling for Nick, Roy, and Johnna to end their calls.

"She's making us hang up," Roy said. "Don't forget, I'm coming collecting when this is over."

"Your peach and navy polka dot dress would be lovely at the calling hours," Johnna said. "I spoke with Reverend Stroup this morning, and he's planning on reading Psalm 121. Is Sue having the funeral over at the new church?"

If I blew an air horn it wouldn't have shut her up. On to the others. "Let's take a break," I said. "Logan, how about a cool cloth for those hives? And I think I've got some cortisone lotion in my handbag."

"I'm heading over to Soapy's for some coffee," Roy said. "Nick Valentine, want to come along?"

Nick got up and strode along behind him. It was good to know that all outsiders were called by their full names, and not just me.

I dug around in my bag and found the lotion for Logan, then left

Anna to help him and Johnna to her personal and marched up the steps to go outside for some air.

I walked the two short blocks down to the canal and watched the mill's wheel turn in the water. My idea had spun out of control just as fast as the paddle wheel was churning. Now I had a group of five self-appointed detectives on my hands and no way to control them.

Back when I worked in a real call center, my employees either followed the script or they got written up and eventually fired. I didn't have to worry at all about Anna. Nick proved he could handle calling the town's residents, but his head might explode in the process. Roy and Johnna were like herding cats, and Logan would need to get in touch with his human side if this were to work.

And it had to work, because despite what Roy thought, I had nothing to do with Jenn's death. I was going to prove it. My five helpers—The Metamora Action Agency—would expedite the process. Or they might expedite me being arrested. Time would tell.

The police were gone from the crime scene today, but the tape had stayed up, enclosing the area where I found Jenn. Old Dan limped out the side door of the grist mill and spotted me. I waved and he smiled with his few remaining teeth and began walking toward me.

He was a mystery to me, believing in the old ways, like dowsing for buried things—water, metal, tunnels—and brewing his own medicines from herbs, berries, and roots. Some cultures would call him a shaman, others witch doctor or hexenmeister. It was folk magic, very different from what Steve Longo displayed at his Odd and Strange shop, and still very much alive and practiced by the older people in town.

Judy Platt, who owned the Briar Bird Inn, swore Old Dan cured the spot of melanoma on her nose a few years back, and I don't doubt he did.

"How are you, Dan?" I called as he neared.

He nodded, still grinning his toothless grin, and held out something to me. "You got them dogs, I hear."

"I do," I said, holding out my hand.

He dropped a metal dog tag in my palm. “Found that down yonder. May go to the missing pup.”

Missing pup? My memory rattled at me. Right. Johnna had mentioned Jenn’s sixth dog, a puppy. There were only the five dogs when I went to the gatehouse.

I rubbed the mud off the tag with my thumb. Bantum Kennel, Connersville, Indiana, was inscribed on its front above a phone number. “Thanks,” I said, dropping it in my bag where it would make its way to the bottom and never be seen again. “Dan, what do you know about a dog’s temperament? Do you have anything I could give a nasty dog to make it nice?”

“No,” he said in his rusty voice. “Gotta take ’em by the scruff when they’re younguns and make ’em know who’s in charge.”

“Is it too late when they’re grown?”

He let out a whoop of a laugh. “Cain’t teach an old dog a new trick, now, can ya?”

I thought of my rushed marriage to Ben, my rushed offer to take Jenn’s dogs, my rushed formation of the Action Agency.

I laughed with him, mostly at my misfortune. “I guess not, no.” Brutus would have to stay in the backyard, and I’d just have to feed him by launching his food out the kitchen window.

“Gotta find that pup ’fore he gets out there in traffic on 52,” Dan said, and with that, he was off again, searching for Jenn’s missing dog.

Roy and Nick were coming out of Soapy Savants with paper coffee cups in hand when I turned to head back up the road to the church. I’d only gotten one block when Ben’s black SUV pulled up beside me and stopped. He rolled down his window, and I knew by the arched brows and disapproving look on his face that I didn’t want to hear what he had to say.

So I started to run. Except my knee had other plans for me, like stopping and preferably sitting on the ground and not moving for a while. But I’d already made a big enough fool of myself without taking a seat on the side of the road. I slowed to a limping walk.

“Good thing you’re not a criminal,” Ben said, shaking his head and easing his truck up beside me. “You’d never outrun the law.”

"Yeah," I said, panting from my quick, short sprint. "Next time I'll hide behind a tree or something."

He got out and stood beside me, put his hands on his hips, and squared his shoulders, like he was readying for battle. "What is it?" I asked. "Just spit it out already."

"My mother sent workers over to the house, and one of them was bit by Cujo in the backyard. He needed twelve stitches and he's suing her. Animal control from Brookville will be picking up the dog. And what the heck is The Metamora Action Agency?"

Oh boy. Somebody flushed this day down the drain. "Animal control?" I said, leaving the Action Agency to be answered for last—or never. "Brutus can't go to the pound. He's already been uprooted from his home. You have to stop them from taking him. I'll figure out somewhere for him to go."

"I don't know if I can do that, Cam. If he's a dangerous animal that's already bitten someone, they'll want to take him and put him down."

"Put him down? No!" I had to get Brutus out of there, fast. "Look, we can talk more later. I have to get back to the church." I took off running again.

"Cam!" he called after me. "It hasn't rained yet. Don't hurt yourself running on that knee."

My knee was the least of my worries. I had to get Andy on the phone and get Brutus out of my backyard.

6

The rest of the afternoon was a wash. Anna was right: if we were going to get anywhere with the Action Agency, we needed to talk to people in person, which left me with a phone bank and nobody to call. I figured I'd check in with Soapy to see if there were any new updates on the play. Plus I was ready to give my good knee for a latte.

"I hear you've got a lot on your plate with that group of yours over at the church," Soapy said while steaming milk.

"Not so much anymore with the play on hold, unfortunately. It's terrible what happened to Jenn Berg."

He nodded thoughtfully while adding the milk to the espresso. "She was a nice girl. I knew her since she was a baby. Theresa and I took Sue flowers to the hospital the day Jenn was born."

Soapy handed me my mug and rested his elbows on the counter. "Sue's ex-husband got into town last night. Staying over at Cass's place where Ben's got a room. Big hot-shot CEO now over in Cincinnati. I hear he complained about everything there was to complain about over there. Like the Fiddle -Dee -Doo Inn can compare to some five -star super hotel in a big city." He scratched his white beard that hung just past his collar then adjusted his glasses. "Andrew hadn't even seen his daughter for going on a year from what Sue tells us. Jenn didn't visit him and he didn't invite her to. He doesn't see Lianne, either."

Jenn's sister, Lianne Berg, was only a couple years younger than Jenn. They had another sister, Stephanie, who was much younger, around Mia's age, but she had a different father. Rumor had it that her dad was Hank Jenkins who owned the BBQ Shack beside the Soda Pop Shop. Going by the looks of Stephanie Nelson, Hank was a dead ringer for the role of daddy.

"Andrew's already been riding Sheriff Rein's rear end about finding who did this. I can only imagine what it's like for Ben living under the same roof with the man. I can sympathize with Andrew—I'd want the person responsible found, too—but they're doing all they can."

I took a sip of my latte and relished the hot liquid running all the way down to my stomach. "Ben stopped by this morning to pick up Mia and told me they ruled it a homicide, but he didn't say why. Do you know?"

"She had a gash on the back of her head, but landed on the front side. Looked like someone hit her with a blunt object and knocked her out, causing her to fall in the canal and drown."

I resisted the urge to rub the back of my head, and willed myself not to think of being cracked in the skull and knocked unconscious.

"For the record," Soapy said, patting my hand, "Theresa and I know you and Ben are both innocent. It's ludicrous to think otherwise."

"Thanks. I wish everyone felt that way. I didn't even know Ben had anything to do with Jenn until after I found her. Of course, there's no way to prove what I knew and didn't know, so I can only hope that whoever did this is caught."

"I hear you've got yourself a team of investigators now. The Metamora Action Agency, is it? Two of them stopped in earlier today."

"Roy and Nick," I said. "I hope they didn't badger you."

"No, no. Roy's harmless, especially when he's sober. There are concerns about the other, though, being that he's a criminal and from out of town. Some people aren't too happy with you bringing that element in from Connersville every day. He was arrested for assault, wasn't he?"

Panic began to rise from my chest, up my throat. I couldn't swallow my coffee. "Yes," I managed to say.

"You trust that he's got nothing to do with this?"

I nodded, having no reason to nod. I liked Nick. I didn't think he had anything to do with Jenn's murder, but I had no idea of his whereabouts outside of nine a.m. to four p.m.

"Well," Soapy said, "the players are meeting here tonight. I don't want to have to cancel the musical after all the hard work your people put in getting tickets reserved. The town needs the revenue. Cass has reservations at her inn, and the Briar Bird is booked, too. Tourists in town will bring business to all of us."

I cleared my throat, happy to be past the subject of Nick Valentine. "I don't want to seem insensitive, but since we're on the subject, isn't there an understudy who can fill in? Would it be in bad taste to use someone else for the part?"

Soapy grabbed a rag and started wiping the counter. "Melody Winkler's the understudy for the part Jenn was playing. It's a difficult situation, because the two were always competing back in high school for the lead parts. Melody always got them. This was the first time Jenn got the lead role over Melody and now ... " He shrugged. "Shame."

"It is a shame."

My mind started buzzing. Was Melody jealous of Jenn getting the lead for once? Jealous enough to kill for the part?

I think I had the Action Agency's first interview. Tomorrow, we'd hunt down Melody Winkler.

When I got home, Andy gave me a sly wink that assured me Brutus got away. I wasn't sure where he'd gotten away to, but as long as he wasn't in my backyard or with Brookville Animal Control, I'd rather not know. There'd be no love lost between the two of us.

Big Gus and Heckle and Jeckle met me at the front door, jumping and barking and licking. Enough fur flew from their coats and rained down on the foyer floor to clog my Dirt Devil beyond repair. I pushed past them and managed to coax crabby old Isobel out the back door where she could do her business, before wrangling leashes on the three most hyper dogs in existence.

When I opened the front door, they pulled me halfway down the sidewalk, wrapping their leashes around my legs. Will Atkins came running out of his antique shop to help me, his glasses askew and long sandy hair flying out behind him. "That black monster was barking half the night. I saw he took a piece of a worker's butt this afternoon."

"So I hear," I said, stepping out of a loop of leash. "Guess Irene will think twice about sending people over to fetch my weathervane."

"You're not someone I'd cross," he said, handing me Gus's leash after untangling it from around my foot. I wondered if he was joking, or if he was hinting about his suspicions regarding Jenn's death.

John Bridgemaker, the leader of the local Native American Council, came out of Will's antique shop next. His long black hair was pulled back and he wore a beaded leather vest over his oxford shirt. His ancestors built many of the covered bridges in the area before the settlers ran them off the land.

"With these three and my gimpy knee, I'm a force to be reckoned with," I said, giving John a wave.

"When did you hurt your knee?" John asked.

"It started bothering me yesterday morning."

"Oh," Will said, taking a step back. "Did you twist it the night before or something?"

Perfect. Now I knew the idea his mind was circling—me sliding on a muddy canal bank and turning my knee after killing Jenn. "No.

It hurts when it's going to storm. We have a big one headed our way, I can tell."

"The leaves are showing their silver sides," John said, gazing up into the trees. I took that as confirmation of the rain coming, even if I didn't completely understand the connection.

The dogs were pulling and whining and doing their best to get me all wrapped up again. "I better let them walk before they drag me down the street. Thanks for the help."

I took off with the dogs, heading for the park by the canal. When they spotted Metamora Mike and his feathered friends swimming in the same spot where I found Jenn Berg, it was all over. They darted past the playground and gazebo, tugging me straight for the water, barking and spinning around each other like a chorus of deranged whirling dervishes. Mike and his pack beat it, posthaste, while I put all my strength and extra cookie weight into attempting to stop our forward momentum. But all my shouting for them to stop, leash burns on my hands, and promises of aching muscles in the morning were in vain. The three hairy mutts plummeted right into the water, to my mortification, taking me and the yellow crime scene tape with them.

I fell and flailed, splashed and kicked, but never let go of their leashes. I *would* get them out of the water, away from the crime scene. I *would* make this right, somehow.

Whistling sounded from the opposite side of the bank, and the trio paused in their thunderous pounding of paws in the water to see who wanted their attention. It was Betty Underwood, record holder of most cookie jars under one roof and owner of Grandma's Cookie Cutter. She was a wiry seventy-something with jet-black hair that faded to a purple hue and more energy than I'd ever had in me, even after a few cups of coffee. She held something in her hand, luring the dogs up the bank. Their paws sank in the mud, ruining any evidence of Jenn Berg slipping down the side. I climbed up behind them as fast as I could, still holding tight. They bounded over to Betty, crime scene tape waving behind them like a bride and groom's car pulling away from the church. All that was missing was old tin cans rattling on the ground.

"Sit!" she said, and miracle of all miracles, they sat. She gave each a piece of a biscuit and turned her eyes to me, dripping, mud-covered, and humiliated. "Well now you've been dragged through the mud figuratively and literally," she said. "I heard you were the brave soul who took Jenn's dogs in. None of them trained a lick, are they?"

"No," I said, futilely wiping at the mud on my shirt. "I don't even know the names of those two." I pointed to Huey and Dewey with their tongues lolling, drooling pieces of biscuit onto the ground. "The big one's Gus."

"They like my homemade dog biscuits, that's for sure." She pulled another from her pocket and broke it in three. "I'll give you the recipe, but you can use oats or flour and anything other than chocolate, or grapes because of the seeds, and onions and garlic can be a problem, too."

"Oh, Betty, I'm the worst baker on the planet. You know that. I'll buy some next time I'm at the store."

"Nonsense," she said. "A monkey could make these. They're Cam-proof, and much better for the dogs. No preservatives or artificial colors or flavors."

"Guess it wouldn't hurt to try." I watched my herd crunch their treats, wagging their tails and beaming up at Betty like they'd do anything she said for another, and resigned myself to becoming the best dog biscuit baker this side of the state line. "Thanks for your help. I better get them home and bathed."

I headed back down the opposite side of the canal from home, walking by the Ben Franklin III, a canal boat drawn from the banks by two enormous draft horses. A tourist favorite. The top of my head didn't come up to the horses' backs. Fortunately they weren't in their stalls, or I'd end up in another battle of wills with the dogs.

Every person I passed—mothers with strollers and little kids with drippy ice cream cones, old couples out walking, men mowing lawns —stared at me like I was contagious. I was sure the filth and canal water had something to do with it, but Betty's words kept coming back. I'd been literally and figuratively dragged through the mud. My reputation as a murder suspect preceded me with every gimpy step I took down the street. I had friends here, but I'd never been a town favorite. Now I was doomed to forever remain the outsider.

A thought glimmered in my mind: I could leave, go back to Columbus, get a job in the real world again. It wasn't like I didn't have a degree and experience. I could make a living and support myself. I could go home and check my email for responses to the resumes I sent out halfheartedly a few weeks ago.

But that would mean leaving Ben. I wasn't sure I'd ever let him move back in, but I wasn't ready to admit defeat, either. I still saw him almost daily. In Metamora, it was almost impossible not to see him. Even if we weren't together, it wasn't like we were apart. If I moved away, back to Columbus ...

I couldn't do it. Not yet, at least.

Doing my best to ignore the steely looks from my neighbors, I crossed the bridge back to my side of the canal and went home. Isobel was asleep in a sunny spot in the backyard. I let the other three inside the fence and got a bucket and soap from inside the house.

Gus loved the hose. He tried to eat it at first, opening his jaw wide and snapping at the water. I had to practically tackle the Wonder Twins to get them washed off. The whole time, Isobel grumbled and growled and retreated behind the Saint Francis birdbath. I had to remember to ask Dennis Stoddard to appraise it for me.

When they were as clean as they were getting, I turned on the sprinkler and watched them run around like little kids with big goofy smiles on their doggy faces.

Since I was covered in mud anyway, I fetched a shovel from the shed to fill in the deep hole Brutus dug the night before. That's when my eyes scanned the roof of the house, and I knew Irene was still undaunted.

The weathervane was gone.

After a hot shower and a dinner consisting of peanut butter cookies and an apple for good measure, I curled up in bed with the paperback Brenda gave me the day before. My knee throbbed and my pride was battered. Unwelcome tears dribbled down my face. With an empathetic whine, Gus bounded up on the bed and lay down beside me, nuzzling his nose against my side. Not to be outdone, the nameless twins hopped up and each pinned one of my feet to the bed.

I closed my eyes and lay my head down on Gus's back, letting the canine warmth spread through my bones.

7

I woke Thursday morning with a nervousness that could only be abated by munching down half a dozen chocolate chip cookies with my coffee. I pushed away Mia's disgust of my million-calorie habit with each and every bite. I was a murder suspect. I was separated from my husband. I'd eat as many cookies as I wanted without guilt.

My sister would be showing up tonight, driving in after work. I'd left her a message about the dogs and hadn't heard back. Hopefully she could deal with them. I'd have to vacuum like my life depended on it to keep her sneezing at bay.

Looking down at my shirt, I made a mental note to pick up a truckload of lint rollers, too.

There was a quick knock on the back door, then it opened and Andy stepped inside. "Breakfast of champions," he said. "Toss me one."

I threw him a cookie and watched him down it in two bites. "Want some coffee?"

I already knew the answer. Andy hated coffee. It was incomprehensible to me how anyone could hate coffee. He held up an extra-large plastic cup from the gas station that I guessed was full of soda. "You need to pick out paint," he said.

"Did you get an estimate?"

"I'm going to do it myself. Everybody else will rip you off."

I had a feeling he meant that nobody else wanted the job of painting the house of a possible murderess, but they'd do it for double the price.

He pulled some paint color samples from his back pocket and slid them across the counter to me. "I'm thinking we should keep with the traditional white," I said. "Don't you agree?"

"WWID," he said, and took a slurp from his straw. "What would Irene do?"

That statement was a prick in my behind. "I don't care what Irene would do. She doesn't live here anymore." I snatched the colors up and dropped them in my handbag. "I'll decide later and let you know."

He grinned and grabbed another cookie out of the box. "Word is the players want to go on with the musical, but Melody Winkler won't do it."

"She won't do it? Why not?" It went against everything Soapy told me about her yesterday. Someone with her competitive streak who was so eager to have the lead female role wouldn't turn it down.

"She said out of respect for Jenn she had to decline."

"Strange." I picked up another cookie and nibbled on it, thinking. "Who talked to her?"

"I'm not sure. Cass told me this morning."

Cass, of the Fiddle Dee Doo Inn, and Andy had been a couple ever since he came to town. They paired off right away and were seldom apart when he wasn't working at my house. Their age difference—he was twenty-one and she was thirty-three—didn't seem to come into question at all. They made each other happy, and that was all that mattered. I had found out the hard way that it wasn't always easy to be happy with the person you loved.

"Where does Melody work? Do you know where I can find her today?"

Andy put up a hand. "Cam, I know you have this whole Scooby Doo thing going on with your group down at the church, but before you go painting your Subaru to look like the Mystery Machine, I think you better take a look at what you're dealing with. Jenn Berg was murdered. Someone hit her on the head and pushed her into the canal. If you go snooping around, don't you think the same could happen to you?"

"You sound like Ben. First you don't tell me about him and Jenn, and now this. Whose side are you on?" I closed the cookie box and shoved it back in the pantry. No more cookies for Andy.

"It's not about sides. It's about a dead woman and a dangerous situation. You're innocent, so leave it alone and let Reins and Ben worry about it."

"Reins doesn't think I'm innocent! He'll be calling me any day now wanting to talk about where I was when Jenn was murdered and what I knew about her and Ben. Now I find out she was pregnant! How is anyone going to believe I didn't know about that and want her dead for sleeping with my husband, which he says didn't happen and the baby isn't his and—" I started panting. My head spun. Spots flashed in front of my eyes. "I need to sit down."

I lowered myself to the kitchen floor and sat right where I'd been standing.

"Cameron!" Andy rushed around the end of the breakfast bar, grabbed a glass out of the cupboard, and filled it with water. "Drink this."

I gulped down the water and a second glass he handed me. "Thanks. Sorry I freaked. It's just that everything in my life is spinning out of control. I don't know how to stop it. If I think about it too much, I can't take it."

Andy plopped down beside me and ran a hand through his auburn waves. "I guess I can understand you wanting to take control. Just promise me you won't get yourself killed—or bring home any more dogs."

"I don't know. They're starting to grow on me."

We both glanced over into the corner beside the fridge, where

Isobel had one eye open glaring at us and a snarl on her lips. "Maybe not her," I said. "But we agree to have a limited relationship based on necessity. I feed her, let her out, and leave her alone."

Andy leaned his head back against the cupboard, laughing. "You take in all us strays. So, how are you going to get that ragtag group of yours to solve a murder case, Velma?"

"First, we're going to talk to Melody. After that, I have no idea. I'm hoping we'll get more leads if Melody doesn't go anywhere."

"I'll keep my ears open. I think Melody works at that clothing store across from the movie theater off 52 in Brookville." He stood up and reached down for my hand to help me off the floor. "You should wrap that knee."

I bent and straightened it a few times, loosening it up. "It'll be better when it rains."

After much back and forth and debate at the church, five of us packed into my Subaru and headed to Brookville to find Melody Winkler. Logan stayed behind to man the phones.

"You stink like booze, Roy," Johnna said, reaching across Nick in the backseat to poke Roy with her knitting needle.

"Don't you jab me with that thing, woman. I told Cameron Cripps-Hayman to drop me off at the Cornerstone. I could do a lot more digging up dirt in there, but would she? No."

"You can't get community service hours sitting in a bar," I said for the hundredth time.

"Who has to know?" He slipped his flask out of his pocket and took a swig.

"That stays in the car."

He stuck his tongue out at me in the rearview mirror.

Logan's hives had gone down and were no more than pink splotches. Anna said she'd talked to him for two hours last night and they came up with the idea of posting signs with our phone bank's number on it for people to call in and leave anonymous tips. They hung posters around town this morning. It was a fantastic idea, one I should've thought of immediately, and it gave Logan a way to help without having to call strangers and ask questions. Or hunt down suspects with the rest of us. I told him if Sheriff Reins or Officer Hayman called in, he should pretend he didn't speak English. He said, "*Sí.*"

"Have you ever been to this clothing store?" Anna asked me. Sometimes she could be a little over prepared.

"No. We're just going with the flow today. We'll talk to Melody and figure out our next move from there." I could tell my answer didn't make Anna happy by the way her forehead crinkled between her brows.

Five minutes later, I pulled into the strip mall across from the movie theater. I felt like we should all put our hands in a pile and chant, *Go Action Agency!* But I kept that notion to myself, and we piled out of the car into the parking lot.

The five of us looked up and down the row of shops. There was a beauty salon, a tanning salon, and a nail salon. A Chinese restaurant, a drug store, and a dog groomer. I made a mental note to remember the dog groomer. On the end was our store. Stature. It sounded trendy. I almost suggested that Johnna and Roy go to the drugstore to purchase more cortisone for Logan, but Johnna might end up in the back of a police car if we separated, and Roy might end up wherever they served alcohol.

"Let's go in," I said, leading my crew to the sidewalk.

A bell on the door tinkled when we entered. The shop was well organized and pop music played on the speakers overhead. "These are kids' clothes," Roy said, holding up a sports jacket.

"I've never seen a little girl with breasts that would fill this out." Johnna poked her knitting needle at the gaping chest of a cocktail dress.

"Can I help you?" a woman said from somewhere in the clothing racks.

Behind me, Nick started laughing under his breath.

"Cameron?" Anna said, trying to get my attention, but I was busy looking for the woman who offered to help us.

"I'm looking for a dress," I called.

"Who is the dress for?" she asked.

"Me."

She appeared around a rounder of men's shirts, and I blinked double time. The sales woman was a little person. Her head barely reached the rack where the hangers hung. Looking around, it came together quickly. Structure was a store for little people.

She took in the five of us, and I've never in my life seen a person so confused.

"Okay," I said. "We're really here to see Melody Winkler. Is she here?"

The woman clasped her hands and shot me with a stern look. "No. Melody runs our online retail. She doesn't work in the store."

"We'll give her a call then. Thanks for your help." I turned and bolted for the door, motioning for the others to follow.

I was barely through the door when I heard the sales lady say, "Ma'am, you have to pay for that!"

"Johnna!" I shouted, pivoting back around. "Put it back."

Busted, Johnna took a sparkly pink headband out of her knitting bag and hung it back up. "Don't look at me like that!" she said. "I thought it'd look nice on Jenn. For the calling hours. I wasn't going to *buy* something that'll end up in the ground."

"Just come on." I hightailed it down the sidewalk. "Where's Roy?"

"He said he wanted an egg roll," Nick said.

This expedition had turned into a disaster, but now that I thought about it, an egg roll sounded really good. "I think I'll have one too. Anyone else?"

The five of us adjourned to Wok and Roll for an early lunch and regrouping session. "What's in these anyway?" Roy asked, examining the meat inside his dumpling. "It looks suspect."

"Wash it down with your moonshine, and you'll be fine," Johnna said, sipping her green tea.

"I'm going to check in with Logan." Anna pulled out her cell phone and retreated to the other side of the restaurant.

"I'm going out to smoke," Nick said, excusing himself from the table.

"That one's probably wondering how he got tangled up in this mess," Johnna said, lifting her chin toward Nick. "Train drops him off in the morning and next thing he knows, he's hunting down murderers."

"Murder*er*. Only one in our town," Roy said, around a wad of dumpling. "Ain't that right, Cameron Cripps-Hayman?"

"That's right, Roy."

"Ha! You know there wasn't no accomplice, do ya? How would you know that?" he asked, pointing a dirty finger at me.

"Knock it off, Roy." Johnna kicked him under the table, making him jump. He groaned and rubbed his knee but kept his trap shut.

I couldn't figure out where Johnna's head was. Did she think I had something to do with Jenn 's death or not? She only seemed to be concerned with funeral plans. Of course, in a town of less than two hundred, a funeral was a big deal. And Johnna liked to have her nose in a little bit of everything. If she didn't, she might miss out on getting her sticky fingers on something good. Dollars to donuts she'd walk away from Jenn's calling hours with "souvenirs" to sell in her shop.

Anna came back to the table pale as a ghost. "Did Logan have news?" I asked.

Her eyes skittered around the restaurant before landing on Nick outside the glass front door. "No," she said, but her voice wavered and she wouldn't look at me. She had news all right, but she didn't want to say what she'd learned from Logan in front of Roy and Johnna. Or maybe it was me she didn't want to tell.

"I'm gonna go bum a cigarette off Nick," Roy said.

"Well, I'll visit the ladies' room before we leave." Johnna gulped down the last of her tea. Before she got up, she slipped the salt and pepper shakers into her knitting bag.

I waited until she was far away enough from the table not to overhear. "What did Logan say, Anna?"

Anna slumped down in the chair across from me. "I don't believe it," she said. "At least, I don't want to believe it."

"What?" I was one second from shaking it out of her.

"Logan said a woman called the tip line. She saw Jenn Berg arguing with a man outside of the Soda Pop Shop the day before you found her."

Oh no. Please, not Ben.

"The caller said they were yelling at each other about money, and when Jenn tried to walk away, the guy grabbed her arm and yanked her back."

I clutched my Diet Coke so hard, the can dented. "Who was Jenn arguing with?"

"Nick."

Relief crashed over me like a cool wave but was quickly replaced with confusion. It wasn't Ben, but Nick? Our Nick? Could the murderer really be one of our own Metamora Action Agency members?

8

By the time we got back to Metamora, the town was abuzz with accusations about the young man Cameron Hayman brought in on the train from Connersville with his black nails and hard rock t-shirts. I heard everything from Nick being a devil worshipper to him being on the run for several murders committed in California.

I was considered as evil as Nick Valentine for introducing him to the community. If the people didn't get a conviction soon, they'd take matters into their own hands and hang us both, Wild West style, in the town square.

I had to talk to Nick and find out what his confrontation with Jenn was all about, but he took off for the train station as soon as we got home. And I still had to talk with Melody. I wouldn't be put off her trail so easily.

Reverend Stroup called me into his office as soon as my foot hit the door of the church. "Sheriff Reins was here looking for you," he said, shifting nervously from foot to foot, his wrinkled forehead even more creased than usual. He crossed his office and sat down behind his desk. "I think you're a nice woman and what you're doing down in my basement to help the town is admirable, yet I haven't known you all that long, not compared to the others in this town. Now, I'm not a man who passes judgment. I leave that responsibility in the hands of our Lord. However, when my parishioners come to me with concerns, it's my duty to listen."

I knew where this was headed. "I didn't have anything to do with Jenn Berg's death, Reverend."

"I understand. I'm certain when Sheriff Reins solves this matter your name will be cleared, but in the meantime I'm afraid I can't allow you use of the church basement for your phone bank."

I stepped backward at the verbal blow. "What about my crew getting community service hours?"

"If you aren't able to relocate, I'll provide them with enough work to cover their hours."

I gave the reverend a stiff nod and stuttered, "O-okay," before leaving his office with my hands pressed to my chest, holding my heart inside. If I let go it would tumble out onto the floor.

Somehow I ended up in the basement even though I couldn't remember walking down the stairs. My crew was doing what they normally did, which wasn't much of anything. "I have bad news," I told them and relayed the conversation I had with Reverend Stroup.

None of them said anything or even looked at me for what seemed like ages. Johnna's lips pursed in a stern expression, and her hands moved her knitting needles fast and sharp. Roy made a hum of disapproval under his breath and took a few pulls of his flask. Logan immediately began disassembling things—unplugging the phones and collecting our stacks of calling cards. Finally, Anna spoke up. "We can get our Action Agency line routed to your house," she said. "We can take turns manning the phone there while the others go out and talk to people, like we did today. Nothing has to change."

"You do have a big house, Cameron Cripps-Hayman," Roy said. "Room for the five of us, I suppose."

A rush of warmth came over me. "I do have enough room for all of you. That's a perfect solution, Anna. Tomorrow we meet at my house!"

If only Anna could give me the solution to avoiding Sheriff Reins.

It wasn't talking about Jenn that made me nervous, it was the fact that he had to know all about the Metamora Action Agency if Ben knew, and I didn't want him putting us out of commission before we talked to Melody and cleared Nick's name.

Hopefully I could clear Nick's name. I prayed I hadn't unintentionally brought a killer into town.

As the Whitewater Valley train chugged away from Metamora toward Connersville with Nick on it, I made my way home to get ready for my sister's arrival. I figured I had a few hours yet to get the house fur free and the dogs worn out from a romp in the backyard.

After I got inside and fended off Gus and my two nameless canine boys, I opened the back door to find Andy planting grass seed over the bald spot where I'd refilled the hole Brutus dug. The three slobbering, hyper monsters rushed him, jumping, barking, and batting him with their paws.

Oh, good gravy!

"Give a guy a heads up next time!" he called, between commands of "Down!" "Sit!" and "No!"

"Sorry, Andy!" I grabbed a soda from the fridge and took it out to him as an apology. "I think they like you."

"They could like me less. I'd be okay with it." He swiped the sweat from his brow and chugged half the can before giving me a regretful smile and saying, "I have something to tell you, Cam."

"I already know about Nick Valentine and how everyone hates me for taking him on as a volunteer."

"That's not it. I was going to wait until tomorrow so you didn't get the news on your birthday, but—"

"My birthday. Holy crap, I forgot!" My mind had completely, totally, 100 percent blocked out the fact that today I turned forty. I was officially over the hill. Half my life was gone—assuming I was lucky enough to live another forty years—and what did I have to show for it? A marriage on the rocks, a house that wasn't actually mine, a job that wasn't a job at all, and, best of all, I was a murder suspect. "I need a drink."

Andy followed me in the house and watched with leery eyes

while I filled a twelve-ounce tumbler with white wine. "It's going to be that kind of birthday, huh?" he asked.

"Do you know how my day went? Let's just say it was the punch line to a joke that starts: A drunk, a klepto, and two murder suspects walk into a store for midgets. And that was the good part of my day!"

"I don't even want to know. Just toss me a beer if you have one so you're not drinking alone on your birthday."

I grabbed a can of Bud out of the fridge. "What do you have to tell me? I'm armed and ready." I held up my wine and his beer can to prove it.

"It can wait until tomorrow."

"Now. I want to know now."

He grabbed an envelope from the mail pile on the table and handed it to me. "It's from Irene's lawyer. She's suing you over the dog bite to her worker."

All I could do was laugh. It was that or cry, and I wasn't going to cry until I at least finished my wine. "This is her way of getting the house back. She'll sue us and we'll have to settle for signing over this house."

"I've been thinking about that," he said and leaned forward over the breakfast bar conspiratorially. "Let's make her not want it back."

"What do you mean," I whispered, like someone might be listening.

"Got those paint chips I gave you this morning?" The grin that overcame his face was Cheshire cat ornery.

"I couldn't," I said, feeling a giddiness I didn't think would be possible to feel after being alerted to the fact that it was my birthday. My fortieth birthday.

I took a healthy drink of wine and relished in the rush.

"You could," Andy said. "I'm not painting this house white."

I scuttled over to my bag hanging on the back of one of the kitchen chairs and started fishing around inside for the paint chips. "Where are they?"

"You really need a smaller bag," Andy said, helping himself to a cookie from the pantry.

"I know. I'm going to clean this one out tomorrow."

Sunk in my bag past my elbow, I finally grasped the little rectangles held together by a metal ring and pulled them out in triumph. "Got 'em! Now to pick a color that will make Irene Ellsworth Hayman's stomach turn."

Andy and I sat down at the table and started flipping through the colors when my cell phone rang. Ben's name showed on the screen. My heart fluttered knowing he remembered my birthday, even if I forgot it myself.

"I have one thing to ask you," he said, when I answered.

"What's that?" I asked, imagining he was giving me a choice between diamonds or pearls, or at very least chocolate or butter cream frosting for the cake he was buying from Betty.

"Why the heck is this aggressive dog back in the pen at Finch's gatehouse instead of with Animal Control like it's supposed to be, Cameron?"

"Oh. Is that where he is?" Every muscle in my body clenched, preparing for the lecture I was about to get.

"Yes! *That's* where he is. And since Finch needs a gatekeeper and I happen to be living like a vagrant, he's given me orders to stay in the gatehouse. I guess that makes this dog my responsibility now. Thank you very much for that. As if didn't have enough to deal with already!"

My fuse was lit and my temper flaring. "Like I don't have anything to worry about? Your dear mommy is suing me! Everyone in town thinks I'm either, A) a murderer, or 2) brought the murderer to town! I have to deal with Johnna Fitzgerald and Roy Lancaster every day. The dogs dragged me into the canal yesterday. My knee is killing me because it won't rain already, and *it's my birthday, you jerk!*"

He was silent while I caught my breath, rage spiraling downward toward an emotional dam of tears. I held them back, swallowed them down, cursed them for even thinking of making an appearance because of Ben.

"I'm sorry," he said and blew out a frustrated breath. "I forgot. But does it even matter if I remember, Cam? Do you want me to remember? You don't want me to live at home with you, so what's my role in this? In your life?"

"I don't know," I said, struggling to keep my composure. "I have to go. Monica's on her way."

"All right. Give her my best. And Cam? Happy birthday."

"Yeah," I said, wanting to go upstairs, collapse in bed, and sleep for the next year or two, or however long it took for my life to be what it should be again. "Thanks."

I hung up. Andy nudged my wine tumbler closer, urging me to partake in the age-old tradition of drowning my sorrows. It was a bad idea. I didn't drink often. The wine I had on hand was left over from a dinner party almost a year ago that Ben and I hosted when Soapy was re-elected as mayor. I'd regret drinking so much when my head was pounding and my stomach was sour in the morning.

But right now I preferred not to think about morning, so I swallowed the rest of the wine in my glass. "My husband's a jerk," I said, standing from the table and wobbling a little.

"He found Brutus, huh?"

"He's living with Brutus." I shuffled my feet, which suddenly felt extra heavy, over to the door to let the dogs in. "Finch has him staying at the gatehouse."

"Oh man," Andy said, slouching back in his chair. "I told Finch I'd take care of Brutus until we could find someone to take him."

"Well, looks like Finch found somebody."

It wouldn't take Ben more than five minutes to have Animal Control on their way to Hilltop Castle. I knew when a dog bit someone and that person had to go to the hospital and get stitches the outcome was never good. But, it was my fault. I should've kept Brutus in the house. I knew the workers were coming over. I couldn't let him be put to sleep. I wouldn't be able to live with myself.

There was a niggling at my brain, like an idea that wouldn't quite form. I sat back down and tried to summon it forward, but all I got was a hazy image of Old Dan limping toward me with his hand out.

Oh! The dog tag! The kennel! I grabbed my overstuffed, overlarge bag and began digging again.

"What are you looking for now?" Andy asked. "And are we having cake or anything?"

"I'll call the kennel where Jenn Berg got her missing puppy and see if they'll take Brutus."

"All right. So ... cake?"

"Only if you're making it." I held my handbag over the table and dumped its contents. Coins rolled, receipts scattered, and my wallet fell with a thunk.

"Holy cow," Andy said, staring in awe.

There was gum and a candy bar, tissues and lip gloss, pens and a check book. There were enough odds and ends to cover over half of the tabletop. In the center of it all was a bone-shaped, brass-colored dog tag. I swiped it off the table and dialed the number.

A man answered on the third ring. "Bantum Kennels."

"Hi, uh, hello. I was wondering ... I have a dog—well, it's not actually my dog, but I took it from a deceased woman—anyway, it has nowhere to go and in the upheaval from its home, it bit someone and now I've got to have somewhere to take it before Animal Control takes him. Can you help me?"

Across the table, Andy covered his mouth, laughing hysterically and turning red.

"You have a dead woman's dog and need someone to take it," the man said, confirming. "And it bit someone."

"Yes." My hopes were low, like below the soles of my shoes low. "I think you might have known his owner. I found a tag from one of her other dogs. That's why I called you. Jenn Berg is the name of the deceased."

The phone clattered around, and the man coughed away from the receiver. When he recovered, he said, "I can't help you," in a rush and hung up on me.

"Well, that was rude." I set my phone on the table and propped my chin in my hand, suddenly very tired. "Guess he didn't like Jenn. Maybe she was dating his husband, too."

"You know what I think?" Andy said, picking up handfuls of stuff and shoving it back in my bag. "You need to go on a date of your own. See how Ben likes it."

"You're a vengeful young man," I said, battling back butterflies swarming inside me at the mention of going on a date with a stranger. "First you come up with a brilliant plan to get back at Irene, and now this. Some would think you have it out for the Haymans."

"Only the ones who mess with you," he said and gave me a wink.

I never thought when I was forty my best friend would be a twenty-one-year-old kid who did work on my house, but there it was. Life's a mystery, I guess.

We both stood up when we heard a car door slam out in the driveway. "I'll wrangle the dogs so they don't maul her," Andy said.

"Thanks. I'll let her in."

My head spun a little when I stood up, but by the time I got to the door, I was feeling good. My sister was here! I hadn't seen her in two months and when I lived in Columbus, I didn't go two days without her.

"There's the old lady," Monica called when I opened the front door. "Happy birthday!" Her smile went ear-to-ear, and she carried a big box wrapped in shiny paper with a fancy bow around it. I ran out to help her with her suitcase.

"I'm so glad you're here!" I said, doing my best not to crush my present while hugging her tight.

"What's on the agenda for tonight?" she asked, climbing the porch steps.

"Andy and I are just hanging out. I have some wine ... "

"No." She spun on her heel. "No, no, no. It's your fortieth! We're celebrating. There has to be somewhere to go, even in this no-stop-light town."

"Amen to that," Andy said, appearing in the doorway and taking my gift and Monica's suitcase. "I'm starving. Let's go to Cornerstone. I'll pick up Cass."

Andy and Monica met last time she was in town and the two of them together was like gasoline and fire. They brought out the obnoxious in each other. "Great idea!" she said, giving him a quick hug. "We'll meet you there in an hour."

"This is a woman with a plan," he said to me, pointing to Monica. "Listen and learn."

"Just go get Cass," I said, pushing him toward the sidewalk.

Monica and I entered the house to a symphony of barking. "I thought you were joking when I got your message," she said.

I shook my head. "I was serious. I hope you can take something."

She waved a hand at me. "I got allergy pills two years ago when I was dating that guy with the cat. I should be fine."

"I have one of those, too. A cat. Well, kind of."

"Kind of?" she asked.

"It's complicated. Anyway, I'm glad you got medication. I didn't want you to have to stay somewhere else when you visit."

"Cam, a *pack* of wild dogs couldn't keep me away."

"Good thing," I muttered.

She plopped down on the couch, picking up my gift. "Come open your present."

I sat beside her, eager as a kid to open the bright, shiny package. I untied the bow before ripping into the paper. I paused when I reached the box. The logo on top was from a lingerie store. Gingerly, I lifted the lid. A rose-colored nightie sat folded in the box. It was silky and came with matching underwear, although I questioned my sister's thought process when she picked out the size. Maybe she was trying not to insult me, but I didn't think I could get them over one thigh, let alone two.

Being disappointed over a gift was childish. It was the thought that counted, even if that thought was a bit sketchy. "Thank you. It's beautiful," I said, giving her a hug.

"There's a gift card from Mom and Dad in the box, too. I thought the nightie would give you confidence. Make you feel appealing."

"Appealing?"

Monica took my hand. "Cam, if you and Ben are apart, you have to face the reality of getting back out there again and meeting other men."

"This seems to be a recurring topic tonight. One that I'm not interested in talking about." I put the lid back on the gift box and patted the top.

"Just tell me one thing," she said. "What happened? You keep skirting the issue every time I bring it up."

Could be because I didn't really know. "When we moved here, it was like he was home and I was an outsider. Sure, the townspeople were nice and welcoming, but there was a sense of putting on airs when I was around. Like a guest who had overstayed her welcome. They put out the good towels and fine china for me, but they were getting tired of it and wanted me to go back home already. Ben said it was my imagination, and I just wanted a reason to move back to Columbus."

"Good idea," she said, grasping my hand. "Move back. This isn't the place for you. You and Ben should've dated longer before getting married."

"Don't," I said, taking my hand back. "We're not discussing this." I'd heard it a million times from Monica and our mother. It wasn't that they didn't like Ben, but I didn't give them much time to get to know him. I guess I hadn't given myself a lot of time, either.

"What should we talk about then?" Monica asked. "What's been going on lately?"

"Lately? Oh, the usual. I found a dead woman in the canal. Ben was kind of, sort of dating her, and now I'm a suspect in her murder."

Monica's jaw dropped.

"Oh, those are her dogs in the kitchen. Well, they're mine now."

She blinked a couple dozen times, rapidly. "I told you moving here would ruin your life."

I wasn't in the mood for I told you so's, but she had a point.

9

The Cornerstone was packed. Andy and Cass were already there, sitting at a corner booth in the restaurant area, which was a good idea, because I needed to get some food in me before any more drinks. Carl Finch was standing beside a suit of armor in the corner by the cash register chatting to customers as they paid their bill.

"You have to try the fried chicken," Cass told Monica as we sat down. "It's legendary."

"Legendary, huh?" Monica looked around and wasn't impressed. True, the restaurant could use some sprucing and updating, but the chicken was incredible.

"You'll like it," I said, smacking her leg under the table to get her to behave. It might not have been Columbus with the chain restaurants and every sort of food imaginable available, but it was what we had and we were proud of it. Besides, it wasn't like Columbus was L.A. or anything.

A high school girl took our drink order and brought my iced tea and Monica's water. "There's Dennis Stoddard," Andy said, edging out of the booth. "I didn't know he was in town again. I'm going to go say hi. Be right back."

"Ask about my birdbath!" I called, but he didn't seem to hear me.

Andy approached a man with salt -and -pepper hair who had joined Carl Finch. He looked to be a bit younger than Finch's mid-sixties. Stoddard's glasses, short beard and mustache, and a camel -colored suit jacket all combined to give him a professorial image. I could picture him on PBS's Antiques Roadshow. I needed to get my hands on him before Irene did.

"It's such a shame about the musical," Cass said, stirring an artificial sweetener into her iced tea. "We worked really hard at rehearsals. I guess I should call my guests who made reservations and tell them it's cancelled."

Cass had the bluest eyes and the sweetest disposition. When she looked at you, you couldn't help but be drawn in. "I haven't even thought about calling back everyone who reserved a ticket over the phone," I said, wondering how I'd manage it with one phone line now. "Maybe Melody will come around."

Monica scrolled through emails on her cell phone, unconcerned with our conversation.

"I can't afford cancellations," Cass said, blinking her glassy eyes. "I'm barely able to keep my inn open."

The town relied on people coming and staying, eating and shopping. So many businesses had gone under in the past few years that there were vacant storefronts. Most of the shop owners now worked full-time jobs and only opened on the weekends. These were necessary changes to make a steady income, but detracted from visitors who were drawn by a bustling crowd and store after store of merchandise packed wall-to-wall.

The musical was what the town needed to pull together. It might not have brought in visitors in droves, but it would bring the town together to rally. It would give them the jolt of enthusiasm they desperately needed to push forward and keep trying to make ends meet.

"Did you order for me?" Andy asked Cass as he scooted back in the booth.

"We haven't ordered yet," she said, giving him a shaky smile.

He kissed her temple and took her hand. "Carl thinks my documentary will bring believers into town on religious pilgrimages."

"Wow," I said, "we could be sitting in the midst of greatness. A future award-winning producer/director." I lifted my glass up to him.

"Here's hoping." He clinked his glass against mine. Cass did the same.

"What are we toasting?" Monica asked, lifting her water glass.

"Cam's birthday," Andy said. "Here's to many more."

We ordered the fried chicken, and it was phenomenal as always. Monica complained that it was too peppery.

After dinner we moved over to the bar area, where Roy was holding court with Frank Gardner and Will Atkins. The four of us sat at a high round table by the windows. It didn't take long for Roy to see me and come over to poke his red nose into my business. "Cameron Cripps-Hayman, did you see who was sitting at the end of the bar?"

I glanced down the bar to where a pretty blonde sat drinking something with a cherry and an orange slice propped on the side of the glass. "Is that Melody Winkler?" I asked.

"That it is. Shall we?" Roy held his arm out to me, like a gentleman, to escort me down the bar.

I smacked his arm away and strode past him. "Come on."

I didn't have a plan or any clue what to say, so I was surprised when I stopped beside her and said, "We're looking for a lost puppy. It belonged to Jenn Berg. Have you seen one around town?"

She looked at me like I was one card shy of a full deck. "No. Sorry."

"It's a shame about the musical," I said. "You were in it, right?"

"Not really." She watched the bartender, who happened to be quite attractive, and sipped her drink.

"Oh," I said. "My mistake. I thought Soapy said you were. It's so awful about Jenn. Were you friends? You went to high school together, didn't you?"

She spun her stool toward me. "Do I even know you? It's a small town and all, and you're Ben's wife, or ex-wife or whatever, but we've never been introduced, so it's kind of strange that you're standing here asking me all sorts of questions about Jenn."

"Here's the rub," Roy said, pushing in between us. "It's no secret you and Jenn hated each other. She gets the lead in the musical, you get angry, she ends up dead. Coincidence?"

Melody shot back away from us and huffed. "Are you asking if I killed her?"

"Yes," Roy said, leaning closer to her. "So, did ya?"

"I did not! I was working all night the night she was killed. If Sheriff Reins wants proof, all of the Stature orders I entered have my computer's IP address and are time -stamped. How is this your business anyway?"

"Ya see," he said, waving his thumb back and forth between he and I, "we're The Metamora Action Agency. That's what makes it our business."

"The *what?*" she asked, indignant.

"The—never mind," he said. "You're free to go."

I followed him back to my table with a new appreciation for how Roy handled people. I would've still been standing there making chit-chat and annoying her without ever getting any real information.

"Guess you're still our main suspect, Cameron Cripps-Hayman," Roy said, leaving me and strolling over to retake his seat at the bar.

Somehow I doubted Ben was getting this much grief even though he had much more motive to get rid of Jenn than I did, even if that motive was pure speculation.

Monica had ordered me a champagne spritzer while I was away. "This looks too pretty to drink," I said, picking up the pink fizzy drink with floating berries.

"I wanted pomegranate, but I was lucky they had any fresh berries at all," she said.

I took a sip. "It tastes wonderful, pomegranate or not."

"I still want cake," Andy said. "Tomorrow, we're having cake."

"I'll pop in to see Betty in the morning," I said. "Maybe she'll have one of her German chocolates on hand."

"This bakery just opened downtown," Monica said, rubbing a

sticky spot off the table with her nose turned up. "They have the most incredible Italian cream cakes. Oh, and chocolate ganache, and this white chocolate cheesecake with white chocolate brandy sauce." She groaned and rolled her eyes like she could taste it on her tongue.

"Why didn't you bring one with you?" Andy asked while I was becoming more and more irritated by her clear intention of one-upping everything Metamora had to offer.

"I should have!" she said. "Next time. Unless I convince Cam to move back with me."

I was just about to let out a groan of my own when my phone rang. It was Mia.

"Grandma Irene is driving me crazy," she said, "and my dad says I have to come stay with you since I'll be eaten alive by the monster you let live at the gatehouse if I stay with him."

Happy birthday to me.

I told Mia to come by in the morning, downed my drink, and was ready to go.

"Party pooper," Cass said. "Come on, have another drink. You only turn forty once."

"Don't remind me." I stood and gave her a hug. "Thanks for celebrating with me."

"See you tomorrow, hotshot director," I said, giving Andy a friendly punch on the arm.

"Tomorrow we paint!" he said.

"And eat cake," I reminded him.

On the way out, I had to make a pit stop in the ladies' room, which was right beside a storeroom where Melody had cornered the bartender. Neither of them saw me, so I took my time going into the ladies' room.

"Can you believe they asked me if I killed her?"

"You did hate her, Mel," he said.

"So what! *You're* her ex-boyfriend who was insanely jealous. You would drive by her house to see if another guy was there! That's stalking! Did you kill her, Zach?"

"I did not stalk her!" he shouted, and bottles clattered like he dropped a case of beer.

I hightailed it into the restroom before I got caught in the crossfire, making a mental note to tell the Action Agency we had another suspect to check out: Zach the Bartender/Ex-Boyfriend.

SOMETIME OVERNIGHT A LITTLE troll took up residence in my head and began mining his way out with a pickax. I knew morning was going to be ugly, but it hurt to blink. Vowing to never drink again, I shoved Gus and the twins out of the way and slipped out of bed to swallow about twenty aspirins and guzzle a gallon of water. I'd have killed for something greasy from McDonald's.

Monica was already up, showered, dressed, and made up with liners and eye shadows—the works. "What?" she said when I gave her a dirty look. "I only had one drink."

"Good. You can be in charge of my life today while I go back to bed."

"You can't go back to bed. It's almost nine. Won't your volunteer group be here soon?"

"I should send them to Irene's," I grumbled, pouring a cup of coffee. "She's the one who got me into this whole phone bank thing in the first place." That's when I remembered Mia was coming to stay, and I leaned over and laid my head on the counter.

"What are you doing?" Monica took the coffee from me.

"Resting. This day is exhausting."

The doorbell rang, the dogs went berserk, and then the door opened. "Cam?" Ben called from the foyer.

"We're in here!" Monica shouted.

"Too loud," I said, easing myself upright.

Ben stopped in the entryway of the kitchen with the canine twins jostling around him, staring at me. He held a bouquet of red and white roses in his hand. "Rough night?"

"Something like that." I could only imagine how I looked

standing there with my tangled hair sticking out on end, wearing old flannel pajama pants that hit mid-calf and my ancient robe with penguins all over it. Not that it was anything Ben hadn't seen a million times before, but after six months of not living together, it wasn't the same. The comfort of having him seeing me first thing in the morning wasn't there. I wasn't used to it anymore, and that thought made my stomach feel even sicker.

"These are for you," he said, handing me the roses. "I didn't know if red was welcome, so I had the florist mix in some white."

I wasn't sure if red was welcome either, but the clenching in my chest told me I didn't really have a choice. If only I knew how to get us out of this mess we'd created. "They're beautiful. Thank you."

We stared at each other for a moment, trying to figure out what should happen between us next. Then Ben cleared his throat. "Mia's out front talking to one of your volunteers. Nick, I believe his name was."

"Oh. Nick." My immediate reaction was to run to the door and yank her away, but I didn't figure he'd murder her on my doorstep. Preferably, he wouldn't murder her at all even if she was a big pain in my rear. I didn't believe he was our killer anyway, so the need to protect Mia from him faded as quickly as it came on.

"I'll put these in water," Monica said, taking the bouquet from me. "Why don't you go get dressed?" She gave Ben a conspiratorial wink. "I'm in charge until she can function again."

"I'll be fine once I have my coffee," I said, turning to grab my big mug, and accidentally kicking Isobel. She barked and snapped at me, catching the toe of my slipper.

"Killer dogs everywhere you look," Ben said, while Gus whacked him in the leg with his tail.

"Come on," I said, darting a hand behind Isobel to grab her by the collar. "Outside." I herded my pack of fur and fangs out the back door where they'd stay for the greater part of the day. Thank goodness it was summer. Winter would be a challenge.

"Can I talk to you in private for a minute?" Ben asked, gripping the back of a kitchen chair like it took all of his strength to ask.

"Sure. What about?" I glanced at Monica, who hustled out of the kitchen.

"I talked to my mom. She's agreed to drop the lawsuit."

"Oh, thank goodness, I—"

He held up a hand. "On one condition."

"Of course. What's her one condition? She gets to move back in?"

Ben bit the inside of his cheek. "Not her. Me."

"*What?* How dare she interfere with our marriage?"

"I know. I know. I told her it wasn't a fair condition. She said she doesn't care if it's not fair, that we can't be separated forever, so we either get back together or get divorced, but we need to figure it out."

"That's not her call to make!" I ran my fingers through my hair, catching on a few knots and pulling, which only made me more upset.

"It's not," he said, stepping closer, "but I agree. I don't want to be separated anymore, Cam. I don't want to be divorced, either, but I'd rather do that than live with my marriage in the balance."

My insides went hollow. "You want a divorce?"

"No. Not at all. I want to move on from this. With you. The dogs I can leave or take, but I want resolution. If we can't work it out ... " He shrugged. "I want to try though."

Temptation latched on to my lips, making me want to agree, to tell him to move all of his things back in and we'd go back to how we were when we were first married. But I knew better. I knew we had areas of our marriage to work on, even though I could only remember the good parts at the moment.

"I know we fought a lot after we moved here," he said, tilting his head and glancing at me through his long lashes. My weakness. He could always wear me down with those lashes. "It was hard for you to move here, and I didn't help. I went to work and figured you'd find your place."

"And your mother," I added, not needing to finish the thought.

"My mother," he said, nodding. "She doesn't help matters. It was definitely easier living two hours away. I should've run interference for you. Told her to back off." Ben took me by the hands and pulled me toward him. "Cam, I'm sorry. I dragged you here and figured you'd be as happy as I was. When you weren't, I didn't want to be bothered with it. I was busy trying to make myself indispensable to Finch and Reins." He shook his head. "I'd rather be indispensable to you."

A warm, sloshy sensation flooded my chest and brought tears to my eyes. Ever since moving here, Ben and I argued relentlessly about the lack of time we spent together and how I felt displaced and abandoned. He never saw where I was coming from. Now he finally had. "I wish it hadn't come to this," I said, as he wrapped me in a hug and squeezed me tight.

"It doesn't have to come to this," he said. "I'll come home."

I wanted him to, but six months apart was a long time. We couldn't just snap our fingers and pretend our problems never happened.

I stepped back, straightened his collar, tried to wipe the wet drops of tears from his shoulder, then finally looked up at him. "Let me think about this. I'm not even out of my robe yet, Ben. I can't think clearly with this headache, and my volunteers are homeless. We're working out of here today. I'm trying to keep a lot of balls in the air, so give me some time."

"Okay. There's no hurry. I mean, as far as the lawsuit, there's a timeline, but as far as I'm concerned, if you're thinking about us, then I can wait."

"Just a day or two."

He took my hand and kissed my cheek. "Call me if you need anything, or if Mia gives you any trouble. Reins will probably stop by today. You can't get out of being questioned."

I slumped down in a chair and watched him stroll down the hall, through the foyer, and out the front door. Monica came back in from the living room, looking sheepish. "I might have listened."

"I figured you would," I said, sorting through the rest of the mail from the day before. There was a birthday card from Brenda and one from Soapy and Theresa.

"What are you going to do? You're not going to stay in this place are you? If you let him come back, tell him it's on your one condition: moving back to Columbus into civilization."

I was really in no frame of mind for her newfound snobbery. Frankly, I felt a little snappish, like Isobel. "There is nothing wrong with this town. Ever since you stepped foot in the door last night you've been putting it down. I'm tired of it, so stop."

She leaned against the counter and tapped her nails. "I thought you were sending out resumes to be able to move back?"

"I have."

"And?"

"And I haven't checked my email to see if anyone has responded."

"Why on earth not?"

It was a good question. When I thought about being in Columbus, I thought about my time with Ben. The dates we went on, walking around the Short North Arts District, seeing shows at the Ohio Theater, dinner and movies at Easton and Polaris. It wasn't a booming metropolis like New York City, but it was home. It was what I was used to. Those were the things I missed.

But Ben was here. I was here. What was waiting for me in Columbus?

Plus, I if I was being honest, I guess this place had grown on me at long last. I'd never met a group of neighbors who were closer, who had lived in the same town from one generation to the next for decades when there was nothing to stay for but nostalgia and tradition. They believed in their town. They loved their town, and I supposed I'd grown to love it, too. I wanted to see it thrive.

"This is home now," I said, meaning it, even if I did have to drive to Brookville for McDonald's.

10

Does working from home mean staying in your jammies all day, Cameron Cripps-Hayman?" Roy stood in my kitchen admiring my penguin robe. Everyone had arrived before I even had a chance to get dressed.

"No, Roy. I woke up a little late. Help yourself to some coffee."

"I'm Cameron's sister, Monica," she said. "I'm in charge until she's feeling better."

"You're not in charge. I'm fine. Just going to get dressed." I hustled upstairs to change my clothes. If I were leaving anyone in charge, it would be Anna. "Mia!" I yelled behind me. "Come up here, please!"

She didn't exactly hurry, so I was fully dressed before she knocked. "What?" she yelled through the door.

I opened the door and let her in, gesturing for her to follow me to the bathroom. "Your dad said you were talking with Nick."

"So?"

"So," I said, tearing a brush through my hair, "he's too old for you, and he's here because he was sentenced to do community service for assault. He's not exactly someone your father or I want you to be hanging around with."

"We were *talking,* Cameron. *Talking*. Okay?"

"As long as it stays just talking. Now, I need you to run to Grandma's Cookie Cutter to get a cake. German chocolate if she has it. If not, let her pick."

"Whatever."

"And Mia? If you keep rolling your eyes they're going to get stuck that way."

She gave me a snort of derision and left the room. If she came back without a cake, I decided I'd toss her out back with the dogs.

Downstairs, Johnna had made herself at home with her knitting in my dining room. I should've locked up the silver before inviting her over. Of course, the upside of Johnna's sleight-of-hand in my house was that there might not be anything left for Irene to take. She'd have to buy all of her cherished heirlooms back from Canal Town Treasures.

Roy had gone outside and was pestering Andy while he set up ladders and got ready to start painting the house. I probably couldn't count maintenance work as approved service hours for Roy, but I had no desire to drag him back inside.

"The Action Agency line will be switched over in a day or two," Anna said, sitting at the kitchen table with Logan.

"I called and said I was you," Monica told me, making another pot of coffee. "I told you I could be in charge."

"Okay, well, thanks for handling that." I wasn't sure I wanted my sister to impersonate me even if she was only being helpful. Her intention seemed to be controlling my life from every angle.

Nick stood at the French doors watching the dogs outside. "Want one?" I asked, sidling up beside him. "They're free. Two for one if you want the twins."

He chuckled but shook his head. "I don't think so."

Anna was staring holes through my back, surely waiting for me to start asking Nick questions about his argument with Jenn. But if there was one thing I'd learned from this whole situation, it was that I was a terrible detective. How does a person ask someone if they're a murderer? I should know, I'd had my share of accusations flung at me over the past couple of days. Maybe that's why I couldn't do it.

Despite my normal lack of tact, I knew what it felt like to be wrongly accused.

But what if I wasn't wrong? Or what if I was right—I mean, what if Nick was the one who killed Jenn? I had every right to ask him. We got a tip on our action line; I couldn't ignore it.

Logan stood up from the table and waved to a stack of poster board. "Anna and I made these in case you wanted us to post them around town to replace the other ones. They have your home number on them, so we won't have any downtime while the phone company switches the tip line over. They say the first forty-eight hours in an investigation are the most critical, and we're past that. I don't think we should take a break because Reverend Stroup disrupted our command center."

"Command center," I said, liking the feel of the words rolling off my tongue. "You're right. We can't afford to lose any more time. You two go hang them up."

If we were really and truly going to make a go of the Metamora Action Agency, then we had to be all in. Nobody could put us off of our goal of finding the killer. But what happened when my crew of volunteers fulfilled their assigned hours? How would I keep them on if the case hadn't yet been solved?

What started out as making calls to reserve seats for the musical become so much more. Anyone could make calls to sell tickets, but it took a lot more dedication to help solve a murder. My crew was irreplaceable now, despite their shortcomings and annoyances. We had to hurry, not just because the forty-eight hour window Logan mentioned was over, but because this case had to be closed before any of them fulfilled their community service hours. Off the top of my head, that gave us about a week until they started dropping from my program—Roy first, followed by Nick and Johnna.

Logan and Anna hurried off, leaving me with a well-meaning sister and Nick, who I somehow had to bolster my courage enough to question.

Maybe after one more cup of coffee.

I'd just poured a cup when Mia's screechy voice met my ears from out front. "Sounds like trouble out there," Johnna called from the dining room. Her knitting needles clattered on the table, and she was hurrying across the carpet. For an old lady, she could move when she wanted to, and there was no way she was missing out on the commotion.

Monica and I followed her to the front door, Nick behind us. Mia stood in the middle of the front yard, cradling a cookie jar in one hand and a cake box in the other. Her eyes and mouth were open wide as she stared, aghast, at my house. "Grandma Irene is going to kill you!" she shouted at me. "How could you do this?"

I stepped farther out on the sidewalk and turned to see the offense. "Oh, she'll grow to love it," I said. "It's pretty!"

Andy had painted one shutter and one board of the siding to test the paint colors: a bright sea foam green for the siding and lavender for the shutters. "It's eye -catching," Andy said. "Much better than that boring white. Anyone can have a white house."

"But ... " For once, Mia was at a loss for words. She was even too horrified to roll her eyes.

"Did Betty have German chocolate?" I asked, taking the cake box.

Mia nodded, still transfixed by my choice of color palette. "She said to give you this, too." She handed me the small cookie jar shaped like a beehive.

"I'll take that," Monica said, swiping the cake box from my hand. "Mia, close your mouth, you're catching flies."

Mia clamped her mouth shut and flung herself around. "I'm going to the Soda Pop Shop to see Stephanie. She's so upset, she needs me to pick out her outfit for the calling hours tomorrow."

"Be back before dinner," I called to her retreating form.

I needed to order flowers to be delivered to the funeral home and find something to wear, myself. Walking into Jenn's calling hours with half the town thinking I was the reason she was lying in the casket would be the most awkward situation I'd ever been in. But if I didn't go, the speculation would multiply like Metamora Mike's progeny. He was one duck whose family tree would never die out.

"What do you want us to do with no phones, Cameron Cripps-

Hayman?" Roy tucked his hands in the pockets of his dirty navy sports coat that he wore no matter how high the temperature climbed.

"Let's go inside and figure something out," I said, carrying the cookie jar up the porch steps and into the house.

"I could go for a cookie," he said, peering over my shoulder.

"Jeez, let me get the lid off." I set the jar on the counter and tugged off the airtight lid. Inside were about half a dozen bone-shaped biscuits and a recipe card. "I hate to break it to you, Roy, but Betty sent these cookies for the dogs."

"I don't mind," he said, sticking his hand in and grabbing one. Before I could tell him to at least wait until I read the ingredients, he had a big hunk in his mouth. "Tasty," he said, spraying crumbs onto the counter.

"Let's see the recipe," Johnna said, snatching it from my hand and looking it over. "All regular, human ingredients in them. I bet they'd be even better with a bit of bacon and cheese though."

She strolled over to my fridge and yanked the door open. "Bacon bits would last longer. You have any of those, Cam?"

"I saw some in the cupboard," Monica said, joining in the fun.

"You need a mold to make 'em bone shaped." Roy nudged Nick's shoulder. "Let's go see what we can find in the shed to jerry-rig together."

Making dog treats was definitely not community service approved work, but we were keeping an eye on Nick, and until I could question him and prove him innocent, I decided that was close enough. Plus we were caring for orphaned dogs, so it was like volunteering at an animal shelter, right?

After justifying baking dog biscuits, I felt much better about the whole operation.

"Where do you keep your wheat flour?" Johnna asked, plopping a block of cheddar on the counter.

"I'm not sure I have any." I wasn't a baker. Every attempt I made resulted in the smoke detector going off. Ben eventually took the batteries out of the one closest to the kitchen.

I rooted through the pantry and found some cornmeal from the grist mill tucked in the pantry. "Will this work?" I asked.

"Dogs can eat corn," Johnna said. "We'll give it a try."

We assembled the measuring cups and spoons along with the ingredients and a large bowl. "Now what?" I asked, my hands starting to tremble.

"Follow the directions," Monica said in a tone like I was a kindergartner.

"It's not that easy for me. I follow the directions and still end up with charcoal."

"Let's preheat the oven," Johnna said, reaching for the buttons on my stove. "What's the temperature?"

"Three fifty." I checked and double-checked the recipe card to be sure.

"Don't hyperventilate," Monica said, patting me on the back. "You're baking for a pack of wild dogs, not the Queen of England."

"Why does it feel like they're judging me already?" I peered out the window to where Gus and the twins were attempting to de-limb my weeping cherry while Isobel snoozed under the picnic table.

"Those dogs would eat the tires off a monster truck," Johnna said, plucking a wooden spoon out of the utensil holder beside the stove. "Now measure out the ingredients and mix 'em all up." She handed me the spoon, and it might as well have been the Olympic torch for as important as it felt in my grasp.

"I'll do my best." I took one more look out the window to my furry tribe and picked up the beef stock.

After all the ingredients were added and a ball of dough sat in the bottom of the bowl, I poured it out onto a strip of parchment paper and used the rolling pin I got for a wedding gift (and never used) to spread the mixture to a half an inch thickness.

"Where are your cookie cutters?" Monica asked."I'm assuming they're at Betty's," I said, "since that's where I buy my cookies."

"You don't have cookie cutters? Even I have cookie cutters."

My sister, the sophisticate. Even *she* had cookie cutters. Where was Mia when I needed a good eye roll?

"We can just break it into pieces," Johnna said. "The dogs aren't going to care."

It was nice having Johnna helping me. My mom was good at a lot of things—mostly things related to being a public relations consultant—but cooking was never one of them. I didn't have anyone to pick up kitchen tricks from or teach me favorite family recipes. I'd hoped I'd find that in a mother-in-law, but all I managed to get was grief from Irene. She gave up on asking me to bring a dish for holidays, or inviting me to potlucks about two months after Ben and I were married. Her enthusiasm for his second marriage was not long -lived.

I transferred the parchment paper with the rolled -out biscuit dough to a cookie sheet, popped it in the oven and set the timer for thirty minutes. "Wait and see," I said. "It'll be black on the bottom when it comes out."

Johnna tapped a finger to her lips, looking over the buttons and dials on the oven. "When you bake, do you use the convection setting or the regular button here that says bake?"

"I usually use convection. Isn't that what you're supposed to use for baking cakes and things?"

"Only if you take some baking time off the recipe and lower the temperature. Unless it says it's the time and temperature to use in a convection oven. It'll cook a bit faster and hotter. That's why you're burning the tar out of everything."

"I had no idea."

The front door squealed opened. "Cam?" Andy called. "Sheriff Reins is here to see you."

"This place is a zoo," Monica said with a sigh.

"It's not normally like this." My stomach did the jitterbug. No more putting off Reins. "I'm coming!" I called to Andy and strode through the hallway toward the door and my fate. When I stepped outside, my life would be in the hands of a man with a badge who was unable to speak aloud about a dead body. How was that fair? What qualified him over me to question suspects and solve this murder case?

Probably something qualified him, but in the midst of bolstering my bravado I wasn't going to admit it.

I squared my shoulders and turned the door handle. The bright sun blasted me, and I had to blink a few dozen times, shading my eyes with a hand. It wasn't exactly the swagger down the porch steps I'd been aiming for, but at least I didn't trip and fall. "How are you, Sheriff Reins?"

"Doing well, thanks," he said, tipping the brim of his hat. "I was hoping you had a few minutes to finish our talk."

"I'm baking biscuits, but I just put them in, so I have a few minutes."

"I'll make it quick," he said. "Nick Valentine wouldn't happen to be volunteering for you today, would he?"

Oh good gravy. I knew I should point Reins in the direction of my shed, but a mama bear protective streak came over me. Nobody was going to get to Nick before I did.

I glanced at Andy, and like always, he got my hint and headed toward the shed to keep Nick tucked away safe inside. "No," I said, willing my voice to stay steady. "He's not volunteering today."

Reins nodded, but I could tell he didn't believe me. Ben probably told him Nick was here. Nick and Mia were talking only a couple hours ago right in this very spot. "Come inside," I said, hoping to get Reins back on the subject of me finding Jenn's body. It seemed the least likely topic to get me arrested today.

"It smells good in here," he said, as we strolled through the door. "What kind of biscuits are those?"

"Bacon cheddar. They might be the first thing I've ever baked that actually turns out edible."

I ushered Reins into the dining room and pulled the pocket doors closed on nosy Johnna and controlling Monica. "Would you like some coffee, Officer Reins?" I asked, pushing aside Johnna's knitting.

"No, thank you. I just had a cup." He sat down across the table from me and took out a notebook. "So, Mrs. Hayman, you knew the um ... the uh ... "

"Dead body?" I supplied.

"Yes. You knew it was a woman. How did you know this?"

"It's not hard to distinguish a female's hand from a male's. From her slender fingers and nails, I assumed it was a woman."

"And your whereabouts the night before you found Miss Berg?"

"I was here."

"Alone?"

"Well, Andy Beaumont was here for a while—Andy's always here if he's not filming—but he probably left around seven."

"Probably around seven p.m.?"

"Yes. But I don't remember that exact evening."

"So it's possible Mr. Beaumont had not been here at all."

I gripped Johnna's ball of yarn tightly under the table. "He's usually here."

Reins tapped his pen on the notepad. "Did you know Miss Berg was dating your husband?"

"They weren't dating. He said they went out a couple times, but that's it. Anyway, no, I didn't know until after I found her in the canal."

"So, you didn't know she was pregnant and seeing your husband?"

"He says they never even kissed!" Heat was creeping up my chest. This line of questioning was making it hard to hide my anger. How could Ben date—go out with, do *anything* with —a girl that young? And after only six months of separation?

"You look agitated, Mrs. Hayman."

"I'm not agitated."

I was seriously agitated. Three days after Jenn Berg is found dead, Ben's giving me conditions to move back in? If she wasn't dead, would he want to come back or would he be taking her to dinner and a movie tonight?

"What is the Metamora Action Agency?" he asked.

"Oh, that?" I swallowed hard, not expecting this swing in direction. "Since the musical is on hold, we're using the phone bank as a tip line to help find the person responsible."

"And what are you doing with these tips?"

"We'll turn them over to you. Of course." I gave him what I hoped was an earnest smile.

"You haven't received any yet?"

I shook my head. Too many lies. I couldn't get my tongue to tell any more.

Reins shot me a stern, narrow-eyed look. I didn't think he'd bought anything I told him since he stepped foot on my property.

He tucked his pen away and closed his notebook. "If you see Nick Valentine, let me know. I need to speak with him."

"Okay." I stood from the table and slid the pocket doors open, relieved to see Johnna and Monica on the other side—polar opposite lifelines in the melee my life had become.

The timer on the oven beeped, and Johnna took the dog biscuits out. "Not burned a bit," she said.

"Those smell so good, my stomach's grumbling," Reins said.

"I'll wrap a few pieces for you to take with you," I said, grabbing my foil.

"That's very kind of you, Mrs. Hayman," he said.

Monica sucked in her lips, doing her best not to laugh, while Johnna broke off a couple flat chunks and slid them on the foil.

"Here you go," I said, handing over the shiny wrapped package.

There was nothing in them that wasn't human food, but knowing I just handed the sheriff a stack of freshly baked dog treats to eat filled me with redemption, because I did not kill Jenn Berg, and it wasn't my fault that my husband was dating—or whatever-ing—her.

"Enjoy!"

11

I'm going for a walk," I said, desperately in need of a few minutes away from my house. Between the dogs and the Action Agency crew and my sister—let's not forget Mia—I had to get away. Reins was the topper to my insane day.

Nick was leaving too. The train was set to depart in twenty minutes back to Connersville. "I'll walk you to the station," I told him. It was now or never.

We made our way past Schoolhouse Antiques and the Cookie Cutter before either of us said a word. Finally, I stopped trying to think of a tactful way to broach the subject and blurted it out. "Nick, we got a tip that you were seen arguing with Jenn the day before she was found."

"I figured somebody saw us," he said.

"I wanted to talk to you about it before Sheriff Reins found out, but he came by today and asked for you. I told him you weren't volunteering today. Since I lied to a police officer, do you think you can tell me what you were arguing with her about?"

"It was nothing," he said, running a hand over his head.

"You don't talk a lot," I said. "You don't like opening up to people. I get that. But I'm trying to help you. What were you arguing about, Nick?"

He rubbed his forehead like he was debating what to say. "She owed a friend of mine some money. That's it. It wasn't a big deal."

"How much money? For what?"

"Five hundred. For a puppy."

"The missing puppy?" My heart sped up to about a million beats a minute. Money owed, a missing puppy—this could be a valid lead.

"I guess. Is it missing?" The lack of concern in his voice piqued my suspicion. Did he not care that a woman he knew, at least in passing, was dead?

"It is missing," I said. "Did your friend take it back?"

He shrugged. "No idea. You can call him and ask."

"Fine. Who do I need to call to get some answers, Nick?" I was two seconds from screaming. There we were—the Metamora Action Agency—traipsing over to Brookville and setting up a tip line, and Nick had information the entire time.

He knew something. His friend was involved—or *he* was involved. Maybe both of them. I had to find that missing puppy. If Nick's friend had the dog, he had to have gotten it from Jenn, and if he did come and get the pup, did he use force to take it?

"She got the dog from Cory Bantum," Nick said and spit over the side of the wooden bridge into the canal.

Cory Bantum. Bantum ... That name was familiar. "How do I reach him?"

"You have the number. You called him to take her dogs."

"I did? I—" Bantum Kennels! The number on the dog tag Old Dan found and gave to me. No wonder the man who answered was so rude when I mentioned Jenn Berg. He might have killed her!

I was breathing so hard, and my heart was pounding so fast, I was light-headed. I had to get it together. If Nick, who had already been arrested for assault, was involved in killing Jenn Berg, he wouldn't think twice about taking me out before I turned him in to Reins or Ben.

I shrugged. "Hmm. I don't remember. Oh well. I guess the Action Agency can look for the dog. That would be helpful."

"Yeah," he said, grabbing hold of the handrail and stepping up into the train. "See ya Monday."

"Right. See ya," I muttered.

I needed to think, get a handle on the situation. Should I turn all the information over to Reins, or would that look like a desperate attempt to divert his attention from me?

It felt too early. I needed more solid evidence. Just because Jenn owed five hundred dollars for a puppy that was now missing, and she was seen arguing with Nick about the money ... okay, it looked bad. Andy would know what to do. He'd at least provide me with an outside perspective. I'd sit on this until I could talk to him about it.

"Cameron?" I turned around, hearing my name called. Roger Tillerman, the train conductor, walked toward me.

"Hi, Roger. How've you been?" Roger was probably in his early sixties. He was starting to get the droopy jowls that older men get, and his blue eyes always looked watery, but he wasn't a bad -looking man. You could tell he was probably a lady-killer when he was younger.

"I've been good. I hear you've been busy fighting crime." His bright smile told me he approved and wasn't making fun.

"We're doing our part," I said. "Since the musical is cancelled, I needed something for my volunteers to do to get their service hours."

"I think it's a great idea. Like a neighborhood crime watch group."

"Exactly!" Finally, someone got it and didn't seem skeptical.

The train whistle blared, making me jump.

"I should board, but I was hoping I'd run into you soon." Roger clasped his hands together like he was about to give a sermon. "Tomorrow, the train is making an evening run through town for a dinner stop at the Briar Bird Inn. I'd be honored if you would accompany me."

It took me a moment to understand he was asking me out. To dinner. Tomorrow. A man hadn't asked me out in over four years.

Ben had no problem in that area, obviously. And because of his escapades, I was a suspect in his little friend's murder.

That settled it. "I'd like that," I said, only feeling slightly sick at the idea of going on a date with a man who was old enough to be my father and had droopy jowls and watery eyes.

"Great!" Roger said, unclasping and clasping his hands again. "I'll pick you up at Ellsworth House at four o'clock tomorrow afternoon."

"I'll be ready," I said, resisting the urge to run. It still hadn't rained, so my knee wouldn't make it very far anyway. I'd end up sitting on the ground stewing in my own embarrassment.

"See you then," he said, giving me another big smile before turning to the train. "Oh," he said, looking back. "It's a Civil War –era dinner, so dress appropriately."

My brain froze. Civil War era? Dress appropriately? Like petticoat and corset? *Good gravy.* What did I get myself into now?

MIA WAS LATE GETTING HOME. It was eight o'clock, well past dinner-time, and she wasn't answering her cell phone. "I should call Ben," I said, popping a chocolate chip cookie in my mouth and tossing Gus a homemade dog biscuit. The dogs loved them. It was my one success for the day.

"She'll show up," Monica said, tapping away on my laptop.

"I thought you took time off. Why are you working?" Monica worked for our mom, coordinating marketing plans for Mom's public relations clients. They used to pass along some of their telephone marketing to the company I worked for. The Cripps women were quite the power trio.

"I'm not working. I'm answering your emails. You have twelve interview requests in here."

"I'm not—how'd you get—I'm not going on interviews!" I rushed over to the kitchen table and slammed the laptop closed. "Don't try to run my life, Monica. I'm doing just fine on my own."

"Is that why you're being questioned by the police, dating a geriatric train conductor, adopting untrained mongrels, and pretending to be Jessica Fletcher? Your life is out of control, Cameron."

"It's not your job to fix it!" I banged my hand on the table, making Isobel bark and growl from beside the fridge. I sank down into a chair and put my head in my hands. "Listen, I know you're trying to help, and I admit, my life is nuts right now, but I need to handle things my way. If I need your help, I'll ask. Okay?"

She took a deep breath and let it out. "Do you promise?"

"Yes. I promise."

She held up her hands and scooted back from my laptop. "Fine. Done."

"Thank you." I sat back and laughed, immediately thinking of something she could do for me.

"What?" she asked.

"I do need your help with something. I need a Civil War –era evening dress for tomorrow."

"For the calling hours?" She cocked an eyebrow, looking at me like my sanity had cracked.

"No. For my date with the geriatric train conductor after the calling hours. He's taking me to a Civil War dinner."

She blinked a few times hard, exaggerating. "Please tell me you're joking."

"I wish I were."

"And where am I supposed to find that?"

"Maybe start next door at Schoolhouse Antiques. I doubt Will will have a dress, but he'll probably know where you can get one."

"Well, I better start searching now if you need it tomorrow afternoon."

"I'll call around while you're next door. Somebody in this town will have a Civil War dress. Trust me."

I got on my phone while Monica went to talk to Will. It was a delicate situation, planning a date on the same day as Jenn's calling hours and having to ask everyone in town if they had a dress and petticoats I could borrow. I figured I'd start with Judy Platt, Cass's mom, who owned the Briar Bird Inn where the dinner was being held.

"I'm sorry, Cam," Judy said, "I have no clue where you could find a dress. Most people get their Civil War clothes from collectors' shows, I believe."

"Would it be terrible if I just wore a regular dress?"

"No, of course not. Especially when you were invited last minute. *Men*."

I hung up feeling a little bit better. I'd wear something long, at least, and put my hair up to try to blend in if Monica had no luck.

Mia came bursting through the door, chattering on her phone a mile a minute and bounded up the stairs. I knew I should go after her and rein her in with some form of discipline, but I had no idea what I could do to her, and I didn't have the strength left to do it anyway. I was sticking with my motto: she was fed, sheltered, and alive, so I had done my job. If Ben wanted a stepmother and not just a babysitter, he should've thought of that before our marriage went off the rails.

I chomped down one last cookie before putting them away and heading upstairs to read in bed. Tomorrow would be another fun-filled day starting with Jenn's calling hours and ending with my date circa 1861.

12

The funeral home was jam packed, wall-to-wall for Jenn Berg's mid-morning calling hours. Mia spotted her dad standing near the front of the room wearing a well-fitted black suit (I could never get him to wear a suit) and made a beeline for him. Her grandpa intercepted her and gave her a big hug.

If Stewart Hayman was around, Irene would be lurking nearby. Knowing I'd be out of the house for an hour or so, she probably took the opportunity to send her workers over to unhinge and confiscate my front door.

I got in line to pay my respects. Sue Nelson stood beside the coffin with her other daughters, Lianne, and Mia's friend, Stephanie. Andrew Berg, Sue's ex-husband, stood on the opposite side of the coffin.

Unable to stand still, Elaina Nelson, hair bright red as ever, dressed in black and white polka dots and black patent leather shoes, paced around all of them accepting hugs and condolences, but by the way she smiled and laughed, it was pretty clear she had very little recollection of why she was even standing there. I guessed that happened when you were over ninety years old. Of course, she would tell you she was only twenty-three, being born on February twenty-ninth of a leap year. Technically, it was true, but she was the only senile twenty-three -year -old member of AARP I'd ever met.

"Quite the crowd," Brenda said, easing in behind me.

"You're cutting in line," I whispered.

"I don't think anyone's going to make a fuss about not getting to the casket sooner," she said. "I hear you're in need of a Civil War dress."

"News gets around fast," I said, taking a few steps forward, following the person in front of me.

"When were you going to tell me about your hot date?"

I gave her a Mia-style eye roll. "As soon as I get a hot date."

She chuckled under her breath. "No, I don't suppose Roger Tillerman and a reenactment dinner can be categorized as hot. Why did you agree to go out with him? Are you attracted to him?"

"Are you kidding? I mean, he's a very nice man, but he's got to be close to my dad's age. And I agreed to dinner before he sprung the Civil War deal on me. Then he got on the train and was gone before I could make up an excuse to back out."

"But why did you agree to a date in the first place?"

My eyes found Ben again. Soapy's wife, Theresa, was giving him a hug. People felt sorry for him because his girlfriend was dead. "I guess because Ben moved on, so I should, too."

"Do you really believe that? That he moved on?"

"I don't know. Maybe not. He did go out with her a couple times though. How can I decide what I want if I haven't ventured out on a date, too?"

"You think you might want Tillerman over Ben?" She chuckled again.

"Stop laughing. It's impolite. A woman is dead up there."

It took us another fifteen minutes to get to Sue and her girls. Elaina was flitting around the viewing room with a coffee pot refilling paper cups and talking everyone's ears off. "How are you holding up?" I asked Sue.

Sue pursed her lips and gazed over my head. "As well as expected," she said.

I got the feeling she wasn't just struggling to hold back tears. She was giving me the cold shoulder. "If there's anything I can do," I said, "please let me know."

"I can't imagine what you could possibly do."

I bowed my head and moved on. There was no saving myself in Sue's eyes. Maybe someday soon she and I could sit down and talk, but the speculation must have gotten to her. I was a suspect in her eyes.

I sidestepped in front of the coffin and looked down at the young woman whose death controlled the puppet strings of my life. Sue had her dressed in a white gown—

Wait a minute. It was a wedding dress. A handmade, old-fashioned wedding dress that I'd seen before in photos of Sue's wedding to Andrew. Her mother had worn it, too. Now she was burying her daughter in it—in the dress she probably would've worn to her own wedding someday.

To Ben?

I gave myself a mental smack for that thought. It was difficult to be appropriately sentimental when battling with possessive feelings over my estranged husband.

Someone gripped my arm and jerked me back. "Don't look at her!" Sue shouted, pulling me away from the coffin. "You hated her! You don't care that she's dead! You were jealous that she was with your husband! You probably killed her!"

The room quickly became a maelstrom of activity. People rushed around us, trying to guide Sue away, but her fingers were still latched tightly onto my arm. "How dare you show your face here!" she yelled, tears streaming down her cheeks. "You didn't even send flowers!"

Oh, good gravy, the flowers.

"I meant to. I forgot. I'm so sorry."

"Let's go." Ben had me by the shoulders, walking me backward as Andrew yanked Sue's hand off me. Her nails caught and left red scratches on my wrist.

I turned and dashed out of the room, Ben beside me and Brenda on my heels. I could still hear Sue wailing behind us. "I have to get out of here," I wheezed.

Ben pushed the exit door open and held it for me, while Brenda grabbed my elbow and shuffled me outside. "I think I'm in shock," I said. "Everything's spinning. Did that just really happen?"

"It did," Ben said. "Cam, I think—"

"This is *your* fault!" I swung my giant handbag around and whacked him in the side. "You couldn't even wait until we were divorced to find someone else! Then she goes and gets killed and everyone thinks it was me who did it in some jealous rage!"

He grabbed my bag so I couldn't hit him again. "I told you, I did not find someone else. We were friends. We went out a few times and talked. About you. You know how people in this town talk. That's not my fault."

"You couldn't have found someone who wasn't a twenty-five -year -old female to talk to, Ben? *Really?*"

He let go of my bag and backed away, shaking his head and holding his hands up in defeat. "There's nothing I can say right now to make this better. I'm just going to go before I make it any worse."

I felt like I might collapse right there in the parking lot. "Let's get you home," Brenda said.

"I can't leave. Mia's still inside."

"Give me your keys. I'll go back in and give them to her. You can't drive in this condition anyway. She can bring your car home."

I dug my keys out of my bag and handed them to her. "You know I didn't have anything to do with Jenn's death, don't you?"

"Would I be driving you home if I thought you did?" She wrapped her arms around my shoulders and pulled me in for a hug. It felt so nice to have someone on my side, I started to weep. "And anyway," she said, stepping back and pulling a tissue from her pocket, "if you were capable of murder, you would've killed Irene a long time ago."

"Don't I know it," I said and blew my nose.

After the disastrous calling hours, it was more important than ever to clear my name. In a few hours, I'd have to go to a dinner at the Briar Bird Inn and have people stare and whisper about me and what happened with Sue Nelson. How much humiliation could a person take in one day?

"Why are your eyes so puffy?" Monica asked, breezing into my bedroom. "I found you a Civil War dress."

She held up a plastic bag on a hanger and untied the bottom. "Ready?" she asked, and whisked the plastic up over a giant Scarlett O'Hara hoop dress in deep crimson.

"Where did you get that?"

"I drove an hour to a costume shop in Cincinnati," she said, confirming my suspicion.

"It's a Halloween costume," I said, realizing she answered the question I'd asked myself right before she came in: apparently a person could take a boatload of humiliation in one day.

"It's the only thing I could find," she said, tossing it beside me on the bed. "I looked everywhere."

"Thanks," I said. "It'll work fine." I had to wear it. She drove an hour to get it for me.

"How were calling hours?"

"I can't even put the experience into words," I said, covering my eyes with my hands.

"That bad, huh?"

"Worse. Worse times a hundred."

"Maybe you need to lay low for a while. Call off this date. Take a hot bath, read a book, go to bed early."

I groaned and rolled onto my side. "I can't call off the date. I don't have his number."

"Well, who cares? It's his job, so he has to be there anyway. It's not like he has to take a date. When he comes, I'll tell him you're in bed sick." She patted my bum knee. "It's not a crime to break a date when you don't feel well, and mentally, you're not well."

"Gee, thanks for the psych evaluation." I grabbed the pillow and stuffed it over my head. "You're right. I'm not mentally well at all. I need to be sent away, locked up. Tranquilized."

"I don't think they have asylums anymore. Although they may have them here. This town is stuck somewhere around 1920."

"If you find one, admit me."

"On my honor," she said.

The dress bag rattled and the mattress sunk where she climbed up beside me. "I should've been around more the past six months. Here you are stuck in Mayberry with no family other than Ben's, and I'm pretty sure they don't count. I should've come right away when you told me Ben moved out. I'm sorry I didn't, Cam."

I rolled back over and scooted up to lean against the headboard beside her. "Today is the low point. I was handling it all, taking it in stride, until today. I thought our separation was a hiccup. No big deal. We needed some time apart, but we'd be back together in no time. At first, the days and weeks went by at a snail's pace. Then, before I knew it —bam! Six months, and I find out he's been hanging around with a girl almost half my age and the whole town knew about it. But I didn't know about it. And now the whole town is pointing an accusing finger at me."

Monica brushed a stray hair back from my eyes and took my hand. She didn't say a word. What was there to say? Nothing would make it better.

"I'm a victim, too." It sounded ridiculous to say after attending the calling hours of a woman who fulfilled the very definition of the word victim, but it felt right.

"The victim of hurt feelings," Monica confirmed, squeezing my hand. "The victim of a marriage going through a rough spot. The victim of a gossipy town. And every day, you do your part. Play your role. I couldn't believe you were doing so well when I got here. I'd be hiding under my bed with a bag of Doritos and a bottle of wine if I were in your shoes."

"Don't look under the bed."

She bent sideways and hung over the side of the bed. "More cookies, Cam?"

"Don't touch. Those are my emergency stash."

"You're like a chipmunk stocking up for winter."

"Don't mock me. Cookies are the only source of happiness I have left." I tugged her back up, and we sat side-by-side.

"You're so dramatic," she said.

"Then the Scarlett O'Hara costume is appropriate."

"If only we were from the south."

"If we lived in the south, I'd have to wear a bathing suit a lot more often. And eat fewer cookies. And the south has big bugs and snakes."

"You're right. This place is much better."

I snuggled down a little lower and rested my head on her shoulder. "I don't think I'm ready for Ben to move back home. I want him to. I want it to work out. I want to stay together, but I can't do it yet. I can't get over the fact that he went out with someone else."

"He should understand that. Maybe after he hears about your date tonight, he'll understand a lot better."

"I'm sure Roger Tillerman will make him jealous." I laughed. "He's such an Adonis."

"He's another man. That's all it takes. Don't discount it."

"I feel bad about leaving you when you're here visiting. I should've never accepted tonight."

"Are you planning a late night?" She gave me a wink and a sly smile.

"Hardly. Anyway, Mia should be rolling in any minute. She was bringing my car back from the calling hours. Since she's been gone so long, I'm guessing she went to Sue's with Stephanie, or she's with Ben or her grandparents. I'll make dinner before I go. She'll probably spend the whole night in her room on her phone."

"Please, don't cook. We'll manage."

"It's no trouble," I said, easing my bad knee off the bed to stand.

"It's not about trouble, Cam. Let's not pretend you can cook."

I whipped my dress bag off the bed and swung it over my shoulder. "Frankly, my dear sister, I don't give a damn."

Gus barked in agreement, bounded on the bed and began licking Monica relentlessly. "Stop!" she yelled. "Down!"

"You got it right," I said. "They're untrained mongrels. Nothing you can do to stop him." The twins came running in, ready to join the action. "Now you're really in for it," I said as they hopped up and landed on her legs, flinging fur and slobber in their wake.

"Remember when I was little and I wanted a dog?" she shouted between all the barks and pants. "I take it back!"

"Well, I'd love to help you, but I have to hop in the shower and get ready for my date."

"Cam! Get them off me!"

Gus, a full-grown male Newfoundland, had to weigh a good one hundred and fifty pounds. The other two were about sixty a piece. Their enthusiasm was going to crush her if I didn't pull them off. "Hang on, let me get a few treats!" I yelled.

I took the stairs as fast as my gimpy knee would let me, grabbed three fresh biscuits from the beehive jar on the kitchen counter, and climbed back up to my bedroom. "Here guys!" I called. "Treats!" The magic of the T word had them off the bed in two seconds flat. I tried commanding them by saying, "Sit!" like Betty had done by the canal, but I only got a few deep knee bends and tail wags in response.

We'd work on it.

13

I look like a Valentine," I said, gazing in the mirror at myself all dolled up in Scarlett O'Hara's red dress. "All frills and ruffles."

"It's very ... wide, isn't it?" Monica said, standing behind me, examining the dress with her head cocked to the side.

I spun around, knocking her back a step with my hoop skirt. "Wide isn't a descriptive word a woman wants to hear before a date."

The doorbell rang, and the dogs went ballistic. "I'll go get that," she said, "so you can make your grand entrance down the staircase."

"Hysterical," I muttered as she strode out of my bedroom.

I was having a shoe crisis. I couldn't wear heels with my knee acting up, and the only flats I owned had thick rubber soles and laces. I could get away with the black ones if I wore pants, like this morning to the dreaded calling hours, but with this dress, I might as well be wearing gardening boots. But I couldn't go barefoot. Not that it would matter with my giant dress on. Nobody would see my feet.

I tied on the black shoes with the thick rubber soles and hoped for the best. At the bedroom door I stopped with the doorknob in my grasp, trepidation knocking the wind out of me.

I was going on a date. *Why* was I going on a date? This wasn't a man I wanted to spend time with. This was getting even with Ben, and it made me sick to my stomach.

Too late to back out now. I rolled my shoulders around a few times, trying to relax, and forced myself out into the hallway. The trek down the stairs felt like a slippery descent into adultery. But Ben and I were separated, and he'd tested out the waters, so why shouldn't I? Anyway, there was nothing more than friendship between Roger and I. I was accompanying an elderly friend to a Civil War dinner. There was no romance in that. No testing of another man's waters—or whatever.

First the bottom step came into view, then the hardwood floor in the foyer, followed by two pairs of feet—Monica's and a pair in shiny black men's shoes. Those men's shoes almost had me running right back up the steps, but my knee kept me from running anywhere. Step-by-step, my view of my waiting spectators grew wider. And then I realized something. The man standing beside Monica wasn't Roger Tillerman. It was Ben.

He burst out laughing when I hit the bottom step. "Isn't it a little early in the year for a Halloween party?"

"Or a little ... *old* for prom?" Mia said, standing off to the side where I didn't see her.

All I could do was stand there and seethe.

"She's going to a Civil War dinner," Monica said. "You try finding an evening dress from that era at the last minute."

"Why are you even here?" I asked, whipping around the newel post and striding down the hallway to the kitchen.

"I brought Mia home," he said, following me.

"Why? She had my car."

"Yeah. We need to talk about that."

I spun, making my skirt flare. "What happened?"

"Well, first of all, she's fine. But she had a little accident," he said, leaning his hands on the back of a chair at the table.

"*How* little?"

"Technically, it's going to be up to your insurance company, but ... " He shrugged.

"But, what?"

"Considering the age of that car and what it'll cost to repair the damage, I'm thinking it's totaled."

Behind my sternum, right between my breasts, a fire of rage ignited. Totaled. My car was totaled. Mia totaled my car. I was glad she wasn't hurt, but the girl had never spoken to me without sarcasm and irritation. She couldn't look at me without rolling her eyes, and her father was about to be sorry for bringing her to me to babysit.

"Cam, stay calm," he said. "You're shaking and turning red."

"My car—I—you—*ugh!*" I couldn't even form words. I was so mad, spots flashed before my eyes.

"We'll get you a new one."

"How much money do you think I'll get from the insurance company? That car was only worth about a thousand dollars!" I'd had it since college. It was ancient, had more miles on it than I thought possible for a car to have, and was pretty much held together by duct tape and prayer.

He winced. "More like five hundred, but don't worry. I already know where I can get one that's only three years old, and I can get it cheap."

"If it's a newer car, then why is it cheap?" He was going to set me up in a car that was used in a drug deal and confiscated by the cops or something.

His hesitation confirmed my fear. This wasn't going to be a car I wanted. "The owner died," he said.

It took me a minute to put this puzzle piece into place, and then I gasped when I got the whole picture. "You want me to drive Jenn Berg's car?"

"You already have her dogs, why not her car? It's a sporty red Kia with low miles. You'll like it."

I wanted to drive that sporty red Kia right up his rear.

"Um, excuse me," Monica said, breaking through the haze of disbelief clouding my brain. "Cam, your date's here."

Roger Tillerman stood behind her with a blue and red kepi hat perched on his head. He was dressed in full Union uniform, and stared at my costume with an amused smile on his lips.

"Rhett Butler, I presume," Ben said, holding out a hand to Roger. They shook, and Ben glanced back at me. I thought he might tell me to have a nice time or beg me not to go, but he didn't. He left the house without another word.

ROGER and I walked the two blocks to the Briar Bird Inn amongst a trainload of other men and women dressed in uniforms and petticoats. Although no other woman sported a shiny, fire -engine -red dress, there were quite a few in hoops. Mine was the biggest by far, probably exaggerated due to the fact that it was a costume and not an historical garment.

I had the distinct impression that my fellow patriots traipsing through town spent more time in their Civil War clothes than out of them. I knew there was a popular culture of reenactors and collectors, but I'd never met any of them before. It seemed like something that was poked fun at in TV and movies and not an activity that real people actually participated in. But here they were!

"Are you sure you want to go?" Roger asked, eyeing me with his watery blue eyes.

"Of course," I said, plastering on a bright smile. "Why wouldn't I?"

After the day I'd had, this dinner was the last thing I wanted to do, but at least I wasn't at home resisting the urge to scream my lungs out at Mia. Roger hadn't said a word about Ben, for which I was grateful.

"Do you do Civil War events a lot?" I asked.

"These train rides, of course, for work, and our yearly reenactment with the Freemasons."

"You're a Freemason?"

"I'm a Shriner, which is part of the Freemasons."

"Is Carl Finch?" I asked. Anytime I thought of Carl, I thought of Freemasons and Knights Templar, the Holy Grail and the Arc of the

Covenant. "My handyman, Andy, is making a documentary about him and all of his religious artifacts."

"Is he really?" Roger lifted his chin with interest. "I hope I get to view it when it's finished."

"Andy's hoping the entire world gets to view it," I said, grinning. I couldn't hold back my pride for my young friend. "He's been working his tail off on it."

"Speaking of tails," he said, "how many dogs do you have?"

"Four. I had five, but one was a biter and now my mother-in-law is suing me." I waved the thought away. "Anyway, I'm searching for a missing puppy, so if you see one wandering around, let me know."

Roger blinked a few times, taking in my rabbit trail of statements. "I'll be sure to."

We entered the Briar Bird Inn and were ushered into a large room with high ceilings and round tables. We were seated with Fiona and Jim Stein, proprietors of the Metamora History Center, where the train depot was located.

"Nice to see you, Cameron," Fiona said. I couldn't remember if she'd been at Jenn's calling hours to witness the morning's fiasco.

"Nice to see you, too," I said, taking in her navy blue, off-the-shoulder dress. It had short, puffy sleeves adorned with ribbons, and she wore her hair up in a knot at the crown of her head.

If I had to guess, I'd place Fiona and Jim in their early fifties. He was bald, boisterous, and big. Santa Claus big. And he was one of the few clean-shaven men in town. When I first met Fiona, she told me she couldn't tolerate facial hair on men and wouldn't allow Jim to have a beard. She ruled their relationship with an iron fist while Jim told jokes and played up to every crowd he could immerse himself in.

"That's a lovely dress," she said, while I stood a good yard away from my chair deliberating how I was supposed to sit with a hoop under my skirt.

"Thank you." I started to sit, aiming to plop myself into the chair and live with the consequences.

"I think," Fiona said, taking my hand before I threw caution to the wind, "you want to lift the hoop a bit in back. Then you can sit."

"Thank you so much," I said, squeezing her hand before feeling around behind me for the hoop.

"Not too high," she said. "Just enough to move it out of the way."

I essentially made a hole between the bands of metal for my rear to reach the edge of the chair through the rest of the petticoats and crinoline. I bent at the waist, sticking my behind out toward the chair and lowered myself down.

To my horror, the chair slid backward on the hardwood floor and I fell off balance, flapping my arms like a wounded bird. I gripped the tablecloth and my place setting came crashing down onto the floor with me. Roger grabbed me from behind, stuffing his hands under my armpits, and hauled me back onto my feet.

For the second time that day, everyone in the room was staring at me. Jim's obnoxious laughter drowned out the whispers and murmurs. "Good thing you have those tennis shoes on," Jim said, "or you really would've gone flying."

"They're not tennis shoes," I muttered.

"What?"

"Nothing," I said, as servers rushed around me, sweeping up shards of crystal and china and replacing my table setting.

"I always thought those things were dangerous," Roger said, nudging my skirt. "I don't know why in the world women ever wore them."

"You know what? I don't, either. Excuse me. I'll be right back." I hustled from the room into the lobby and through the door marked Ladies. My dress wouldn't fit in a stall. I stood in front of the sinks and lifted my dress, shedding the bell underneath and leaving it in the corner. I'd pick it up on my way out after dinner.

Without the hoop, my dress dragged on the floor. I gathered it up and strode back into the dining room, not even trying to hide my black rubber-soled shoes.

The servers were swooping around the tables delivering the salad course when I sat down. "You look much more comfortable," Roger said, offering me the breadbasket.

I took a roll and passed the basket to Fiona. "Much more."

Roger was nothing short of a gentleman. Having your date fall on her rump, break plates, and ditch her hoop skirt in the bathroom had to be trying for a man. Ben always said I was a handful. He used to say it made life interesting.

I'd really like to make my life less interesting and more un-humiliating. I didn't remember being so prone to disaster. It seemed to get worse every year, like a symptom of aging. But instead of gray hair or needing glasses, I kept falling knee-deep into trouble and couldn't avoid it.

As if he disembarked from my train of thought, Zach, the bartender from the Cornerstone, reached in and set a salad plate in front of me. Melody Winker's voice buzzed through my ears, calling Zach a stalker, talking about Zach driving by Jenn's house.

A jealous ex-boyfriend made for a tidy suspect—as tidy a suspect as I was, at least. I had to find a way to talk to him.

Dinner continued with Roger offering to dress my salad with the Briar Bird Inn's own tangy red French. Their salad dressing had been my favorite since Ben brought me here for dinner on our first anniversary. I could forego the lettuce and shredded carrots and dip a crusty buttered roll in the dressing. I would have if I were at home. I'd weaseled the recipe out of Judy and made it when I had vegetables in the house, which was rare for a woman who lived on cookies and coffee.

The main course turned out to be Judy's chicken and dumplings, a well-guarded family recipe she refused to share with me. It wasn't on the inn's regular menu, but guests could request it. When there was a town potluck, everyone crossed their fingers that Judy would bring her chicken and dumplings.

Halfway through dinner, while I was cursing the corset squeezing my mid-section and considering ditching it in the ladies' room alongside my hoop skirt, Fiona made me lose my appetite. "I see you've made a daring choice with the paint colors on Ellsworth House," she said. "Irene's just sick about it."

"Good thing Irene doesn't live there," I said.

"She's an Ellsworth. It's her family home," she said. "Unfortunately, your colors break the town code for historical accuracy, and you did not seek approval beforehand."

"Approval?" I asked, pressing my hands against my constricted rib cage. "From who?"

"The Daughters of Metamora have to approve variations to the code."

"So, Irene," I said and couldn't keep the smirk off my face. It figured. As President of the Daughters of Metamora, she had the final say in all of their pesky, pesty matters.

"We all vote," Fiona said, "but yes, her opinion weighs heavily on our decisions."

"Is everyone in this town afraid of that woman?" I wiped my mouth and set my linen napkin on the table.

"What woman?" Roger asked, catching the tail-end of our chat.

"My mother-in-law."

"It's not fear," Fiona said. "It's respect."

Good gravy. Respect, indeed.

"The woman who's suing you?" Roger asked.

I'd nearly forgotten that Roger didn't live in Metamora and might not be as up on town gossip as the rest of us. "One and the same," I said.

"Is she your *ex*-mother-in-law?" he asked.

Our conversation thus far had been limited to polite pleasantries. That's a lovely necklace. Thank you. Is that an authentic military badge? I didn't think he was harboring the illusion that this date was going anywhere.

"No," I said. "I'm separated from my husband. We aren't divorced."

"Oh." Roger scooted his chair back and tugged at the bottom of his uniform jacket. "I was misinformed."

Guilt for not making that point clear swam around with the dumplings in my stomach. "I apologize. He's moved into the world of dating, so I didn't think about clarifying before accepting your dinner invitation."

"I can see how that would be a confusing situation."

It shouldn't be confusing. What was a separation anyway? A trial to see if divorce agreed with you? I didn't need a trial. I knew it didn't work for me. I wasn't ready to accept Ben waltzing back into our marriage and our home, but I wasn't anywhere near ready to go on a date again—even with a geriatric Civil War reenactor.

Dessert and coffee were served, and no matter how stuffed and constricted I was, there was no way I was missing out on fried apple pie a la mode. Another of Judy's specialties, the individual pie fold-overs were filled with apples and fried golden, then sprinkled with cinnamon and sugar and topped with a scoop of vanilla ice cream.

When all else failed, there was comfort food. Not the healthiest motto to have, but it was working for me at the moment.

I scooped up a spoonful, realizing Zach wasn't the server who brought our dessert. As surreptitiously as possible, I searched around the room for him, but he was nowhere in sight. Given my luck all day, missing an opportunity to talk to him might not be a terrible thing after all. The odds for a good outcome were not in my favor.

"I need to get back to the train before the riders board," Roger said, before I'd finished my coffee.

We said our good-byes to Fiona and Jim, and I fetched my hoop from the bathroom. Roger held the door open for me and we stepped outside into the darkening evening.

"I had a nice time," I said. "Thank you for bringing me tonight."

"The honor is mine," he said. "It's always nice to make a new friend."

Yes, friends. But the way he said it made me feel guilty, like I had lead him on.

We walked down the sidewalk to the road. A car was parked on the side and loud music throbbed through its rolled-up windows. It was a red Kia. A sporty red Kia.

My instincts sharpened and I craned my neck trying to see who was inside. When he turned and looked out the passenger window, I almost dropped my hoop. It was Zach. The driver turned the wheel to pull out, and I got a quick peek at her. My world was rocked. Lianne

Berg. Jenn's sister was driving her car and picking up her ex-boyfriend from a serving gig at Briar Bird Inn.

14

The next morning I fought to stay asleep. I was having the kind of dream you don't ever want to wake from. It was Christmas, and Christmas in Metamora was nothing shy of magical. The shop windows shined with twinkling lights. Pine garland and red velvet bows scalloped the railings of the wooden bridge. Sleigh bells jingled from the draft horses, and fat snowflakes floated down from the sky. The air smelled of cookies and warm sugar frosting.

In my dream, Ben and I walked hand in hand through town, stopping to say hello to neighbors and friends. Little kids made snow angels and chased each other with snowballs, squealing in delight. I carried a shopping bag with a gift from Ben inside—a new weathervane for our house. Ben led Brutus on a leash. He'd somehow trained the crazy animal to behave.

Then he turned to me and smiled. It was the slow, lazy smile from when we were first dating. The one filled with longing. Ben's "in love" smile. "Cam," he said, "what do you think I should get Jenn Berg for Christmas?"

I shot up in bed, shaking off the dream -turned -nightmare. My subconscious refused to believe Ben was telling the truth about not dating Jenn. It wouldn't let me forget for one second, not even while sleeping.

It was hot, and the sheet was twisted around my legs. My hair was damp with sweat, but all I wanted was a big cup of coffee. Today I was doing nothing. Not one single thing. I wasn't stepping a foot out of my yard, not even if Monica was bored out of her mind and begging me to leave. Well, maybe we could see a movie in Brookville and go out to dinner. Cooking wasn't on my agenda, either.

I took a quick shower and dressed before heading downstairs. Coffee was in the pot and Monica was sitting on the patio drinking a cup, petting Isobel, who stood beside her chair. What the heck?

I poured my coffee and took the mug outside. "How'd you get her to be nice?" I asked, fending off Gus and the nutso twins.

"She likes me." Monica smiled, like it was a grand achievement, and it was—not just because it was crabby old Isobel, but because Monica was allergic to dogs and therefore not a fan. Isobel lifted her muzzle and growled at me.

"She doesn't like me," I said, sitting down at the patio table. I picked up a stick at my feet and threw it for the three amigos. They ran after it, tumbling over one another, which distracted them from retrieving the stick and started a game of chase around the yard.

"You don't understand her. She doesn't like to be stuck with those three young males and all their energy and barking."

I considered this. "I don't blame her, I guess. But she has her spot beside the fridge and they seem to leave her alone."

Monica nodded, watching Isobel tip her face to the sun and close her eyes. "I suppose."

"Has Mia been down yet?" I asked.

"No. But she's planning on going to Irene's with you."

"I'm not going to Irene's. Why would I go to Irene's?"

"Because she called last night to summon you to the Daughters of Metamora meeting this afternoon, where you will have the opportunity to present your case for the 'appalling'" —here she made air quotes—"colors you've painted Ellsworth House, and they will determine if you are required to repaint."

"*What?* That's insane! You think that's insane, right? I'm not the only one who sees that this woman is out of her mind?"

"Out of her mind or not, that's how things work here." Monica stroked Isobel's head, and the dog put a paw up on her lap.

Everyone was against me. Even the dog.

MY WEATHERVANE SPUN on top of Irene's roof. "Climb up there and take that down," I told Mia, pointing to the trellis standing against the enormous brick colonial.

"Why would I do that?" she asked, with her perpetual frown.

"Because you totaled my car, and you owe me."

"My dad's buying you a new one, so I don't owe you anything. It was an accident, okay?" She let out a huff and strode past me up the brick walk to Irene's front door.

One of these days, karma would find her. Or she'd grow up and learn from life kicking her in the pants. One or the other. I didn't wish Mia misfortune, only lessons that would make her a nice person. If that was possible. But people won the lottery, so why not?

Irene swung the door open and smiled her caked -on pink lipstick smile. She smelled like -old -lady lotion (lilacs maybe?) and wore a crisp pink skirt and jacket. "Mia!" She grabbed her granddaughter's shoulders and gave her a kiss on the cheek. "Your first Daughters of Metamora meeting. I'm so proud. Stewart!" she yelled. "Get the camera!"

Then she turned her attention to me. "You got my message."

"Apparently."

"You think this is ridiculous, I suppose?"

"Apparently."

"It's called respect, Cameron. Respect for the history of this town. Respect for the legacy of the founders and their families. That's what the Daughters represent. That's why the historical code is in place—to protect tradition and honor our past."

It was a nice speech, I'd give her that. "What will the town do when nobody can pay their bills? When the town is abandoned and everyone leaves to find work? How are the Daughters working to improve tourism?"

"I recognize your contribution," she said, ushering me into the living room where the other Daughters were sitting around in similar pastel suits, drinking tea and coffee. "It's a shame the musical had to be canceled. I know that has to be hard for you."

From the sofa, Cass waved at me. She sat between her mom, Judy Platt, and her grandma, Betty Underwood.

The room was filled with mothers and daughters and grandmothers. Sue Nelson perched on a chair by the window, looking out into the front yard. Next to the fireplace, Mia chatted with Stephanie. Sitting on the opposite side of the window from Sue, Lianne tapped on her cell phone. And the Nelson matriarch, Elaina, in a hot pink polka dot dress with matching hat, chatted Fiona Stein's ear off.

I took a seat on the fireplace hearth, close to Cass. "I'm sorry about this," she said. Then she leaned close and whispered in my ear. "Once the old women are gone, this club will exist for girls night out only."

"With Mia involved, I believe it," I whispered back.

"I heard about your car." She shook her head.

"Sergeant-at-Arms," Irene said from the front of the room, "bring this meeting to order."

Fiona untangled herself from Elaina's stream of babbling and stepped up beside Irene. "Madam President, I give you the daughters of our founder Graham W. Nelson."

Sue, Lianne, and Stephanie stood for recognition. Elaina remained seated but waved and blew kisses, drawing titters of laughter from her fellow Daughters.

"Madam President, I give you the daughters of our founder Samuel L. Jackson."

Samuel L. Jackson? The actor? Probably not. Decidedly not.

Cass, Judy, and Betty stood up, and Irene nodded her acknowledgement.

"Madam President, I am the daughter of our founder Paul S. Brooks, and I call this meeting to order."

"Thank you, sister Daughter."

Sister Daughter. I held in a chuckle.

"I am the daughter of our founder Elijah Levinsworth Ellsworth, and President of the Daughters of Metamora."

Levinsworth Ellsworth? This kept getting better and better.

"I would like to welcome my granddaughter Mia to her first Daughters meeting. Stand up, dear!"

Mia stood awkwardly while everyone clapped politely, then she retook her seat and resumed whispering to Stephanie.

"The minutes of our previous meeting have been read and approved," Irene said. "Now on to new business. Our first item on the agenda is the painting of Ellsworth House, now owned by my son, Benjamin Hayman, and occupied by his estranged wife, Cameron Cripps-Hayman."

"I wouldn't say estranged," I said, prickling at her word choice. "Ben and I talk daily, or almost daily."

"Nevertheless," she said, "the issue today is the painting of Ellsworth house. Purple and green." She closed her eyes, like it physically hurt her to think about it.

"Lavender and sea foam," I corrected. "But actually, I think it's more of a sage."

Fiona stood up. "The chair must recognize you before you speak."

I drew my pinched forefinger and thumb across my lips, zipping them. After this business was finished and I left, they'd probably all sit around getting a good laugh from Fiona's stories of my Civil War dinner misadventures.

Who was I kidding? The whole town had probably already heard all about it.

"Do any of our Daughters have an opinion to share on this matter?" Irene asked.

Fiona stood, and Irene nodded in recognition. "I think it's an eyesore," Fiona said vehemently. "It's right across the canal from the train depot. What will visitors think of our town? It looks like it's turning into a ghetto."

Well. Fiona had done a good job of suppressing her wrath the night before.

I glanced around the room, afraid of who might blast me next, and caught Mia's eyes. She smirked, like this was the most fun she'd had in a long, long time.

Cass stood up and waited for Irene's go -ahead. "I like it," she said. "It's not bright or gaudy. The colors are muted and coordinate well. Cameron hired local help and bought her paint and supplies in town."

"Your boyfriend," Sue Nelson said, standing. Fiona didn't utter a word about her needing recognition from the chair to speak. "Of course you wouldn't take issue with Andy getting paid. And going by your taste in interior decor, I'm not surprised you think the colors are muted and coordinate."

"Susan, that's not nice," Elaina said, wagging her finger at her daughter. "You're in no frame of mind to pick out house colors."

Sue pressed her shaky lips together and sat back down, turning her eyes out the window again.

Irene pounded a gavel on the coffee table in front of her. "I think we've heard enough. Let's vote. All in favor of Cameron Cripps-Hayman repainting Ellsworth House white?"

Everyone but Cass raised her hand. Judy and Betty gave me apologetic looks but held up their hands as well.

"By an overwhelming majority," Irene said, "Cameron, you have thirty days to paint the house white again. Thank you for attending our meeting. You're dismissed."

Dismissed. Wonderful. "What happens if I don't repaint the house?"

"Fines begin accruing at thirty days, Ms. Cripps," Irene said, purposely leaving off the Hayman. She lifted a penciled eyebrow at me. "Any other questions before you leave?"

Giddiness bubbled up inside me. This was all so absurd. I couldn't hold back the tickles of laughter in my throat. "No," I said and did my best to look dignified as I dashed from the room and out the front door so I could burst into a full-blown fit of hysterics.

I drove Monica's car home with tears streaming from my eyes from laughing so hard. I don't know what was so funny. I was being sued and had no money for a lawyer. I had to borrow my sister's car because mine was crushed, and now I had to come up with more money to buy new white paint to repaint the house I had just started painting purple.

Wait until Ben found out about this.

I parked in my driveway and dug through my handbag for my cell phone to call him. After pulling out a dog bone, a bottle of hand lotion, and the case for my missing sunglasses, I finally found it and dialed his number.

"Your mother's making me repaint the house," I said.

"Before or after you go to jail for aiding and abetting a felon out on bond wanted for questioning in a murder case?"

"Aiding and ... " Nick! Maybe it wasn't a good idea to hide him from Sheriff Reins in my shed.

"I'll be over to talk to you in ten minutes, Cameron. Don't go anywhere or I'll have you arrested."

Oh good gravy.

15

Did you forget that I was here Friday morning?" Ben asked, hands on hips, pacing around the kitchen. "I even told you Mia was outside talking to Nick Valentine." He stopped and threw his hands in the air. "You knew I saw him here! Then you lied to Reins about it. Do you know what kind of position that puts me in?"

Sunday was turning out to be just as terrible as Saturday. I stuffed a cookie in my mouth and muttered, "Sorry."

"Sorry?" He ran both hands over his head and got those wide, wild eyes he got when he didn't know what to do with me. "What am I going to do with you, Cameron?"

"What are you going to do with your mother? That's the question," I said. "She's costing us a fortune. First the lawsuit, and now repainting the house. I've got five-gallon pails of purple and green paint that I can't return, you know."

He stepped toward me and looked down at me with hard, all-business eyes. His mouth was a tight line of anger. "I can't afford to pay for a lawyer and get the house repainted on top of buying you a car. If you weren't always waging war with my mother, you wouldn't be getting sued or repainting the house. You have to admit that. Take some of the blame for the mess you're in."

"I can admit it! Okay? Your mother is a giant pain! She hates me and goes out of her way to drive me crazy."

"Can't you ignore her?" he said, dropping his chin, like he was exhausted with this subject that had been an ongoing source of conflict for us for four years.

"No, I can't. I won't tuck my tail and hide in the corner when she smacks me on the nose with a rolled -up newspaper. I'm not her dog to train and order around. I won't let her treat me like that, Ben, and you shouldn't want me to."

"What can I say, Cam? I'm a terrible husband. How was your date last night?"

I clenched my fists at my sides. "The most interesting part was seeing your dead girlfriend's sister driving her car—the car you want to buy me—and picking up Jenn's ex-boyfriend from work. Very curious, don't you think?"

He started pacing again. "Zach Kennedy and Jenn went out for a couple years. It got physical a couple times, and I was called out to break it up. She never pressed charges. She broke things off about the same time you and I separated, and he went ballistic, said she'd regret it. Swore he'd get her back."

Ben knew everything I'd overheard at the Cornerstone and more. "He's a suspect, right?" I asked. "I mean, he's the most obvious."

"He's been questioned, but he has a solid alibi for that night. He's been taking community college classes, and the professor recorded him as present that evening. After class, the professor and a handful of students—Zach included—went out for a few beers. He was drinking so he stayed overnight with one of his female classmates instead of driving home."

"The guy gets around if he's with Lianne less than a week later."

"We don't know if he's *with* Lianne."

"Still," I said, "it's weird. Why would she hang out with a guy who was so terrible to her sister?"

Ben shook his head. "I don't know."

I didn't either, but I wanted to find out.

He opened the fridge and took out a Coke, hopping back when Isobel snapped at his foot.

"Don't look at me," I said, avoiding what I knew would be a dirty look. "She's only nice to Monica."

"Maybe she should go home with her then." He pulled the tab to open his can and took a drink. "Speaking of coming home ... It's been a couple days. Did you think about me moving back in here?"

"Of course I thought about it." I wanted to tell him yes, but I knew the right answer was no. I wasn't at the right place, mentally, to have him come back yet. Still the words battled on the tip of my tongue. *Yes, no, yes, no ...*

"And have you decided?" He sat down and touched one of the red roses he gave me for my birthday, sitting in their vase in the center of the kitchen table.

"Nothing's really changed, has it?" I said, sitting across from him. "I'm the aimless wife with nothing going on for herself, and you're the cop who gets frustrated and bossy."

"I'm not bossy," he said. "Frustrated on occasion, but not bossy. And what do you mean aimless? I don't think you're aimless."

"I need my own identity here, Ben. I had one in Columbus. I think that's one of the things you liked about me, isn't it? I haven't found who I am here, though. I'm getting there."

"So, I wait until you find yourself, is that it?"

There was a moment between us where I felt something break, a connection being snapped in two. Whoever we were together before, we couldn't be again. I wasn't the woman I used to be, and the new me would eventually have to decide if she could take Ben back, even though he'd always be in my heart.

"Yes," I said. "If you want to be with me, you need to wait until I know who I can be here. This was your place, Ben. We moved here, and you were given a house and a job. The prodigal son returned. I've made some friends, but it wasn't easy. Now I need to do more and find my place."

"I wouldn't say prodigal son. It's not like I left and raised hell."

"You know what I mean."

He sighed and tipped his Coke back, drinking deep. "The last four years, Cam ... has it been terrible for you here?"

"No," I said, reaching across and taking his hand. "If it was terrible, I'd leave. Monica is mystified that I want to stay, but there's something about this town. And you're here. I don't want to leave. I want to figure out how to fit in here."

He squeezed my hand. "You fit with me, you know."

"I hope so," I said, meaning it.

Bittersweet emotions constricted my chest, like the corset had the night before. I didn't want to cry. Crying was for defeat, and I wasn't defeated. This was a new start. He could get to know the new me, too. I didn't have to grow and find myself without him. "Ben? Would you like to see a movie with me Wednesday night?"

His smile made the corners of his dark eyes crinkle. "Like a date?" I nodded. "Only if there's popcorn and Peanut M&M's involved."

"Come on, you know me! Are popcorn and M&M's ever not involved?"

He laughed. "So, we're dating. Should I refer to you as my girlfriend or my wife? Or something else?"

"Hey now, don't get ahead of yourself. Just because I have a ring on my finger doesn't mean you automatically get a second date."

We laughed together, and it relieved so much pressure. All the agonizing I'd done over the past six months faded. I didn't know where we'd be in another six months, but for now, this would work.

LIANNE AND ZACH huddled in my mind and wouldn't leave. There was something going on there, and I had to figure out what it was. Were they a couple now? Were they up to something? Did they whack Jenn over the head, despite Zach's alibi?"

"Hello? Earth to Cameron," Monica said, sitting next to me on the couch. We'd hunkered down in the family room all day to watch a marathon of home -improvement shows on HGTV. Somewhere between using chalkboard paint to make fancy jar labels and carving birdhouses from gourds, I had zoned out.

"Sorry, what did you say?" I asked, shaking my head to get Zach and Lianne to clear out.

Monica pointed to my lap. "I *said,* where'd the cat come from?"

I glanced down to where I mindlessly petted Spook, curled into a tight black ball on my lap. "He shows up sometimes."

"From where?" She looked around like she expected a whole clowder of cats to emerge from the air vents.

"The attic, I think."

She threw her hands in the air and jerked her head back. "You think?"

"I told you the cat was complicated."

"How have the dogs not noticed him?" She and I both leaned to look over the back of the couch, where Gus lay snoring on the floor. The twins were chewing on raw hides in the hall. Isobel was where Isobel always was when she wasn't nuzzling Monica's leg—the kitchen beside the fridge.

"I named him Spook for a reason," I said. "He has a lot of ghost-like qualities."

"Let's hope he keeps them, or it's going to be pandemonium in here."

"Good point. I'll get him some food and put him back outside just in case."

I picked up Spook and tucked him under my arm. Never once had I heard my silent feline specter meow, and I prayed this wasn't the time he chose to become vocal.

Out in the kitchen I opened the back door, flipped on the overhead light, and plopped him down on the patio. "Stay here."

They say when a cat narrows his eyes at you, it's a sign of affection, but when Spook did it with his unnatural, alien-emerald eyes, it gave me the willies, like he was cursing me. "I'll bring you some tuna," I said, backing slowly into the house.

Monica filled a plastic dish with water while I scooped tuna out of a can onto a paper plate. "I'm surprised the dogs didn't scare him away," she said.

"Did you see the missing chunk out of his right ear? I think he's been in some vicious fights. And he has crazy sharp claws. I don't think there's much of anything that scares Spook."

I'd had the misfortune of meeting Spook's claws when I tried to bathe him. It was a futile task I gave up before I got one furry paw into the water.

I served my prowling tomcat his dinner and scratched him behind the ears before going back inside, where Monica was pulling fruit out of the fridge. "Care for a healthy snack?" she asked. "I stopped at a fruit stand off of Route 52 yesterday while you were on your date. I can't eat one more cookie or I'll die."

"I think one of us was adopted," I said, picking up a carton of blueberries. "I've never eaten one of these that wasn't in a muffin, pancake, or cobbler."

"Don't forget pie," she said, poking me in the hip. "You'll like this. You mix plain yogurt with some oats and blueberries and, let's see ... " She poked around in my fridge some more and pulled out some strawberries. "This should work."

As she spooned all the ingredients into glass juice cups—bemoaning the fact that I didn't have footed dessert dishes—old, crabby Isobel shuffled over with her nose in the air sniffing. "You want some, too, sweetie?" Monica asked her in a baby talk voice. "Can dogs eat this stuff?"

"Hang on," I said, pulling the recipe Betty sent me with the beehive cookie jar. "There's a list of things dogs can't eat jotted on the back of this. No garlic, onion, avocado, chocolate, raisins, grapes ... " I read through the list and didn't see blueberries, yogurt, strawberries or oats listed. "Looks like it would be okay, but it'll be a mess. She'll get it all over the fur around her mouth and it'll get on the floor."

Isobel whined, then sat at Monica's feet, panting. Monica, in turn, shot me her best puppy dog eyes. "Come on, Cam."

"What if we freeze it first? At least it'll be solid then."

Monica gazed down at Isobel. "Can you wait for a little while? I promise you'll get some."

Isobel licked Monica's hand and hobbled back to her spot by the fridge to lie down.

"Yeah," I said, "one of us was adopted." I couldn't get near that dog without her trying to take my toes off.

"Where are your ice trays?" she asked, mixing up more of her yogurt-berry mixture.

"I don't have any. The freezer has an icemaker. What about a mini-muffin tin?"

"You don't have cookie cutters, but you have a muffin tin?"

"It was a wedding gift with the rolling pin. Never been used." I slipped it out of a drawer and handed it to her.

"Let's line it with plastic wrap so they come out easier."

Once she got the pan the way she wanted it, she spooned in the yogurt, oats and berries and popped the pan in the freezer. "Much healthier than bacon and cheese treats."

"These dogs are starting to eat better than me," I said, spooning a bite into my mouth. I wasn't much of a yogurt fan, but it was pretty good. "You know, I bet we could make these with all kinds of things dogs would like. Bananas, peanut butter, probably even sweet potatoes."

"Dogs eat sweet potatoes?" she asked.

"Well, Betty's list doesn't say they can't. Maybe we should pick some up and try it."

"What do you think?" she asked in the baby voice, turning to Isobel, who twitched an ear.

"I think she says to leave her alone."

Monica took her dessert to the table and sat down. "Do you think it's strange that neither one of us ever had kids? I mean, I've never even been married."

"I don't know, Mon," I said, sitting across from her. "We were kind of brought up to strive for professional success, not to be domestic goddesses."

"Millions of women do both, though," she said.

"Oh, it can be done. I just think we skipped over the marriage and children part when it came to making goals for ourselves. I wasn't thinking of getting married when I met Ben, it just kind of happened."

"Why didn't you two have a baby?"

"A baby? Well, I didn't ... " Wait. A baby. Lianne and Zach raced around inside my brain again. Jenn Berg was pregnant. She'd broken up with Zach six months ago. Was the baby his? I had to find out how far along she was, and if Zach knew. Was he angry? Did he think the baby was Ben's and kill her in a jealous rage?

His alibi was the only problem with my theory. Who was this mystery girl from his class he spent the night with?

"Cam, you're zoning out on me again," Monica said, dropping her spoon in her empty glass. "What's your deal?"

"I need to find out what classes Zach—the bartender at the Cornerstone—is taking. Then I need to find a way into one to see which girl he's interested in."

"Yeah ... " She stood up and rounded the counter, placing her empty dish in the sink. "Good luck with that."

"We need to go to the Cornerstone and talk to him. It's the only way to find out."

"When? Not now."

"Yes now."

"But it's Sunday night."

"Do you have something else to do?" I asked, coming up beside her and rinsing out my glass. "It's not like you have to work in the morning. We'll go have one drink. A coffee and liqueur drink. I'll make small talk with Zach, find out what I need to know, and we'll be home in an hour."

"What if he's not working tonight?"

"Then we skip the drink and come back home." She didn't look convinced. "By the time we get back, Isobel's frozen yogurt should be ready."

She let out a long sigh. "Fine."

"And while we're there, maybe I'll fill out an application."

"A job application? Why? And to do what? Wash dishes?"

"No, not wash dishes. Maybe hostess or something. I don't know. Ben says he can't afford to buy me a new car, paint the house again, and hire a lawyer to deal with Irene's lawsuit."

"Maybe he should call the old dog off!" she said, laughing. "I can't believe she's suing you."

"I don't know if he can call her off. When Irene gets something in her head, she's like a dog with a bone."

"Well, dog gone it!" she said, laughing.

"Okay! Stop!" I made myself quit laughing and caught my breath. "No more dog quips."

"Not even one more?" She held up her index finger, grinning. "One?"

"No. Not even one. We need to get changed and head to the Cornerstone."

"Alright, I'll save it for later, then."

Monica's dose of goofiness was what I needed to get me energized and in a better frame of mind. Irene could sue me. She could fine me for my paint colors. Mia could total my car. But they couldn't take away my sister. They couldn't take away my adopted bark machines or my phantom cat. They couldn't take away my laughter. Only I could do that, and I chose to keep my sense of humor about the domino effect of crazy situations falling around my life.

16

The Cornerstone bar was practically empty. Other than Andy sitting with Carl Finch and Dennis Stoddard, taking notes while they yakked, only one couple sat at a table by the windows drinking wine from a local vineyard. Ben and I had gone there once for a tasting. We ate cheese and crackers and sampled about a dozen different kinds of wine. Well, I sampled about a dozen. He was driving. I passed out in the car on the way home. Who knew a Dixie Cup–sized swallow of wine could go right to your head?

Ben had carried me in the house and, apparently, upstairs, because I remember him taking my shoes off while I lay on the bed. There's a foggy memory of him brushing my hair back and kissing my forehead and chuckling about me overdoing it.

Thinking back on the good times with Ben made me anxious. What if I was doing the wrong thing? What if I should let him move home and forget about finding myself first?

But there was Wednesday. We'd go to a movie and make a new memory. I still had him, and we'd figure this out. We'd be okay.

Zach came out of a swinging door behind the bar, carrying a rack of beer mugs. "Be right with you ladies," he said.

Monica and I sat at the bar, and I caught my reflection in the mirror behind the bottles of booze. Who was that woman looking back at me? That forty-year-old woman? At a size 16, she was heavier than she'd ever been. She'd found a few rogue strands of gray around her temples. She kept telling herself to get her eyes checked; printed words weren't supposed to be blurry. And she was obsessed with solving a murder that she should have nothing to do with.

What was I trying to prove, and who was I trying to prove it to?

"What can I get you two lovely ladies?" Zach asked, flashing us a million-watt lady-killer smile.

"I'll take an Irish coffee, please," Monica said.

"Make it two."

He knocked on the bar. "Coming right up. I'll put a fresh pot of coffee on."

"Thanks," I said.

He turned to a coffeepot beside the booze bottles on the end near the swinging door to the back room. I scrambled, trying to think of what to say. "I was thinking about maybe taking a college class or two," I said to Monica. "I'm just not sure where to take classes around here."

"You have a graduate degree from Ohio State," she said. "Why would you—"

I kicked her. *Play along* I mouthed, tipping my head toward Zach while eyeing him sidelong.

Oh! she mouthed back. "I mean, I forgot that you wanted to go back for those, um ... real estate classes—"

"Business!" I said. "Business classes. You know, so I can open my own business here in town."

"Right." She shrugged and widened her eyes, helpless. My sister was terrible at playing along.

Zach turned around and leaned his hands on the bar. "What kind of business are you wanting to open?"

I couldn't believe my awkward attempt to lure him in to our conversation worked. But what kind of business? What kind ... what kind ... I couldn't panic.

"Dog treats," Monica said.

"Dog treats?" Zach and I both said at the same time. He looked at me, confused.

"It'll be so much more than just treats," I said. "Eventually. Treats are just the launch pad products."

"People around here love their dogs. My ex had five of them."

"Wow, five. That's a lot." There were graduating classes in high schools with double Metamora's population. Even if Zach and I had never been formally introduced, with a little under two hundred people in town, everyone knew who everyone else was. I wondered if he'd forgotten the other night when Roy and I questioned Melody. Or was bringing up his ex—Jenn Berg—some kind of test?

"Not a lot of people buying their dogs fancy things like designer collars and organic treats, though," he said. "This might not be the best place for a store like that."

"She was thinking about a website and catalog for national orders," Monica said. "Marketing, advertising, PR, we already know how to do all of that. It's the business side of things—accounting and inventory, that kind of thing—that we need to learn."

We? Monica was fully invested in our act now. "I was looking to take a few classes. Is there a community college or somewhere you know of?"

"I'm taking a couple of classes at Ivy Tech over in Richmond. Business administration and accounting. You should check it out." Zach turned to get our Irish coffees, and I grabbed Monica's hand, shaking it before I exploded from excitement that this haphazard plan was working. "Here you go," he said, setting our mugs in front of us.

"Ivy Tech, huh?" I took a sip of my coffee, willing myself to sound casual. "Think they'd let me sit in on a class to see what I think before I sign up?"

"I don't see why not," he said. "My business admin professor is a cool guy. Let me text him and ask."

"Really? Thanks!"

"No problem," he said, holding up his cell phone.

Monica tapped me with her foot, both of us wondering at how

well this spur-of-the-moment trip to the Cornerstone was working out.

A minute later, Zach had my answer. "He said it's okay by him for you to sit in on his class. It's Mondays and Wednesdays from six forty-five to eight."

Since I found Jenn's body on Tuesday, my goal was to punch holes in Zach's alibi after eight p.m. last Monday night. "Great!" I said. "I'll be there tomorrow evening."

Monica and I finished our Irish coffee and headed home. With Mia at Irene's for the night, the dogs were the only ones there to greet us when we walked in the door. The carpenter bees were tucked into their hive inside the porch column for the night. Spook was nowhere to be found. He'd turn back up when I least expected him.

"You know," Monica said, popping a frozen yogurt round from the mini-muffin tin, "maybe selling dog treats isn't a bad idea."

I shook my head. "You heard Zach, there isn't a big enough demand for something like that around here. Maybe if tourism regenerates it would work."

"But you could sell them over the phone, distribute them to sell in dog boutiques in big cities, and take Internet orders. It could work."

She knelt down and held the yogurt treat out to Isobel, who sniffed it once before snatching it out of Monica's hand.

"I don't know," I said. "It seems risky to invest in a business selling something anyone can make in their kitchen."

"But it's not about being able to, it's about having the time to. It's about the pretty packaging and pampering your pet. It's about buying a special treat for your special friend when you're out shopping for puppy sweaters."

"I see your marketing gears turning, Monica. Don't get ahead of yourself—or me."

She tapped her fingernails on the countertop. "I could help you. So could mom. It could be a Cripps business venture."

"How would you have time for that with your job? You work like eighty hours a week as it is."

"It's just me at my place, Cam. I have all the time in the world."

"I have the time, too, that's for sure," I said, considering her points. "It would be fun doing something like this with you and Mom, if she's interested. I don't think it would bring in enough money to pay for a lawyer or more paint, at least not at first, but I could probably get a job somewhere in the meantime."

Thinking about it more, it didn't sound like that much of a risk if we kept it small at first. Maybe Betty would let us set up a little table in Grandma's Cookie Cutter. We could put together an inexpensive website, and the Metamora Action Agency could make some calls to dog boutiques while they manned the tip line. I could pay them on commission, ten percent of every treat they sold.

It could work. The new Cameron Cripps-Hayman could be a Metamora business owner.

"I HEAR you had an interesting weekend, Cameron Cripps-Hayman," Roy said, standing in my kitchen the next morning drinking coffee. "What with the fistfight at the calling hours and performing a striptease at the Civil War dinner."

"There was no fistfight or striptease, Roy. Those are exaggerations."

"It was more like a catfight," Johnna said from her spot at the kitchen table where she was knitting, as usual. "The claws came out."

"Sue's claws," I said. "Not mine."

I checked my cell phone for a text or email from Nick, who hadn't shown up on the train. There was no word from him.

"The phone lines have all been switched over," Anna said, hanging up my landline phone. "They all route through your home phone number. Guess we should switch the posters again so we have the right number."

"That's a good idea," I said, "but first let me fill you in on a new lead I got over the weekend."

I told the four of them about Zach and Lianne in the car. "Do any of you have information about the two of them?" I asked when I was done with my story. "Are they dating? Friends? Co-conspirators of some kind?"

Johnna's knitting needles stilled. "You know, Lianne and Jenn weren't close. They were when they were younger, but they started growing apart in high school. Lianne was a wild child, always giving Sue grief." She tutted. "I did hear that recently she's been trying to turn herself around. Make something of herself. Don't sound like she's making a good job of it if she's hanging out with the likes of Zach Johnson."

"Eh, he's not so bad," Roy said. "Pours a nice, healthy shot of whisky, he does."

"Well, he couldn't possibly be part of a murder then," Anna said, flipping her hair over one shoulder.

"Hey now, girlie," Roy said, shaking his finger at her, "don't discount the merits of a man who's honest with the bottle."

Logan had his laptop on the table, and his fingers typed away. "What are you doing, Logan?" I asked.

"I'm inputting all of our suspects and evidence into a database so I can create a graphical chart and map the progression of each lead."

"Oh," I said, not exactly following. I wasn't technologically unsavvy, but I couldn't conjure a visual of what he meant. "Can't wait to see it."

"We don't need no computer network to tell us who killed that girl," Roy said. "We only need what the good Lord gave us up here." He poked the side of his head.

"This takes all the bias out of the equation," Logan said. "We're humans. Humans have emotions and opinions about other humans based on past experiences. This program only considers what's logical."

"A lot of great detectives relied on their gut instincts," Roy said. "Sherlock, Monk, Columbo."

"Don't forget Magnum," Johnna said with a sigh. "Tom Selleck could really pull off facial hair."

Anna sat forward in her chair. "Jessica Fletcher and Miss Marple represent great female detectives. We can't forget them."

"The program doesn't take sexism into account either," Logan said. "One more way it's superior to human thinking."

"Now, I won't sit here and be subjected to dirty talk, young man." Johnna waved a knitting needle at Logan.

"Okay," I said, stepping firmly into the generation gap before they bridged it themselves, and I ended up prying Johnna's needle from up Logan's nose. "We have a lot to go on. I'm headed to Ivy Tech tonight to sit in on Zach's class and try to find the girl he stayed with the night Jenn Berg was murdered. If I can figure out who she is, I can talk to her—see if she's lying about him spending the night."

"You think the sheriff didn't do his job, Cameron Cripps-Hayman?" Roy slurped another sip of coffee, eyeing me over the mouth of his mug.

"I think Sheriff Reins is following all of the leads he gets," I said, avoiding a line of questioning that would lead to me admitting my lack of confidence in our sheriff.

"Cameron needs the class anyway," Monica said, breezing into the kitchen. "She's starting a business."

"You are?" Anna said, sounding way more excited about this prospect that I was. "What kind of business."

"Specialty dog treats," Monica said.

"Just what this town needs." Roy shook his head. "At least it's not another antique shop."

"Are you sure this is a good idea?" Johnna asked. "Friday was the first time you ever baked something that you didn't turn to coal, remember?"

"That's a good point," I said, twisting my lips. "It's not definite. Monica and I were talking last night about it, but the idea needs a lot more thought first."

"Sounds like it needs a lot more practice," Roy said. "That reminds me, Nick and me finished the dog bone –shaped cutter. It's out in the shed. I'll go fetch it."

"You're going to need a vendor's license," Logan said. "And you'll want insurance. Maybe set up an LLC."

I held up a hand. "I think that's putting the cart before—"

"Packaging is going to be a huge sales point," Anna said. "What's on the outside is as important as what's on the inside."

"You're exactly right," Monica said, sitting down beside Anna. "Branding is ninety percent of making a business successful."

I slumped down next to Johnna and let go of my attempts to stop their brainstorming session. Logan was already talking about website hosting and setting up a distribution hub in my attic.

"Sounds like they've got this all figured out," Johnna said, looping yarn around her needle. "It's not a bad idea, and it's not like dogs are picky—most of 'em anyway. You don't need to be a Paris -trained chef to make dog treats, and there aren't many ingredients involved. Betty's got that big oven over there. I bet she'd let you bake up a few good-sized batches if you asked."

"Oh, look at this one!" Monica said, pointing on her tablet screen to a pink -and -white striped paper bag with a clear window on one side. "They'd look so cute packaged in these."

"No pink," I said, but nobody was listening. The business we may or may not be starting was already out of my control. My crew really did put the first A in Action Agency. They got a whiff of an idea and latched on to it for all they were worth.

Now if we could only find our killer.

17

I hadn't been to a college class in about fifteen years. Monday night I parked Monica's car in one of the student lots and hiked across campus to the business administration class Zach was in. I was one of the first people to arrive and sat off to the side in the back of the room where I could observe and, hopefully, not be noticed. The room was smaller than I expected. This wouldn't be a lecture to a hundred students. The room might hold about forty, which would make it easier to figure out which girl he went home with a week ago.

I opened my handbag and took out a notebook. Somewhere in the bottom, about a dozen pens were rolling around, but I'd be darned if I could find one. I took a mental inventory of every item I touched: travel-sized tooth paste, a hair clip, a baggie of Cheez-Its, a long screw I found on the road and picked up so it didn't puncture anyone's tire. Ah ha! A pen.

The professor whisked in and plopped his briefcase on the desk up front. Zach strolled in not long after and took a seat in the middle of the room with an empty chair on either side of him. Surely, if he'd stayed overnight with one of the women in this class, he'd sit with her. Unless I was giving him too much credit for being a decent person. I was suspecting him of murder, after all.

The professor looked up at the clock and cleared his throat. "Good evening, class. I hope you're all ready to have a lively discussion on quantitative methods for decision making."

Class was started. She had to be in this room. Unless she didn't come tonight.

"But first," the professor said, "let's make sure we're all here."

I scanned the room as he began going through last names. "Anderson?"

There was a cute, petite brunette sitting diagonally to Zach's left, but she hadn't turned around and he didn't seem to be paying her much notice.

"Baker?"

There was a rustling behind me, but I had my eyes on a redhead up front, with long legs and willowy arms.

"Berg?"

My ears perked up. The rustling in the back came nearer as someone rushed down the aisle beside me.

"I'm here!"

Lianne Berg shot into the chair beside Zach with a smile and an armful of loose papers and notebooks. "Sorry. My bag broke in the parking lot."

The professor moved on with attendance as I scooped my jaw up off the floor. Lianne Berg was the girl Zach was with the night her sister was killed.

AFTER CLASS, which was enlightening from the parts I heard—when my concentration wasn't scattered on thoughts of Zach and Lianne's motives—I introduced myself to Professor Hudgeons.

"Thank you so much for letting me sit in on your class tonight."

"I hope you enjoyed yourself and join us on a permanent basis."

"I think I might," I said, if for no other reason than to keep an eye on Zach and Lianne until the killer was found.

"Wonderful. We sometimes go to a local pub after class and continue our discussions. You're welcome to join us tonight."

"Maybe I will," I said. "That would be interesting."

He gave me directions, and I set off to the parking lot. Driving to the pub, it struck me that signing up for a college class was adding another debt that Ben and I couldn't afford. I'd have to find a stream of income fast.

Hudgeons was getting out of his car when I parked at the pub, so we walked in together. "You're starting a business?" he asked. Zach must have told him.

"Yes," I said. "A line of specialty products for dogs, starting with treats."

"My mother used to make our dogs sweet potato chips, God rest her soul. We had a pair of Blue Weimaraners. Betsy and Duke. Best behaved dogs you can imagine."

"I'd love the recipe," I said. "My monster dogs will eat anything, but if they've been taste tested by two well -trained dogs, they must be good."

He took my cell phone number and agreed to text me the recipe.

A group of eight students, including Zach and Lianne, sat at a long table against the wall. A pitcher of beer was already being poured into frosty mugs. Zach took notice of me for the first time that night. "Cameron, right? How'd you like the class?" He sat a full mug in front of me.

"I think I'll benefit from it a lot," I said. "Thanks again for asking if I could sit in tonight."

"No problem."

Lianne wore a poker face. In a million years, I couldn't guess what she was thinking as she stared at me from across the table. Finally, she spoke. "How'd you like the Daughters meeting? Irene takes it so seriously. It's a joke."

"I wish it were a joke. I can't afford to repaint my house, but I don't want to be fined, either."

"So don't pay. It's not like she can send you to a collections agency and ruin your credit."

I'd never thought of it that way. I guess because she was my mother -in -law, and the other women in the club were influential in town, I didn't want to cross them. "Seems like they could make life miserable if I don't do what they want."

"Not if you ignore them."

I wanted to tell her I was sorry for the loss of her sister, that I was sorry for what happened at calling hours between her mom and I, but I couldn't get the words out while sitting at a table of strangers. It didn't seem like the right time or place.

I took tiny sips of beer, not wanting to drink and drive home but wanting to appear as though I was joining in on their fun. At the end of the table, Professor Hudgeons was leading a riotous debate about something. I didn't catch what the topic was. I watched Zach and Lianne interact as inconspicuously as possible.

Every now and then, while they were talking, she'd touch his arm, or he'd turn his body in his chair and brush against her. They were certainly friendly, but it was a leap to say with any authority that they were more than that. And if they were, what did that mean?

All I knew for certain was, A) Lianne was driving her sister's car, and 2) Zach and Lianne were friends. So far, that didn't lead me anywhere other than suspecting Lianne was who Zach was with the night Jenn was murdered. Would Lianne lie for him? Would the two of them be in on it together?

"Do you guys always drive home after coming here?" I asked, digging.

"It's only about twenty minutes from my apartment," Lianne said. "Sometimes I let Zach drink more and I drive and sometimes he drives. He usually stays at my place when we meet up like this after class."

Bingo! "Oh. It must be convenient to live close. I didn't know you two were together."

Zach was embroiled in the conversation at the end of the table when Lianne glanced his direction before replying. "We've been off and on for years. I'm sure you know he was with my sister for a while, but he and I go back further than they did. We've just never been able to get it together and make it last."

"Oh." I took a sip of beer, swallowing all of this information down. "That's got to be difficult. Having a sister dating someone you care about."

"It was," she said. "I mean, I was fine with it." She ran her fingers down her neck, clamming up, perhaps suspecting she'd said too much.

"Well, anyway, I'm very sorry for the loss of your sister."

"Thank you." She picked up her beer mug and took a few big gulps.

"I feel terrible for forgetting to send flowers. The week was crazy, and I forgot. There's no excuse for it."

She gave me a faint smile. "Flowers don't change anything, anyway."

"I guess not." Sue would still think I was to blame for her daughter's death no matter how many bouquets I sent, and there wasn't a flower on earth that could bring Jenn back.

Being that it was a Monday night and most of the students in Professor Hudgeons's class had day jobs, nobody stuck around too much longer. I made a show of taking my time and visiting the ladies' room before leaving, so I could follow Zach and Lianne out.

From the back corner of the pub, I watched them. Zach stumbled a little, then laughed and gestured to his shoes. They looked new, so maybe he wasn't stumbling around from drinking, but from his stiff soles. Lianne tucked her arm through his and rested her head on his shoulder, and they pushed through the door.

I hurried through the bar, darting in and out of tables and chairs, my handbag banging off the backs of people sitting in them. "Sorry," I said. "Pardon me." My knee still gripped with a spasm of pain if I put too much pressure on it or bent it too fast, but I was determined to get out to the parking lot before they pulled away.

Pushing through the door into the dark night, I scanned the row of parked cars under the dim light on the corner of the bar. Nobody was around. Everyone had already left.

I shook it off. It wasn't like I'd overhear Zach's confession, and after spending time with them, I wasn't convinced that they had anything to do with Jenn's murder anyway.

18

By noon the next day my kitchen was cluttered with people, dogs, baking ingredients, and the mingled scents of various dog treats being tested. To my horror, Roy came prepared with his own apron sporting the saying *Keep Your Hands Off My Buns.*

"I think we're getting ahead of ourselves," I shouted over the sound of barking and Roy and Johnna arguing about theh amount of carrot shavings to add to their dough.

"The sweetie chips are a winner," Monica said, watching Isobel chomp a handful of baked sweet potato slices. Professor Hudgeons had texted me the recipe like he promised, and I'd handed it over to Monica.

Nick had bailed on his volunteer hours for the second day in a row, and I was beginning to suspect he'd found somewhere else to complete them since I'd pretty much accused him of murder. Or maybe he was guilty and playing it smart by not coming back.

Zach and Lianne weren't off my radar yet, but Nick's friend Cory Bantum was taking a prominent spot in my mind. I had to make my way out to the kennel in Connersville today to pay him a visit. Maybe if I solved Jenn's murder, my mother-in-law would drop her lawsuit and let me keep my house painted the colors I wanted.

Who was I kidding? She'd probably fine me for doing police work without a badge.

Anna and Logan sat at the table working on a website. The two of them, along with Roy, Johnna, and Monica, had taken the liberty of naming the business Dog Diggity. It was cute, I'd give them that, but I was still on the fence about the whole idea of a dog treat business.

Johnna put a hand on my shoulder. "I called and talked to Betty last night. She says if you're wanting to test how your treats will sell, to let her know. She'll help however she can. Why don't you run down and chat? Oh! And look!" She picked up a square knit pouch the size of a sandwich bag. "A treat cozy!"

If ever there was a time to lay my forehead—smack my forehead—on the counter, this was it. "It's cute," I said. "I'll go talk to Betty." I hurried and made my escape from the crazy Dog Diggity overlords who had taken control of my kitchen.

Outside, Andy battled bees. "Why don't I call an exterminator?" I said, watching him dart across the yard with a handful of buzzing black and yellow balls after him.

"Don't you dare. I got this." He swatted his hand and dodged one. "I picked up a bottle of this powdered stuff that you shoot in their hive. It's the same stuff exterminators use."

"Okay, if you say so, but do me a favor and don't end up in the hospital."

I left him to wage war and headed down the road past Schoolhouse Antiques, where Will was outside jabbing rusted lawn ornaments into the ground—big metal cattails and flowers on the ends of rods that bobbled around when the wind blew. I was certain that at one point in their lives the ornaments were painted, but it was hard to tell with all the rust. I was also certain that Will would call it an antique patina.

"Hi Will," I called, waving, remembering that the last time I saw him he wanted to run away, like I was about to bash him over the head and make him my second victim.

He looked over and smiled, then hastily shoved his lawn ornament into the ground and retreated inside his shop. I'd have to talk to

Brenda about her boyfriend's crazy, misplaced ideas. I hadn't talked to her since the disastrous calling hours. I pulled my cell phone from my pocket and sent her a text, asking if she was able to meet for coffee in ten minutes. I got a reply right away: *Meet you at Soapy's*

I'd chat with Brenda and stay away from Ellsworth House a little longer. Two birds, one stone.

Betty was sweeping her front walk, and I scared her when I said, "Hello!" from only a few feet behind her.

"Oh!" she said, placing a hand over her heart. "I didn't hear you walk up."

Her short hair was shiny blue-black today. "Cass color your hair again?" I asked.

"You know I can't tell that girl no when she insists she can do as good a job as my beauty parlor."

I wanted to ask if her beauty parlor used shoe polish as hair dye, because it looked like Cass did. "She sure does a good job." Nothing wrong with stretching the truth a little to make someone feel good. Plus, Cass's heart was in the right place. With business down, it was surely hard for Betty to part with her money at the beauty parlor.

She propped her broom by the door. "I hear you're not only making dog biscuits, but interested in selling them?"

"Johnna and the rest of my phone crew have taken to the idea like fish to water. I'm not so sure it'll work, but I'm thinking about giving it a shot."

"What do you have to lose? What you don't sell, those dogs of yours will gobble up."

"True. There's still the investment of packaging and advertising to consider."

"Well, let's cross our fingers that the Canal Days Festival this fall brings in a crowd since the play was cancelled." She opened the door to the Cookie Cutter and beckoned me with a wave to follow her. Inside it smelled like vanilla and cinnamon and the walls were lined with shelf upon shelf of collectible cookie jars.

"That's four months away," I pointed out. "There has to be a way to get the musical rescheduled before then. The town needs it."

Betty rounded the counter and pulled her oven door open, releasing a waft of steam and a heavenly aroma that made my mouth water. "Grandma's Snicker Doodles," she said, "with cinnamon chips."

The grandma of Grandma's Cookie Cutter was Betty's Grandma Underwood. Although she'd been gone for decades, her cookies were still legendary.

"Hot from the oven," Betty said, sliding one onto a napkin and handing it to me.

"These are my second favorite after your chocolate chip."

"You're a traditional girl. No fancy, newfangled cookies for you. But I bet I could get you to change your mind. My cousin Tillie just sent me a recipe she found in one of Grandma's old photo albums—no idea how it ended up in there. Cheesecake cookies." She shrugged her eyebrows up and down suggestively.

"I think I could go for that," I said. "I do love cheesecake."

Who was I kidding? I loved all sweets. Pies, cakes, cookies—I was an equal opportunity dessert eater.

"You know," Betty said, as I nibbled on a snickerdoodle, "we don't have to put on a play about murder. It wouldn't be inappropriate to choose a different one and start rehearsing."

It was a great—and perfectly logical—idea. "Why has nobody thought of that? We don't need to fill in Jenn Berg's role if the players put on a whole new play. I'll ask Soapy about it. I'm headed there next."

"Well, then you best get to the reason for your visit. Dog treats, right? I have a spot right up front where I can put a round table for you to set up a display. I'm not too busy to sell them for you. I can tuck your money under the register and keep it safe."

"Wow, that sounds great. I guess I don't have any reason not to then, huh?"

Betty tilted her head, appraising me. "Unless you don't want to. That's a valid reason. Don't let anyone talk you into doing something you don't want to do. You have to be committed to it, or it won't work."

I nodded. She was right. And I wasn't committed yet. "I'll think about it some more and let you know."

"My offer stands. No rush." She patted my arm. "Take another cookie for the road," she said and scooped up another with her spatula.

GAZING at the churning water in the canal on my way to Soapy's, it was hard to believe it had been a week since I found Jenn.

One week and no murderer.

Loud, persistent barking and quacking grabbed my attention. I could hardly believe my eyes. Ben was walking along the road with Brutus on a leash. Brutus was engaged in a quarrel with Metamora Mike. The duck flapped and quacked, not leaving the big black brute alone. "Maybe next time you won't try to eat him," Ben said to the dog, tugging on his leash. He saw me and raised a hand, smiling.

"How'd you manage to get near him without losing a leg?" I called, waiting by the wooden bridge.

"Bribed him with a steak bone. I wouldn't say we're friends, but we put up with each other."

"And you're walking him," I said, taking a step back as they approached. "I don't have a steak bone, so don't let him bite me."

"I think you're okay. He's only tried to eat ducks so far." He looked back to where Mike was waddling, huffily, to the bank of the canal.

We strolled across the bridge, and I kept my distance from Brutus even though I was featherless. I didn't trust him not to take a piece of my backside. "Anything new with the investigation?" I asked.

He looked at me, then at the ground. I could tell he was weighing his options. To tell me, or not to tell me ...

"Reins's men found two set of prints in the mud. One matched Jenn's tennis shoes. The other prints were a man's."

"What does that mean?" I asked, grabbing his arm. "Am I off the suspect list?"

"Don't get excited. Nobody's off the list yet."

"But if a man was with her ... " If a man was with her—and it wasn't Ben—who was it? Zach? Nick? Cory Bantum?

"Don't go poking around anymore, Cam," he said, catching the flash of adrenaline in my eyes. "Disband your Action Agency and stay out of trouble before you really get Reins after you. Or worse."

"Worse? What's worse than Reins thinking I killed someone?"

He jolted to a stop. "Being killed yourself. This isn't a joke, Cameron. Going after bad guys isn't a game. How would you feel if one of your crew was hurt?"

"I'd feel terrible. Obviously." I walked on ahead of him. I didn't need a lecture.

"Cam," he called, behind me. "I'm not trying to be condescending, but you need to think about these things. You have two teenagers and two senior citizens along with a felon working for you. It's not exactly CSI."

"I don't even watch CSI," I said, spinning around to glare at him. "If you remember, you watched that upstairs in the bedroom while I watched my shows in the family room."

"That's right, I'm the villain because I didn't want to watch reruns of Parks and Recreation."

"It's funny!" I said, adamantly defending my favorite show to him for the millionth time.

"Well, this isn't. I want you to stop whatever it is you've got going on with that group of yours before you end up hurt or worse."

"Worse, like dead? I'm not going to end up dead, Ben."

He ran a hand through his dark hair and lowered his head, looking up at me with those dark eyes through thick lashes. "I don't know what I'd do if something happened to you."

"Don't," I said.

"What?"

"The eyelash thing. Don't do that."

"Fine," he said, resting his hands on my shoulders. "Can you do me one favor, though?"

"What's that?"

"Don't go searching the closet of every man in Metamora for canal mud, okay? We all have canal mud on our shoes."

My lips cracked into a smile. "Oh, that. I guess I can do that. For a minute, I thought you were going to tell me Mia was headed back from Irene's."

"That reminds me," he said, cringing.

I decided to take pity on him. Darn eyelashes. "Okay. I guess it's no big deal since I don't have another car she can wreck. As long as she's not plotting a hostile takeover with your mother."

"I doubt Mia has any interest in hostile takeovers."

There was a lot he didn't know, or care to see, where Mia was concerned. One of these days, he'd figure out she wasn't the angel he thought she was. Soon she'd be back with her mom, sunning herself on a beach, and all would be right with my world again. Or at least on its way to right-side-up again.

"I'll pick her up and take her out to dinner," he said. "I'm glad she's spending time with my mom and dad, but I need some time with my little girl, too."

"I'm sure you do," I said. I knew how much he wanted to spend more time with her during the year. It was hard on him to live over two hours away, but at least it wasn't farther.

"Hey, Cam! Ben," Brenda said, strolling out of her shop, Read and ReRead. "You joining us?"

"No," he said. "I'm just walking this guy." He nodded to Brutus.

"That's brave of you," she said.

"I'll talk to you later," I told him.

"Are we still on for tomorrow night?" he asked.

The movie. "As long as you're nice to me."

"Popcorn and M&M's," he said. "My treat."

"Pick me up at seven."

Soapy brought our cappuccinos to our table and sat down with us. "How are things, ladies?" he asked, stroking his beard.

I wrapped my hands around my mug and sat back, eager to relax into coffee bliss. "Well," I said, "I've got a kitchen full of people making dog treats and trying to talk me into opening a business. I'm not off the hook for Jenn Berg's murder yet, and I have more dog hair in my house than a whole herd of Shop-Vac's could suck up. On the bright side, Betty gave me a snickerdoodle on my way here."

He chuckled. "Sounds about right for you."

"Business is slow," Brenda said, "even online. Will's holding a tag sale next week to get rid of some of his bigger pieces. We're hoping it draws a good-sized crowd. How're you and Theresa doing, Soapy?"

"Hanging in." He leaned forward, resting his forearms on the table. "Used to be a time when summer meant late hours and running out of stock. Now we're lucky to get ten customers a week in here."

"Something has to give," I said. "The town can't falter like this for much longer before completely falling apart. Let's do a different play." I shifted toward him in my chair. "Betty and I were talking, and we both agree that picking another play—one that doesn't have a murder in it—wouldn't be insensitive or disrespectful. The town was relying on the play to bring in customers. We need to see it through."

"I agree," Brenda said. "Our town's been through a terrible tragedy, but we're going to face even more—financial tragedy for all of us—if we don't try to get people here somehow."

"Okay, okay," Soapy said. "I can see your point. So if we do put on a different play, which one?"

"I'm not familiar with plays and musicals," I said, "but I'd be happy to help pick one out if there's a list or a book to look through."

"Here," Brenda said, taking out her phone. "I'm sure there's a list online. You have to buy the rights and the scripts and music."

"There's a website," Soapy said. "That's where we found *Oh Horrors! It's Murder!*"

Brenda searched around online with her phone and finally found a website that looked promising. She started reading the titles and descriptions, and nothing stood out to me until she came to *A Dog's*

Life, a musical comedy that cast a few actors as dogs. My mind went into high gear.

"That's the one," I said, banging my hand on the table like a gavel. "We can tie in the play with Jenn's dogs. Well, my dogs now. It can be put on in memoriam to her. A tribute. We can even collect donations for the Brookville Animal Shelter if we wanted. She's gone, but she's still a part of the program."

Soapy rested a hand on my shoulder. "I like it. It'll be a nice gesture from the town. Good thinking, Cam. I'll give the players a call, and we'll get to work right away."

"I'll get my crew back on the phones!" I said, jumping out of my chair. "You better add a third performance, because this play is going to be standing room only."

Maybe I'd even get the Action Agency out of my kitchen.

19

Back at home, Andy wasn't lying listless in the front yard, and the bees seemed to be gone, but it looked like a cyclone picked up a bakery and dropped it in my kitchen. Banana peels, melon rinds, and apple cores littered the floor, while the remnants of dough and what I hoped was cottage cheese dotted the countertops. "Is this a green bean?" I asked, plucking the object out from between my toes.

Next time I'd leave my flip-flops on.

"I'll clean it all up," Monica said, taking a sip of iced tea and wiping her forearm across her brow. She had flour in her hair. "We came up with some good recipes today. Dog -approved!" she said, giving me a thumbs up and a big smile.

I poured myself a glass of tea and motioned to her to follow me out onto the patio. The dogs were chasing each other around in circles in the yard. Well, Isobel growled and nipped at their legs when they ran by her.

"You're really getting into this," I told her. "It surprises me."

"I like dogs. And cats. I should've gotten allergy meds sooner, I guess."

"But Mon, you're baking. I've never seen you do anything domestic in my life."

She grinned. "I never knew I was good at it before! Good by dog standards, that is. I'm going to take vacation days to come back and help you when you open Dog Diggity."

"About that ... I'm not sure it's something I want to do. I like the sound of having a business, but what gives me the most satisfaction is sharing my successes. If I'm the only one benefiting, I'm not sure it'll be as fulfilling as helping the town build itself back up. Soapy's putting on a different play, and I want to keep promoting it, and everything else that's to come. I love the dogs, but my heart's not into making up recipes."

She sat back in her chair and sighed. "No Dog Diggity?"

I studied her and wondered if she saw herself the way I did. The way she was when she let down the big -city professional -woman facade. "There's nothing saying *you* can't open Dog Diggity."

She laughed. "I think the overhead would be way too high in Columbus. Plus, there are already tons of gourmet pet boutiques in the city."

"I didn't say in Columbus. Do it here."

"Here? Like stay here? I don't know." She shook her head, but I caught the gleam in her eye.

"We've grown on you," I said. I pointed a mock accusing finger at her. "This place and the people do that, and you don't even realize it's happening."

"No," she said, still shaking her head. "I mean, sure, I've gotten used to your crazy bunch, but I don't think I could live here. There's no mall. Where would I get my nails done?"

"Brookville. It's not *that* far to civilization. Although whoever decides to open a McDonald's in Metamora will have my undying devotion and probably ninety percent of my money."

"Tired of fried chicken?" she joked.

"Never. I love the Cornerstone's fried chicken. Which reminds me, when did Andy leave? He hasn't been around much lately."

"About two. He said he had things going on at the castle. I didn't ask what."

"Film -related, I'm sure. Stoddard's probably making him the next

Spielberg. " I waved the subject away. "Anyway, instead of you taking vacation days to come here and help me, why don't we do it together? I'll work during the day promoting the town's events, and in the evenings, I'll be your lackey to boss around."

"I do like the sound of that," she said. "And being single and somewhat frugal, I have a bit of money saved up to put into a business. Mom can help with advertising and PR."

"Between the three Cripps women, we can make Dog Diggity the biggest dog treat supplier in the state."

"I thought you were going to say in the world." She pretended to give me a dirty look.

"I didn't want to overreach. And you can stay here. There's plenty of room. Think about it."

Monica drummed her fingers on the table. "Would I get to fight with Irene?"

"Yes! If she tries to take the doorknobs off, I want you to tackle her. Take her down in the flower bed."

"Done," she laughed.

"Speaking of Irene, she should be dropping Mia off soon. Ben's taking her to dinner later."

"Mia's trouble, you know. I was trouble at her age, so I know trouble when I see it."

"You don't have to tell me," I said. "Ben won't believe it, but I have a feeling he'll learn the hard way."

Gus tromped over and dropped a tennis ball dripping with dog spit in my lap. "Thanks," I told him, tossing it into the yard. He loped off after it.

"Would you mind staying with the Action Agency team again tomorrow?" I asked Monica. "I have to run to Connersville."

"What's in Connersville?"

"Possibly a murderer, but we'll see." Gus brought the ball back again, and I threw it.

"Cam, I don't think this is a good idea. Why don't you tell Ben and—"

"And have it be nothing? And have him lecture me? I don't think so. I'd rather go check it out myself. It's not a big deal. Jenn owed this guy, Cory, five hundred bucks for her puppy. I'll say I'm there to pay the debt. I doubt he'll bash someone over the head if they're offering him money."

"Why don't I come with you?"

"I really need someone to stay with the gang. They need to start calling again. We're putting on the play after all."

She looked skeptical. I didn't need my sister giving me a hard time. "How about I take Andy with me?" I said.

"If you have to go at all, I guess that sounds better than you going alone."

The dogs started barking and running toward the gate at the side of the house. "It's just me, you dummies!" Mia shouted.

"Shoo!" Irene yelled. "Get back!"

Monica nudged me with her knee. "Are you going to go hold your beasts back?"

"I don't know. I'm kind of wondering where this might go."

"Umm, another lawsuit, if I had to guess."

"You're probably right." I got up and strode across the yard. Monica followed, calling to Isobel.

I held the twins by their collars and was figuring out what to do about Gus when Mia opened the gate and he charged toward Irene, tongue flapping in the wind with a giant doggy grin on his face. "Oh my!" she cried, stumbling backward as he jumped on her, leaving two big, muddy paw prints in two very strategic locations on her chest. It looked like she was wearing a paw print bikini top.

"That's it!" she yelled. "I want these dogs—" Gus licked the words right out of her mouth. Sputtering, Irene stormed back through the gate and slammed it shut. "I'll be sending you my dry cleaning bill!"

"I'll put it in the pile," I called. Paying for her dry cleaning wasn't going to happen.

Then a police siren blared out on Route 52, and the dogs began to howl. It wasn't often that a siren was heard, and this made two Tuesdays in a row. I couldn't stop the goose bumps from popping up on my arms. Living in this small of a town, it was likely I knew whoever was having an emergency.

Good gravy, not another body.

At least I had witnesses this time. I was nowhere near wherever that siren was headed.

Ben was late. He hadn't given Mia or me a time, but he liked to eat dinner around six in the evening. It was a quarter till eight and we hadn't heard from him. "I'm calling him," I said, grabbing my cell phone from the kitchen counter.

It rang three times, and his voicemail picked up. "Ben, Mia and I are wondering where you are. Please call us."

"You sound worried," Mia said, picking at her cuticle. "My dad's a cop. He carries a gun."

"So, nothing ever happens to police officers because they carry guns?"

She gave me an eye roll and walked down the hall. A second later, I heard her stomping up the stairs to her bedroom.

"I'm sure he's fine," Monica said, unloading the dishwasher.

"I know. It's just not like him." I plucked a few sweetie chips out of a plastic container and the dogs came running. "I think they can smell these a mile away."

"Those are their favorite. I improved the recipe from Professor Hudgeons and glued a thin slice of sweet potato to a thin slice of apple with a little egg white then baked them."

"You came up with that?"

"I did," she said, lifting her chin and smiling with pride.

"I think you've found your calling."

"We'll see."

The twins gobbled their chips down, and I gave Gus extra for being a good boy and defending me from Irene. Monica fed one to Isobel, who took dainty bites like she was a princess and not an old crab who could separate you from a limb.

The knock on the door came as I was sealing the treats back up. "Ben," I breathed, rushing down the hall to the foyer with barking dogs racing around my feet. I whipped the door open to find him standing there with his arm still up, hand in a fist from knocking. *"Where have you been? We were worried."*

He dropped his arm. His shoulders slumped. "The police station. The gatehouse got broken into."

"That's what the police siren was about," I mused, pushing dogs back to let Ben inside. "You weren't there when it happened, were you? Was anything stolen?"

"No, I was up at the castle talking to Finch and Andy. They were getting ready to film, waiting for Stoddard. I was helping Andy with his audio, changing the batteries in his microphones. Brutus was caged and started going ballistic. It's a long way to the castle from the gatehouse at the bottom of the hill, and I could hear him all the way up there. By the time I got to down to the house, the door was standing open and whoever broke in was gone. There was no sign of forced entry, but I usually lock the door. I guess I must've forgotten to."

"And they didn't take anything?"

"Not that I could tell. There isn't much to take in the first place, though. I had my wallet on me. The TV is an old one not worth much. My laptop was locked in my truck. I left it in there after working in Brookville this morning. Living in that gatehouse is a step above camping."

Mia jogged down the stairs. "Daddy!" She rushed into his arms. "Can we go somewhere vegetarian?"

"Sure we can."

"Good luck with that," I said.

"Stephanie said there's a Chinese restaurant in Brookville," Mia said.

I held back a laugh as the day with the Action Agency at Stature and Wok and Roll sprang to mind. It was good to know I could look back and laugh at my disasters.

"Chinese it is," Ben said. "Cam, would you like us to bring you back anything?"

"No thanks. Have a good time."

I watched them go, reminiscing about the early days of my relationship with Ben. Mia had been twelve, and while she'd always had an attitude, it was cute for a girl her age to act so grown up. Now, it was irritating. But there was still a bit of that little girl inside her. She loved her dad, that much was true. Sure, she knew how to play him to get whatever she wanted, but there was no lack of real affection between them. I was sorry Mia and I hadn't been able to grow close. Maybe if she'd spent more time with us, we would have. Maybe it wasn't too late.

THE NEXT MORNING, Andy and I left behind the cacophony of the Action Agency and the pack of dogs in my kitchen. I owed Monica an expensive purse or shoes or something for this.

"Cass got the lead in the new musical," Andy said, sitting in my passenger seat eating an Egg McMuffin. There would be no road trip without stopping at the golden arches, even if said trip was only ten minutes up the road.

"That's great! Is she excited?"

"They're all excited. Nobody wanted to cancel the play."

"As soon as we get back, I'm going to be the bossiest boss on the planet and get every ticket reserved."

"Put me down for four. I'm making Finch go, and Stoddard will bring his wife."

"Four tickets it is. How's the documentary going?"

"Really well. I've got the footage I need to get started editing, but the project is going to be bigger in scope than I thought."

"How's that?" I asked.

"I'm going to bring the town into it more. If this is where the Arc of the Covenant is buried, I want to dig into the town and its history, answer the question: Why here?"

"Sounds like you need—cue the horror music—the Daughters of Historical Metamora."

"It's in the works. Irene cornered Stoddard coming out of Odd and Strange. She made him a deal. She'll give him information—on camera—in exchange for an appraisal of two antique wall sconces."

"Those are *my* sconces!" I said, turning to him in astonishment. "She can't keep taking parts of my house, Andy!"

"Eyes on the road, Cam!" He reached over and jerked the wheel to the right.

"Sorry." I settled down and made sure my hands were at ten and two on the wheel, eyes locked on the road. "Good gravy, that woman makes me mad."

"Look," he said, pointing up ahead on the left. "Bantum Kennels."

I signaled and turned into the parking lot. It didn't look open. "Maybe we're too early."

"There has to be someone here to let the dogs out and feed them, right?"

We got out of Monica's car and walked through the empty lot. "I don't hear any dogs," I said. The quiet was almost eerie.

Andy tried the door. "Locked."

I cupped my hands and peered in the window. There was a front desk bare of any office equipment other than a few scattered pens. A chair was turned over in the waiting area. "I'm not sure they're still in business." I dug around in my handbag looking for the metal dog tag with the kennel's phone number on it. "Hang on. I'm going to call and see if there's a phone inside that rings. Maybe there's a message that will give us a clue."

House keys, reading glasses, paperback—where was that stinking little tag?

Andy tapped his foot, waiting impatiently. "I'm going to run around back while you search the small universe living in your purse."

"I need to downsize."

"You need a yard sale," he said, taking off around the side of the kennel.

My fingertips identified something cool, smooth, and bone-shaped. "Gotcha," I said to myself, pulling the tag out. I dialed the number and put my ear to the window. Inside, a phone rang. Maybe they were still in business if the phone line was active. I peered inside again as another ring echoed through the window. That's when I saw a computer monitor lying on the floor beside the desk.

Something strange was going on here.

"Cam!" Andy shouted. "Call 911!" He came sprinting back around to the front of the building. "There's a man back there lying on the ground, unconscious. I can't get past the fence to see if he's breathing."

Was it Cory Bantum? I hung up on the phone inside then dialed and reported the incident to the operator. Two minutes later, a squad car and an ambulance sped into the parking lot.

"Back here," Andy said, running to show them where the man lay.

Alone, I walked to Monica's car and sat in the driver's seat. If the man was Cory, then who did this? And where had Nick been the past couple days? Was he involved? Did he do this?

I dialed Nick's number, ready to ask him straight out if he knew what was going on here, but his voicemail picked up. "Nick, it's Cameron. Call me." It's not like I could go into details on a phone message. Most of me hoped he'd call back, and I could get to the bottom of this. Another part of me wanted to drive far and fast and never look back. They found the men's shoe prints at Jenn Berg's crime scene. Obviously, it wasn't me who killed her and everyone would know that soon enough. I could stop all of my detective work now. I wasn't even very good at it.

"Cam?" I turned in my seat to see Andy walking up to the car. "Look who was inside the fence." In his hands was the smallest ball of white fur I'd ever seen. "He has a tag." He held up the heart-shaped dog tag attached to a red collar. "It says Marshmallow on one side, and on the other there's Jenn Berg's name and a phone number."

"He was there that night," I whispered. "Cory Bantum. He took the puppy back."

"*Someone* was there. This is the only dog she was missing, and she had that red leash around her wrist."

"Was that him back there? Cory Bantum? The owner of the kennel?" I reached up for the puppy. He had to weigh all of two pounds. His fur was thin, still growing in.

"I didn't hear anyone say his name."

I looked away from the puppy up to Andy. "Is he dead?"

He lifted his shoulders and winced. "It didn't look good. I don't know."

"Do we need to stick around? I want to get this guy home." Translation: I wanted to get *myself* home. My crazy kitchen sounded pretty appealing at the moment.

"Let me go talk to the police officer and find out."

While he was gone, I snuggled the micro-puppy, wondering how long he'd been without food and water. When did Cory—if that's who it was—get attacked? It must have started inside since the reception area showed signs of a confrontation.

I debated calling Ben. Even if this was Connersville and out of his jurisdiction, we found Jenn 's puppy on the property. Cory, whether he was the unconscious man or not, should be questioned. Someone had to answer for how her puppy got here when she was walking it at the time of her murder.

My cell phone rang. The caller ID read Nick. I hurried and answered. "Nick!" I said. "Where are you? We need to talk. I'm at—"

"I didn't do it," he said. "And neither did Cory."

20

Nick was panicked. I could hear it in his voice. "Neither one of us killed that girl," he said. "I swear."

The puppy whined and licked my hand. "How did Jenn Berg's puppy—I'm guessing the one she owed your friend, Cory, five hundred dollars for—end up back at his kennel?"

He didn't answer me.

"Nick, I'm sitting in the parking lot at the kennel right now with the puppy on my lap. Andy and I came to talk to Cory. We found a man lying on the ground unconscious when we got here and the police and paramedics are here now. I don't know if it's Cory or not, but something went on here. What do you know about it?"

He swore and groaned. "Listen, I don't know if it's him you found or not. I'll tell you what happened the night that girl was killed, though. Cory asked me to come with him to get the dog back since she didn't pay him for it. When we got to the gatehouse, she wasn't home. It was late and dark, but we heard the pup yip from about fifty yards away, she was walking him down 52. We followed her around the corner and down the road toward the canal. That's when Cory called out to her. We jogged to catch up. She said she didn't have the money, he said he wanted the dog back. They argued, but I swear, he didn't touch her. He grabbed the dog and jerked off the leash. Then we left. That's it. She was alive, and we weren't at the canal yet. We were still on the side of the road."

"There's only one problem, Nick, and it's the same problem I've got: nobody else saw you two that night."

"No! Someone did. There was a man there in his car when we got back with the pup. He was looking for someone to open the gate and let him through. He was an older guy. Said Carl Finch was expecting him. We told him the gatekeeper girl would be right back."

"That doesn't mean you didn't kill her, though. You could've killed her and walked back with the puppy and told him that."

"But we didn't!"

I took a deep breath and closed my eyes for a second. I couldn't think straight. "All I know is that there are signs of a struggle inside the kennel and a man, who I'm not sure is alive, outside in the yard. I don't know how close you are with your friend, but you might want to find out if this man is him."

In the side mirror, I saw Andy approaching. "I'm going to hang up now," I said. "Find out if it's him. I'll call you back later."

Andy climbed in the passenger side. "I gave the police a statement and our phone numbers in case they need to ask anything else. I told the guy Ben was your husband. He knows him, of course."

"Of course. It's not like any of these little towns are really separate from the others." I started the car with the puppy snoozing on my lap. "Maybe I should look into buying my own kennel since I seem to be running one. Did you find out anything about the man? Was he alive?"

"Barely. They think he was out there for a couple days."

I headed down 52 back toward Metamora. "They didn't say who it was?"

He shook his head.

If it was Cory Bantum, he was too close to too many bad things happening, and I was going to find out why.

"So, let me get this straight," Monica said. Andy and I were back from our road trip, sitting in my kitchen. "Nick admitted to being with Jenn Berg only minutes before she was murdered, but he and his friend—the guy she owed five hundred bucks to—had nothing to do with it?"

"That's what he says." As a suspect, I was too close to the murder. I needed Monica's perspective. Maybe I was overlooking something obvious. Something she'd be able to point out and say, Duh, Cameron. You practically stepped in it.

Andy tinkered with his camera. "Nick says Cory Bantum repo'ed the puppy and they got out of town."

"And how do we know this?" she asked.

"He claims there was some old man at the gate waiting to be let into Hilltop Castle," I said. "Some friend there to see Finch."

"It had to be Stoddard," Andy said. "The day after Jenn was murdered was when I filmed him talking about Finch's artifacts. He said he'd gotten in late the night before."

"Then I need to talk to him," I said. "Something's not right with Nick's story. He said when they took the puppy, Jenn hadn't yet reached the canal. But she had the leash with her when I found her, and Old Dan found the dog tag in the same place. So she must have kept walking. I need to ask Ben if there were puppy prints in the mud. If not, that confirms their claim that they never got to the canal."

"Stoddard will be back in town to interview Irene on film this weekend," Andy said. "You can ask him about that night then."

"If Cory or Nick killed Jenn," Monica said, "Nick wouldn't come right out and admit it to you, Cam. You need to be careful. It sounds like you're closing in on what happened, and that's not a good thing unless you're trying to get yourself killed. Whoever it is, he didn't bash that girl on the head accidentally. Tell Ben about this and let him and Sheriff Reins deal with it."

"Nick's not going to hurt me." I was sure of it. At least, 75 percent sure.

Who was I kidding? I was maybe fifty-fifty. But curiosity, and adrenaline from finding another victim, had me wound up to solve this case. I was so close I could taste it, and it was as good as Betty's chocolate chip cookies.

The back door opened and Mia stepped inside from the patio where she'd been lying out tanning. "I hope you had sunscreen on," I said. "Even an SPF 15."

"How am I supposed to tan if I've got sunscreen smeared all over me?" She shot out a hip and flung her hair back.

"Overexposure to the sun is dangerous, Mia." I didn't figure her teen sense of invincibility would be penetrated by lectures of melanoma, so I went for her vanity. "It causes premature wrinkling. You want to look like Elaina Nelson when you're twenty?"

"I will *never* wear polka dots," she said and flounced out of the kitchen with the puppy bouncing at her heels.

Point missed entirely.

At least the little white ball of fuzz took a liking to her, and her to him. She'd proclaimed Marshmallow to be a stupid name and started calling him Liam, because apparently that was a much better name for two pounds of yappy white fur. She said it was an actual name, which was true, but I suspected it was also the name of her current pop star crush.

Gus and the twins also wanted to crush on Liam, literally. But not intentionally. They didn't realize they weren't the same size as the munchkin pup. One swat of Gus's paw had sent Liam careening across the kitchen floor. Mia was now keeping the puppy with her at all times.

"How many tickets did the Action Agency reserve today?" I asked, hoping Monica would drop the topic of Nick and Cory Bantum.

"Another fifteen," she said. "Roy got a group of ten, if you can believe it."

"Roy did?" Wonders never ceased.

"It was a bit of a mess after you left this morning. We had to spread out through the house to each have a phone attached to the landline. It's a good thing Ellsworth House has been around forever, and Irene hasn't shown an interest in the old rotary phones. You might want to look into finding office space somewhere. When I went around the house to check on how they were doing, I found Johnna asleep on your bed."

"What? No. She probably stole my pillow."

"I can't account for everything in your room, but your pillows are still there."

"I'm going with Cass to watch rehearsal tonight," Andy said. "And I have an idea that the players will go for, but first, you have to go for it."

"What?" I asked. "It sounds ominous."

"Not ominous. It's a way to get Dog Diggity off the ground in the town and a way to have the volunteers hours making dog treats count for community service."

"So spill it," Monica said, leaning forward in her chair.

"Dog Diggity sets up a booth at the play. During intermission, the Action Agency passes out complimentary dog treats, and you two sell them in the back for people who want to buy more to take home. It's legitimate hours spent serving the performing arts community in Metamora."

"That's brilliant," Monica said, beaming from ear to ear. "What do you think, Cam?"

"I think if you're in, I'm in." I couldn't remember the last time I saw my sister so invested in an idea. She might not see it herself yet, but she would. Focusing her time and attention on a project that made her happy and at the same time, enabled her to employ her business savvy ... it was a no brainer. She'd soon realize Dog Diggity was her calling, just like I'd slowly come around to admitting that promoting the town that had grown on me like a wart was my true ambition. Even Irene couldn't run me out of town now.

"Are you filming the play?" Monica asked Andy.

"Of course. I film everything. I was lucky enough to get a few shots of Old Dan dowsing before he put his rods away again. I'm thinking of opening the documentary with that."

"The day I found Jenn's body?" I didn't say, Isn't that kind of insensitive?

"As a documentarian, it's my duty to portrait the town in all its shades of light and dark," he said, flicking a switch on his camera back and forth.

"Please tell me you didn't record the body being retrieved and the police searching the crime scene."

Andy put his camera down and looked at me across the table. "I'm a fly on the wall. I see all. I film all."

"Okay, but will you *use* all? Metamora doesn't need bad publicity. The business owners—our neighbors and friends, Andy—don't need any more obstacles to keeping their doors open." I had the overwhelming urge to dive across the table, grab his camera, and smash it on the floor in to a million tiny pieces. "What do you think we've been working for with the play? With all the phone calls?"

"What you've been working for, Cam. Not we. I've been working on a documentary that will launch my film career. That's why I'm in this town to begin with. I'm going to make it the best it can be."

All I could do was stare at him and hope my chin didn't hit the table. Here I was thinking gushy thoughts about how the town and the people here snuck up on Monica, snuck up on me, but all along, Andy thought of himself as a traveling documentarian and not one of us.

"What will you do when you finish filming? When this whole project is said and done? Leave? What about Cass?" The last part was none of my business, but I had to ask. She was my friend. And I was nosy.

"I don't know," he said. "I'll find another project that needs documenting on film. I've always been interested in abandoned buildings. Schools, malls. What happened to them? Why did humanity turn away from these places that were once an iconic gathering place in their town?"

His wistful expression told me he was no longer mentally at the kitchen table. He was off in his mind being the urban explorer/documentary filmmaker he always aspired to be. I suppose I couldn't fault him for that.

"I guess I thought you'd stick around," I said. "You seem to fit in with us. I thought you liked it here."

"I do," he said. "But there's only so much to film, isn't there?"

I shrugged. "I don't know. Is there? I mean, we have the Native American mounds. There could be a story there."

"Those are Native American mounds?"

Now I had his interest. "Yes. Fifty earth mounds were documented and thirteen stone ones. Most were destroyed when the highway came through in the thirties, but I'm sure you've seen some right there off of 52."

"Yeah," he said, nodding, gears turning behind his eyes. "I have to think about this. It might work with the film I'm already working on, but there might be enough to document in a new project."

"There's a ton," I said. "Drive an hour or two east into Ohio and there are more. Serpent Mound, Fort Hill, all kinds. You could keep working here while you shoot."

He grinned. "You're trying to get me to stay, aren't you? You're going to miss me."

"Well, other than Brenda, who I don't see as often, you're kind of my best friend here—which is strange, but I've gotten used to it."

"Monica's staying," he said.

"I am not," she said, but her smile gave her away. "Okay, well, I might. I haven't decided."

"Anyway," I said, "she's no help to me. When she sees a bee, she runs away screaming. Who's going to keep those little buggers out of my porch columns?"

"I hate bees," Monica said. "When I was in fifth grade, I was riding my bike and smacked into one. It latched onto my bottom lip and stung the crap out of me. My lip swelled to the size of a kielbasa and stayed that way for a week. I hate bees. I even hate honey just because bees make it. Beeswax candles? Forget it."

"Okay, we get it," I said. I had to stifle a laugh, because I could vividly remember Monica's bottom lip hanging down to her chin, all puffy and red. She couldn't talk and had to carry around tissues to catch the drool. The kids at school called her Mush Mouth.

My cell phone rang, veering me off memory lane. It was Ben. "Calling to tell me which movie you want to see?" I asked, answering.

"Calling to ask what business you had in Connersville this morning where you, *once again*, stumbled upon a dead body."

"He's dead?" *Oh, good gravy.* "He was alive when the ambulance came. Was it Cory Bantum?"

"How did you know the name of the deceased?"

Ben was mad, and when Ben was unhappy, he made sure I was unhappy. "Well, it's interesting, actually. Um, why don't I tell you when you pick me up?"

"Why don't you tell me now."

"Okay. See, Old Dan found a dog tag on the canal bank near the spot where Jenn was—where I found Jenn." Great, I was becoming Sheriff Reins, unable to say the word murdered. "It had the name of the kennel on it. I figured it belonged to her missing puppy, so I went to Connersville to ask if it was there."

"Cameron," he said, followed by his deep, annoyed sigh. "How would a puppy get from Metamora to Connersville? Would he take the train? What made you drive to the kennel on a dog tag that a crazy old man found in the mud?"

"Because Nick Valentine told me Jenn owed Cory Bantum five hundred dollars for her puppy." I closed my eyes and grit my teeth in anticipation of the crap storm I'd just unleashed.

But there was silence on the other end of the line.

"Ben?"

"I don't know where to start, Cameron."

"How about with which movie you want to see tonight." Bait and switch was my only hope, but I didn't think he'd fall for my tactics.

"I'm going to be a little busy tonight picking up Nick Valentine and hauling him in for questioning. That is, if you don't have him hidden on our property this time."

"Nope. Not here."

"Good. Let's keep it that way. Is there anything else I should know about?"

"No. Nothing."

"After work tomorrow, I'm taking Mia back to her mom's. I'll be by to pick her up around five."

A flash of disappointment rippled through me. I had been looking forward to our first date as a separated married couple. "I guess I'll see you then."

He hung up without another word. Something told me disappointment was rippling through him, too, but for a different reason.

21

I woke up at the crack of dawn the next day so nobody would see me prowling around the bank of the canal where Jenn Berg was killed. I had to see for myself if what Nick told me was true.

So far, lots of duck prints, but not one puppy paw print.

There were two distinct footprints, one smaller, and narrower. A female tennis shoes. The other print was larger, a man's print. Not an athletic shoe, but not a smooth dress shoe, either. There were some treads on the bottom, but not from a heavy sole, like a work boot. The shoe type was hard to identify.

It had been late that night. Dark out. Most of the light that night would've come from the town's lights atop the utility poles. A calendar would tell me the phase of the moon. If it had been a full moon, Jenn might have been able to see ... see what? Her attacker?

I backed up and took in the scene from another angle, as if I had been walking along the canal that night. What would I do if I heard someone approaching?

I'd run. I'd run like a pack of wild dogs was chasing me. Of course, Jenn had owned the only pack of wild dogs in town—and now I did—but regardless, the footprints of a person running would surly look different than those of someone walking.

Would she run flat footed, or on her toes? Heel first? The stride would lengthen, that was a fact. Suddenly I wished I'd joined Ben for a few more *CSI* episodes.

Studying each footprint, the depth of the imprint, the method of each footfall hitting the ground (heel first, I found), and the stride, I had to conclude that Jenn wasn't running.

The second set of prints, the man's prints, joined hers in front of Nelson's Knitting Needles. He was someone she knew. I was no detective and had no training in crime scene forensics, but her footprints looked like they stopped, turned a bit, got deeper as she waited for his approach. Then the two of them walked on together. This wasn't a story of fear and panic. This was a person she felt safe walking with in the dark.

So who was he? And why would he be out here late at night after Jenn got off work? And why had she continued walking if the puppy was gone?

I liked to take walks when I had a lot on my mind. She would've had a ton on her mind since she was pregnant (by whom?) and had an ex-boyfriend who wouldn't leave her alone. Did she work with Zach that night? Did they argue? Cory was demanding his money. Nick was confronting her here in town. And there was Ben. What would Jenn be thinking about Ben?

Where was Ben that night? The Fiddle Dee Doo Inn was a stone's throw from the canal. Well, if you were good at throwing stones. In all actuality, it was probably half a city block or so away. Ben could've seen her from the window in his room and come down to join her. He never would've let her walk alone.

My head spun with information overload. How did any of it fit together? Which pieces could I get rid of? The answer was in there somewhere, mixed with all of the misdirection and dead ends.

"What are you doing out this early?" Brenda called from the door of Read and ReRead. "The sun's only been up for an hour."

"Just taking a stroll." I ambled over to her shop, wishing I hadn't been spotted. Brenda, of all people, would know I'm not the early morning walk type of person.

"Without even one dog?" she asked, as I followed her inside to where well-worn pages held stories waiting to be discovered.

I took a deep breath, the scent of old books comforting me, and decided it was best to come out with the truth and not look suspicious. "To be honest, I was examining Jenn Berg's crime scene, and they'd trample all over it with their big furry paws." I held a stack of books for her while she took them off the pile one by one and shelved them alphabetically. "I can't make sense of it."

"That's why you don't get paid to solve crime," she said, taking both of my wrists while my hands were still full. "You don't need to prove anything to us, Cameron. If there was any evidence that you were the person responsible for Jenn's death, Sheriff Reins would arrest you."

"I can't stop now, though."

"Why? There's nothing you can do."

I didn't want to tell her I was close, way too close to figuring this out to quit. So I changed the subject. "Is Will in the new play?"

Her shoulders stiffened as she pushed a book into its spot. "Will left town for a few weeks. He's taking what he calls a tag sale road trip to find antiques for the store." She crossed her arms and turned to me, leaning against the shelf. "He never goes antiquing for weeks at a time, and he's never not asked me to come along. This whole murder has him acting so odd."

"He thinks I did it."

"He thinks everybody did it," she said, patting the bun on the back of her head. "He's gone off the deep end. Hopefully getting away for a while will help."

"I'm sorry he's taking it so hard."

"The sooner whoever killed her is found, the better."

"Have you seen Sue? How's she doing?" Brenda's shop was between Soapy's and the Soda Pop Shop.

"She's been relying on Lianne and Stephanie to run the shop. Lianne isn't around much, though, and Stephanie's only fifteen. She can't run a business, even when business is slow. I've been splitting my time between here and there, helping out. We all have. Cass,

Fiona, Mia, even Elaina tries and makes a bigger mess, but she has good intentions."

"Mia?" Maybe my ears were playing tricks on me.

"Yes, Mia. She's behind the counter next door with a red -and - white striped apron on most days."

I tapped my foot. "She's up to something. It's not like her to be helpful, or nice, unless she's getting something out of it."

"She needs a new car, right? Maybe she's saving money."

"That's even less likely, but I guess maybe she's doing a good deed for a friend." Although I was highly skeptical. "Who runs Nelson's Knitting Needles while Elaina's at the Soda Pop Shop?"

Brenda laughed. "Elaina hasn't sold so much as a ball of yarn for as long as I can remember. Her husband left her a nice bank account and she stocks the store like it was still Metamora's heyday. Then she gives her friends whatever they want. Johnna hasn't paid for yarn or needles there for years."

"Why does she keep it open?"

"Because it's what she knows, and the list of things she knows gets smaller and smaller every day."

An idea hit me. "Do you think she'd lease the building, or share it?" Monica would need a space if she went forward with Dog Diggity.

"I think she could be convinced, as long as she keeps the pretense of the yarn shop. Elaina's used to love an adventure, and it's hard to find something exciting in this town. Other than murder, I guess. Why? Are you looking to open a shop?"

"Not for me. I think my sister might be sticking around." I could picture it now. A polka dotted awning, polka dotted lettering, polka dotted dog treats. It could be worse.

"Wow, another Cripps to give Irene a run for her money." Brenda laughed. "Better get that house repainted white. The Daughter's fines are no joke. She once charged me fifty dollars because I left a trash can outside the shop for two days."

"*Fifty*? She's an evil overlord and she must be stopped. What does she do with the money she gets from these fines?"

"I wish I could say she was buying Botox treatments or throwing lavish parties, but she gives it to Reverend Stroup for the food pantry."

To say I was shocked would be an understatement. "Oh, Irene, you have a human side after all."

Brenda laughed again. "Except I hear she's not going to fine you money. She wants a pair of wall sconces from Ellsworth House."

"I take it back. She's the devil."

When I got back home, Ben was sitting on the front porch step waiting for me. He patted the spot beside him. "In the last four years we've lived here," he said, "never once have you stepped foot outside this door before eight a.m. What's got you out of bed so early today?"

I would not be trapped by a man who interviewed criminals for a living. "Couldn't sleep," I said, "so I thought I'd take a walk."

"Isn't it strange that someone who owns four dogs wouldn't take even one with her?"

"Five," I said, and instantly wanted to staple my lips together.

"Five?" He stood up and brushed off his pants. "Where did you stumble on another dog?"

I was confused. Didn't we talk about the puppy and the kennel on the phone? "The puppy, remember? It was at the kennel."

He stepped up to me, and I swear there was smoke coming out his ears. Ben was flaming mad. His hands hit his hips and his forehead crinkled up, making his eyes harsh slits. "Let me get this straight. You took evidence from a crime scene where a man was barely hanging on to life and didn't hand it over or report it?"

"It's a puppy, not a murder weapon. He needed food and water. Somebody had to take care of him. I couldn't leave him there. I thought I told you."

"Cameron! You told me Jenn Berg owed Cory Bantum money for that dog, not that you found it at his kennel. She ends up dead and he ends up with the dog. You don't see the connection there?"

"Of course I do. I'm not stupid, Ben! I thought Nick Valentine would've explained it to you when you questioned him."

"Nick doesn't seem to be around anywhere. I talked to his neighbors, I talked to his parents, and I talked to his parole officer. You were the last person to speak with him, so why don't you tell me everything you know."

"I have no problem telling you everything I know. Let's go inside."

That wasn't entirely true; I did have a problem telling him everything, because he'd get even angrier with me for not going right to him with the information.

The dogs pounced on Ben, jumping and barking and licking, while I stalled, making coffee and setting out a plate of Betty's cookies to try to sweeten him up. "First of all," I said, "Nick didn't do it. Neither did Cory."

"Is that right?" He sat at his spot at our table, stretching his long legs out. It was like deja vu seeing him there in the morning with coffee brewing.

"Yes," I said, and told him the story as Nick told it to me. How they got the puppy back, how there were no paw prints in the mud with Jenn Berg's, and how Dennis Stoddard had just arrived when Nick and Cory were leaving. "So that proves it," I said. "Stoddard can confirm they didn't do it."

Ben started laughing. Then he started rubbing his head, like he was in pain. "Okay, let's go back to, *first of all.* First of all, we don't know the man at the gate was Stoddard. Second of all, how does a witness placing Nick Valentine and Cory Bantum at the scene clear them of committing the crime? And third, Nick—a man who has a record of assault—flees after Cory Bantum is attacked and dies from the inflicted injuries. Not the actions of an innocent man, Cameron. If anything, it makes me more convinced than ever that one or both of them murdered Jenn."

I lifted my coffee mug, trying to hide behind it. "When you say it like that ... "

He pounded his fist on the table. "For the love of all that's holy, Cameron, why couldn't you do what I asked and stay out of this?"

My coffee wasn't sitting well in my stomach. Arguing with Ben always made me nauseous. "I wanted to make sure the puppy was okay," I said.

"You wanted to prove that you could solve this case." He stood from the table. "I know you too well to believe you accidentally stumbled into information while searching for a missing puppy."

He was right, of course, but I was determined to keep my big mouth shut and not get him more riled.

"I'll be back at five for Mia. Reins and his team are doing another sweep of the gatehouse. Whoever broke in must be looking for something that belonged to Jenn. I'll make sure to tell him all about Nick Valentine and Cory Bantum's involvement."

I nodded, figuring silence was the best response.

THE DAY WENT on with the Action Agency arriving and setting up all over my house. I made sure Anna was in my bedroom and Johnna was in the kitchen, where I could keep an eye on my belongings. Roy spent the first hour and a half coaching Logan on how to schmooze with ladies over the phone. Since he'd landed a big reservation, he deemed himself the expert.

"I don't like that old guy being in the spare room upstairs," Mia said, making kissy faces at Liam, the puppy.

"How do you think I feel?" Monica said, pointing a vegetable peeler at Mia. "It's *my* room."

"I'm going to sort this out soon enough," I said. "The best solution is that the murderer is found, I'm no longer a suspect, and Reverend Stroup lets us back into the church basement. In the meantime, we have to make calls from here. The town needs as many visitors as possible for this weekend."

Remembering what Brenda had told me about Mia that morning, I pulled her aside. "I want to talk to you about something."

I got an eye roll, of course, but no smart-mouthed retort as we stepped into the dining room.

"I heard you've been working at the Soda Pop Shop, helping out Stephanie."

She lifted her eyebrows. "And?"

"And I think it's great that you're pitching in to help out a friend."

"Thanks, I guess."

"Are you getting paid, or volunteering your time? Either way is fine, I'm just curious."

She shrugged. "I don't know. Steph said she'd get her mom to give me something, so I guess I'll get money."

"Do you like it? It's your first job, isn't it? Does your dad know?"

She ticked off her answers on her fingers. "It's okay. Yes. No. Anything else?"

"No, I guess not. Your dad said he's picking you up at five to take you back home. I hope you had a nice visit."

"Yeah." She bit the side of her cheek. "I guess I better get over to Steph's, since it's my last day."

Liam bounced around her feet, looking up at her with his round, black eyes. They'd miss each other for sure. "Would your mom let you keep him?"

"No way." She shook her head and frowned. "Mom's not an animal lover."

"Well, I'll take good care of him for you."

"Don't let the other dogs use him as a toy." She knelt down and picked him up, cuddling him under her chin. He licked her and she laughed, making him bark his tiny puppy yip.

"I think Liam will be just fine," Monica said, coming up beside Mia. "Isobel seems to think she's his mama, or maybe his grandma. She won't let those other dogs harm him."

"Good," I said, hoping it made Mia feel better. "Oh, Mon, if you decide you want to stay and give Dog Diggity a go, you might want to talk to Elaina Nelson about sharing her shop. Brenda says she doesn't actually sell anything anymore."

"She's batty," Mia said. "Steph says her mom wants her grandma to sell the knitting shop. She's too senile to run it."

Monica pursed her lips in thought. "Huh. I'll have to think about that. It's a great location."

"One of the best." I could imagine it now, my sister and I having coffee every morning before she opened her shop. It would be like old times.

The phone in the kitchen rang, and I heard Johnna answer it. "Cameron?" she bellowed. "It's Ben. He says it's an emergency."

I ran in with Mia right behind me and grabbed the cordless house phone from Johnna. "Ben? What's wrong?"

"I get one phone call," he said, "so I figured it better be to you."

"One phone call? What are you talking about?"

"Sheriff Reins arrested me, Cameron. I'm in jail."

22

W*hat do you mean you're in jail?"*

Beside me, Mia whimpered and covered her mouth with both hands. Monica came around the end of the kitchen counter and put her hands on Mia's shoulders. Johnna was in all her glory. This was the best gossip she'd gotten first hand for a long time.

"They found a pair of shoes in the closet that match the imprint of the men's shoes at the crime scene."

"The footprints in the mud match the soles of your shoes? Why? How?"

My heart was going to break my ribs and jump right out of my chest. It pounded so hard, I felt it in the back of my throat.

"I don't know. The only shoes I own are my black dress shoes and my work boots. Neither have the type of tread the shoes that made those prints would have."

"So how can they arrest you?"

"They say they found the shoes with the matching prints in my closet at the gatehouse."

"What are you saying Ben? The shoes aren't yours, so how did they get there? Were they there when you moved in?"

"No. The house was cleaned out. Finch hired someone in to clear it out and take all Jenn's belongings over to her mom."

"Well then, if they aren't yours, what were they doing there?"

"I didn't check the closet after the break in," he said, like he was gifting me a clue.

"Are you telling me someone planted them there?"

"Makes sense."

I figured Reins or one of his deputies was standing nearby, listening to Ben's conversation. "I know you don't want me involved in this, but now you can't keep me out of it. I'm going to get you out of there."

"Finch will need someone at the gatehouse," he said. "He's expecting Mr. Stoddard tonight." I took that as Ben's approval to snoop. "Be careful," he said, and after a longer than needed pause, added, "Brutus bites."

"I understand. I'll be careful, and not just with Brutus. I won't do anything stupid."

His only answer was the sigh of annoyance. He knew me too well. Stupid followed me around like planets circled the sun.

"Finch has the key. Can you do me a favor and run Mia home?"

I looked at Mia, standing beside me, stricken. "Of course, I can run her home."

"I'm not going anywhere!" she said. "I'm staying here until my dad's released!"

"Okay. Okay," I said. "Stay calm. It won't help him if we lose our cool. You can stay as long as you want, as long as your mom's okay with it."

"Do *not* let her go to the gatehouse, Cam," Ben said. "I mean it."

"I already told you, I won't do anything stupid." And having Mia around would be stupid. "Monica's here. Mia can stay with her while I go over there."

Monica nodded and patted Mia's shoulder. "Everything will be fine," she told her. "Don't worry."

By this time, the commotion had lured the rest of the Action Agency—and all the dogs—into the kitchen to find out what was going on. Johnna was giving them the lowdown while keeping one ear on my phone call for updates.

"There will be a hearing to decide if I can be out on bail," he said, "but it might not be until Monday."

"Do you need anything? Books or magazines?"

"No. Don't worry about me. Tell Mia I love her, and this will all be over soon."

"Okay." I didn't know how to end our call. I wanted to tell him I was sorry. I should've let him move back home, then he wouldn't have been at the gatehouse in the first place. I wanted to tell him everything would be okay, but would it be?

"Okay," he said.

"Ben?"

"Cam, you don't have to say anything."

"I'm going to get you out of there."

"All I want is for you to stay safe. You and Mia."

We hung up, and half of me wanted to charge through town on a mission to find whoever planted those shoes in the gatehouse. The other half of me wanted to curl up in a ball in bed and cry under my blankets. I took the middle road and went to the pantry for cookies.

"Sounds like the Metamora Action Agency has a job to do, Cameron Cripps-Hayman," Roy said, tugging on the lapels of his grungy navy blue sports coat.

"No," I said. "There's no job. This is serious business. Two people are dead and one skipped town. Ben's been framed and falsely arrested. I won't have any of you harmed. Our job is to get ticket reservations, not to solve murders."

"That's not what I was led to believe," Logan said. "I broke out into hives because we were suddenly crime fighters. Now that I've gotten used to the idea and found a place for myself as the Agency's tech guy, we're not following up on this?"

"I think you're right to be apprehensive," Anna said. "At the same time, the four of us have reach in the community where you don't. Johnna and Roy have relationships with the older members of the community. Logan and I have an in with the younger people.

Between us, we can ask a lot of questions to a lot of people in a short amount of time."

"Don't forget me," Mia said. "I'm Irene Hayman's granddaughter. I have some pull in this town."

"You will stay in this house and not leave it," I said. "I promised your father I'd keep you safe."

"I'm helping!" she said and stomped her foot. "At least let me go to the Soda Pop Shop and talk to Steph and Lianne. They might know something."

Lianne, who'd been cruising around in her dead sister's car with her dead sister's ex-boyfriend. Even if she and Zach didn't strike me as guilty, there was something going on that I couldn't put my finger on. "Okay," I said. "But if you suspect anything at all, call and tell me. Don't try to free your dad on your own."

"If she's helping, we're helping," Anna said. "Logan and I are older than her."

"He's *my* dad," Mia said, indignant.

"Fine! Fine. You can all help. Let's report back here at five, then I'll have to go to the gatehouse."

"What is all the commotion?" Andy asked, bustling in through the back door. He took a look at all of our faces and stopped in his tracks. "Something bad happened, didn't it?"

"Ben's been arrested for Jenn Berg's murder," I told him, filling him in on all the details with the shoes and suspected setup at the gatehouse.

"That's serious business," he said. "What are we going to do about it?"

"We're going to find out who framed him."

Andy glanced around again. "How do we know it wasn't someone in this room?"

Johnna let out a hoarse, rattle of a laugh. "You caught me. I usually do all my murderin' with a knitting needle through the eye, but went for something a little different this time around."

Anna jabbed a thumb toward Roy. "This one's too drunk every night to do anything that productive."

"Hey!" Roy said and then shrugged. "You're right."

"Nobody in this room did anything," I said, ending it. "But if we want to find out who did, we should get started."

"I'll head over and talk to Finch," Roy said. "Pick his brain a bit."

"I figure Elaina might know something she doesn't know she knows," Johnna said. "People talk around her, think she doesn't have any sense left anyway. She doesn't, but if you know how to fish for information, you can get it out of her."

"I'll pick up Cass," Andy said, "and we'll see what we can dig up."

"Good luck," I said. "And thank you."

Anna and Logan went to talk to their principal, Mr. Stein. Principals always know things. I hoped he wouldn't get mad at them for showing up at his house during summer break.

When they were all gone, I turned to Monica. "I can't believe this is happening. Ben's a police officer. One of the good guys. How can he be in jail?"

"Don't fall apart on me now." Monica shoved me down into a chair. "Your job is going to be going back over everything you know and writing it down. Then we're going to see if we can find any connections that we missed."

I grabbed Johnna's pen and one of the phone records with past visitors' names on it and flipped it over to the blank side. Then I started from the bitter beginning, with a sandwich and a duck.

Cass came back to the house with Andy at five o'clock, joining the rest of the Action Agency in the kitchen. "I'm so sorry," she said, hugging me. "Ben's innocent. They can't keep him in jail."

"Unfortunately," Andy said, "we didn't find much to prove it."

"Finch confirmed that Stoddard fella was the one at the gate the night Jenn died," Roy said, pointing to the corresponding bullet point on my list. "Said Stoddard mentioned seeing two other fellas with a pup."

"That confirms what Nick told me." I drummed my pen on the paper.

"Mr. Stein wouldn't talk to Logan and me about the murder," Anna said. "He thinks it's too vulgar for people our age to think about." She rolled her eyes, making me realize for the first time that even mature teenage girls weren't immune to eye rolls.

"He did suggest we keep our distance from you, though," Logan said without apology. Anna smacked him in the arm. "What?" he said, looking confused. My all -logic no -emotion robo-boy.

"All Elaina kept chirping about was Lianne driving that little red car of Jenn's," Johnna said. "I couldn't get anything else out of her."

"Wait." I ran down my list. "There's something ... I don't ... "

"Well, I think—"

"Shh!" I said. "It's coming to me. Just give me a minute."

I stopped and ran my finger under the phrase *no forced entry* on my list. "That's it."

"What's it?" Monica looked over my shoulder to see what I was pointing to.

"Lianne has Jenn's keys! The gatehouse showed no sign of forced entry." I set the paper on the table and looked at the faces around me. "Lianne broke into the gatehouse."

"What?" Johnna said. "No."

"Why would she do that, Cameron Cripps-Hayman?"

Mia appeared in the doorway of the kitchen. I expected her to launch an irate protest against my accusations of her friend's sister. Instead, she took a few steps father into the room and crossed her arms, waiting for me to continue.

"What about the shoes?" Anna asked.

It all rushed back. The night at the bar. Watching Lianne and Zach leave. Zach stumbling. "He had new shoes," I said. "Zach had new shoes on a few days after the murder. Where were his old shoes? They planted them in Ben's closet!"

Mia took another step forward and picked up my list of clues. "Nice theory, Sherlock," she said, "but there's one problem." She tossed the list back on the table. "Jenn was always locking her keys in her car, so she gave Lianne the spare. The car key is the only one Lianne has."

"What about Zach's shoes?" Monica asked.

"If owning more than one pair of shoes makes a person a murderer," Mia said, "then you better put me on your list."

"Maybe Zach has a spare key to the gatehouse?" I said. "If she was always locking herself out of her car and gave a second key to Lianne, why not give Zach one to the gatehouse when they were dating?"

Logan shook his head. "We have nothing to support that. The evidence points to Nick. It's the most logical conclusion. He and Cory Bantum were seen fleeing the area. Then Cory ends up dead, and Nick disappears. Nick has a record of assault. The obvious solution is that Cory was threatening to come forward and Nick silenced him. He's most likely on his way to Indianapolis to make sure Mr. Stoddard doesn't talk, either."

Oh God, I didn't want to believe that, but it made a lot of sense. "Someone should warn Stoddard." I turned to Andy. "Do you have his number?"

He nodded. "I'll call him. He'll be in town this evening. As long as he's locked up with Finch in Hilltop castle, he'll be fine."

"Right." I paced to the patio doors and looked out at the dogs romping around. Isobel stood guard over Liam, having designating herself as the puppy protector when Mia wasn't around. Anytime Gus and the dingbats got too close, she bared her teeth, growling and barking her warning. "So how do we find Nick?"

"We don't," Roy said. "We let Sheriff Reins handle it. We've come to the same conclusion the police have. That tells me our sleuthing days are over."

"I'm not giving up yet," Logan said, and we all stared at him in astonishment. "Give me tonight to find Nick. If he's using his cell phone, I'll have his location."

"Are you a hacker?" Mia asked. "Because it sounds like you're a hacker."

"I don't do anything illegal," he said. "But I know ways around regulations."

"Work your magic," I said, crossing my fingers. It was our last hope of finding Nick and freeing Ben.

As Logan tapped away at a laptop and the other Agency members packed up to head home, my mind wouldn't stop racing. There had to be something to my theory about Zach having a spare key to the gatehouse. It made sense—if Jenn gave a car key to Lianne, she'd have a spare for her house, too. Plus, there was still the pesky piece of missing information regarding the paternity of Jenn's baby. Connecting Zach to the shoes, key, and baby was a short jump in my mind. All I had to do was prove it somehow.

"I've got a sudden craving for Cornerstone chicken," I told Monica after the gang left.

She scrunched her nose. "Not a fan."

"I need to question Zach. He has the motive to plant those shoes, and he's the most likely person to have the means."

"The key?"

"The key." I grabbed my handbag. "I'll pack a bag for the gatehouse. You can drop me off after we eat and I get answers."

"I hope you know what you're doing."

"Do I ever? Don't worry. I have a feeling that before this night is over, we'll know who killed Jenn."

Upstairs, I packed a bag and poked my head into Mia's room. "Hey," I said, waving my arms around. She had earbuds in and couldn't hear me. When she saw me, she jumped and pulled her earbuds out. Liam hopped off her pillow and yapped.

"Why didn't you knock?" she said, all huffy. "I could've been changing my clothes!"

"I'm sorry. I'll remember to knock from now on." Having a teen under my roof was going to be a big learning curve. Little kids didn't care about privacy, but I had to remember Mia wasn't a kid, even if she acted like one most of the time. "We're going to the Cornerstone for dinner. Grab your shoes."

She turned up her nose like Monica had. What did people from Columbus have against fried chicken? "I'll make a salad." She tucked her earbuds back in, dismissing me.

Okay, then.

I shut her door and made my way down the stairs, gritting my teeth against the pain in my knee. I wondered if John Bridgemaker knew any of his ancestors' rain dances. I'd try anything at this point.

Monica sat forward in the driver's seat and tapped her fingers on the steering wheel the whole way to the Cornerstone, not saying a word.

"There's nothing to be worried about," I said when she parked and turned off the car.

"I don't like the thought of you in that gatehouse by yourself. I'm going with you."

"You can't. I need someone to stay with Mia. Please, don't worry. I'll be fine."

She made an irritated, growly sound as she got out of the car but didn't argue.

The Cornerstone was busy. The new church held all of its small group meetings on Thursday nights, and many of the members came for chicken afterward. There was a line of people at the door waiting for tables.

"I'm going to take a look in the bar and see if Zach's here," I said. "Be right back."

Monica grabbed my arm before I could dash away. "Why don't we order to go? Then you can talk to him while we wait for our order."

"Okay," I said, agreeing since Monica didn't want to be there in the first place.

I left her at the cash register to order and strolled into the bar. Zach was bartending. There was a decent -sized crowd, and a baseball game played on the TV. Getting him away from his customers for a minute or two would be difficult, so I decided the best way, other than dragging him outside by his ear, was to be direct. He wouldn't want to discuss Jenn, the baby, and the break in within earshot of a bunch of people.

I picked an empty stool between two men at the center of the bar and sat down. "Be right with ya," Zach said, popping tops off beer bottles. He lifted his chin in recognition and smiled. He sure didn't look like a murderer, but I couldn't let his good bone structure distract me from getting to the truth.

"What can I get you?" Zach asked, sliding a beverage napkin in front of me on the bar. If I was going to question him during this rush, I'd have to take the bull by the horns.

"Answers," I said. "Were you the father?"

Zach's face went red, and he looked away. "I've got a job to do, so tell me if you want something to drink."

"Ben's in jail. Were you the baby's father?"

He cursed under his breath then turned and strode to a swinging door. He pushed it open and bellowed for someone named Diane to come out. I scurried over.

"Listen," he said to me, "I can give you five minutes, but that's it."

I followed him to the storeroom by the restrooms where I'd seen him talking to Melody. My body buzzed with adrenaline. I couldn't believe I was about to confront him on this. Who was I to make such claims? Not the police. Not the victim's family.

He shut the door behind us. I'd never been claustrophobic, but I developed a sudden case of it. "How do you know about the baby?" he asked. "Only Jenn's family knows, and only because the cops told her mom. Let me guess, your ex-husband told you?"

"We're not divorced," I said. "And yes, he told me because there's a rumor going around that he and Jenn were dating. He didn't want me to hear that she was pregnant and think it was his baby."

He laughed.

"Why is that funny?"

"People are so bored with their lives in this microscopic town, they latch on to anything and make it a big deal so they have something to gossip about. Jenn wasn't dating your ex-husband. He's an old man. She could be his daughter. She was going out with some guy named Cory who she got her last dog from. The baby was his."

"Cory Bantum?" *Oh good gravy.* I was going to kill Nick Valentine for leaving this little factoid out of our conversations.

"Yeah, that's the guy. Real loser. He didn't want the kid. Broke up with her when she told him she was pregnant. So you're cornering the wrong guy."

"Too bad that one's dead," I said.

"What?"

"Cory Bantum's dead," I said, "and I hear you had a problem with being jealous of Jenn dating other men."

"Are you accusing me of killing Jenn *and* this Cory guy?" Zach laughed again. "I don't have time to play Nancy Drew with you." He pushed by me and opened the door.

"Are those new shoes?" I asked.

Zach looked at his feet. "Yeah. What of it?"

"What did you do with your old ones?"

"Stuck them in the charity bin at church. You're welcome to go dig them out if Reverend Stroup doesn't mind."

The charity bin. Very convenient. "Did Jenn have a spare key to the gatehouse like she did for her car?"

Zach's face got all red again. "I had a key. I gave it back. I don't know what she did with it after that. You can't be back here anymore."

He strode down the hall and back behind the bar. The baby might not have been his, but that didn't clear him from my suspect list. If anything, he was even more suspicious due to his alleged jealousy issues. But Cory Bantum was the person I needed more information on, and finding Nick Valentine was on the top of my to do list for tomorrow.

Monica was waiting by the door with greasy white paper bags full of chicken. "I think we got buffet chicken," she said, crinkling her nose. "God knows how long it's been sitting around in its own grease under a heat lamp."

"They go through it so fast, it doesn't have time to sit. Let's go." If she didn't want hers, I'd take it.

I pushed the door open and held it for her. She took a few steps and froze, making me run right into her. “Mon!” I said, stumbling back. “Why’d you stop?”

“My tires,” she said, nodding toward her car. “Someone slashed my tires.” She spun around to face me. “This is a message for you, Cam. You can’t go to that gatehouse tonight.”

“Don’t be ridiculous,” I said, but my shaky voice gave me away. Slashed tires could very well be a message for me to stay away tonight. “I’ll call Andy to come help us change the tires.”

We walked to the car, and Monica set our bags of chicken on the hood while I dialed Andy and told him what happened. “I think there are spare snow tires in the garage,” I said. “Can you help me out?”

“Be there in a few,” he said, and hung up.

“I don’t know what I’d do without that kid,” I said, tossing my phone in my handbag. “I can’t let him leave when the documentary is finished.”

Monica sighed. “I know there’s nothing I can say to keep you at home tonight, so I’m just going to stand here and be irritated.”

“Better than constipated,” I said, grinning. Nothing like fifth grade boy humor to break the tension.

She shook her head and held up a chicken bag. “I don’t think that’ll be an issue after eating this.”

Ten endless minutes later, Andy pulled in with Mia in tow. “What are you doing here?” I asked her. “Are you hungry? Do you want me to get you chicken after all?”

“No,” she said, wringing her hands, stress audible in her voice. “I don’t want you to go to the gatehouse.”

“Mia ... ” Stricken by the first display of emotion she’d ever shown me besides apathy, I was speechless. I hugged her, and she hugged me back, holding on tightly.

“I know you want to find out who did this and free my dad, but what if something happens to you?”

“I promise I’ll be careful,” I said, holding her back by the shoulders so I could look into her eyes, so much like her father’s. She even had those darned long lashes. "If I sense anything is wrong, I'll call 911, just like your dad would do. Okay?"

Monica came up beside us. "We'll call her every hour, Mia. We'll make sure she's safe."

Reluctantly, Mia nodded. "But if you don't answer, we're coming over there and getting you."

"Fair enough," I said, warmed by Mia's affection, and hugged her again to start making up for lost time.

23

The gate at Hilltop Castle was open when Monica and I got there at a little after six p.m. She drove up the steep incline to the top and parked in front of Finch's massive front doors.

"This place is nuts," she said, leaning her head out the window and looking up to the pointy turrets. The castle had always creeped me out. I couldn't understand why anyone would want to build an enormous castle on top of the highest hill in town. Carl Finch didn't strike me as a vain man, only eccentric. Owning a castle must have been on his bucket list.

"Be right back," I said, getting out of the car.

An echoing gong sounded from inside when I rang the bell. Who would answer? A busty woman in a French maid uniform? A stuffy old butler? Lurch?

It turned out to be Finch himself who opened the door, without a single hair of his comb -over out of place. "Hello, Cameron," he said. "I'm so sorry for all the nasty business with Ben, but it's good to have you here."

He didn't suggest that Ben was innocent, I noticed. "Thank you," I said. "I'm sure it will all be sorted out soon. Do you have a key for me while I'm staying at the gatehouse?"

"I do." His mustache twitched as he dug in his trousers pocket and pulled it out. "Here you are. I'm not expecting anyone until later this evening when my good friend, Dennis Stoddard, arrives. If anyone unexpected shows up, press the intercom on the gate and let me know who it is."

"Okay." It seemed easy enough. "Anything else?"

"Stay vigilant down there. I'd like to think the town is safe and nothing will happen to you, but the past week has proven otherwise."

Nothing like the power of positive thinking, I wanted to say, but didn't. "I'm sure it'll be quiet and peaceful tonight."

On the drive back down the hill, I thanked my lucky stars that it wasn't the middle of winter. I couldn't image navigating the roller coaster driveway covered in ice. Monica dropped me off beside Brutus's fenced in pen.

"Call me if you need me," she said. "I'll be here in thirty seconds flat. And for the record, I don't think this is a good idea. I don't like it one bit."

"It's already on the record. Several times. Don't worry. I'm going to read and relax."

Her eyebrows were still tilted with concern. "I'll be here at eight in the morning to pick you up. Not a minute later. Be ready."

"Eight a.m.," I said, giving her a thumbs -up.

She waved and drove away as I turned to the big, black, growling beast of a dog in the pen beside me.

"I'm prepared to make friends," I said, waving my bag of chicken and French fries around.

I pulled a hunk of meat off a chicken leg and stuck it through the fence, trying not to look like I feared for my fingers. Brutus let out a low growl and then lunged for the food. I let go and jerked my hand back, almost becoming part of his meal. "Are we friends now?" I asked him, watching him lick his chops. He sniffed and nosed the fence, eager for more. "Fine. I'll give you a handful of fries, but the rest are mine. And I never share my food, so you better like me after this."

He wagged his tail as I opened the bag and grabbed a handful of salty fries. "This isn't good for you, you know, but I'm desperate." I tossed them through the fence. He gulped them down before they hit the ground then nosed the fence again, tail still wagging. I held my hand out to him and hoped for the best. Brutus licked the salt from my fingers and pressed his nose against my palm before turning and retreating into a wooden doghouse in the corner of the pen.

I guessed that meant we were friends. Maybe this day hadn't gone completely to the dogs after all.

THE GATEHOUSE HAD ONE BEDROOM, a bathroom, a tiny kitchen, and a sitting room. Ben hadn't been exaggerating when he said it was like camping. The size made it easy to cover every corner, nook, and cranny, searching for anything that would tell me who framed him. I wished I had a way to dust for fingerprints, but the place was spotless, and I probably wouldn't have found any anyway.

After turning out all of Ben's pockets, confirming there weren't even dust bunnies under the bed, and finding only expired barbecue sauce in the cupboard, I plopped down in the recliner in the sitting room, defeated. How would Nick have gotten in to leave his shoes? Did he take Jenn's keys when he was seen arguing with her?

This was like having a puzzle with too few pieces. Or the wrong pieces. Something just wasn't fitting.

Deciding the picture might be clearer on a full stomach, I took my chicken dinner out of the bag and settled back into the chair with the book Brenda gave me. It was a mystery about an old castle, of all things. Being distracted by a house full of people and dogs all week, I hadn't gotten too far into it yet.

By the time I popped the last fry into my mouth, I couldn't put the book down. At the same time, the suspense was killing me. I kept looking over my shoulder every other page and considered that it might not be the best book to read while sitting in the gatehouse of a woman who was murdered.

The fictional castle in my book had secret passageways and a locked room harboring an ancient artifact. The artifact was stolen, the butler was murdered, and, by my calculations, the gardener was the killer. Not that my suspicions could be trusted.

I took a break from reading when my eyes got tired and the room grew dark. Thunder rumbled overhead, promising the storm my knee had been foretelling for the past week.

I turned on a table lamp and scrounged around inside my handbag for a teabag I knew was in there somewhere. I really had to do something about the size of my bag and my organizational skills.

Finally finding the teabag, I started filling a pan to boil water when my phone rang. It was Andy. "How's it going over there?" he asked. "Is Stoddard there yet?"

"Not yet. Things are quiet. Brutus and I are friends, so that happened."

"Nice. Well, if Stoddard gets in soon, will you give me a call? I had a breakthrough idea. I need to get him on film with the bronze Templar Cross. It's the heart of Finch's collection. Finch doesn't want it on film, but I have to have it. It's going to make the whole movie's premise of Metamora being the site of the Arc of the Covenant."

"Sure. I'll let you know when he gets here."

I hung up with mixed emotions. I wanted Andy's film to be successful, and if it were, the town would get a boost in tourism, but at what price? Finch's privacy? The castle had already been broken into once, which was why there was the big gate and nobody was allowed on the property. I'd hate to see the castle made into a target once people found out what's inside.

I grasped the edge of the counter as a lightbulb moment struck. In my mystery book, the castle held an ancient artifact that few people knew about, and one who did stole it. All the time I'd spent wondering who murdered Jenn, I never considered access to the castle, and what might be inside, and who would want to take it.

Dennis Stoddard!

Stoddard was here the night Jenn was murdered. Cory and Nick were the witnesses, not the other way around. They could place Stoddard near the crime scene. Stoddard killed Cory, and Nick left town to save himself.

If Nick and Cory last saw Jenn alive, then someone killed her after they left. Someone who needed her keys to get inside the castle. Stoddard wanted Finch's Templar Cross!

Stoddard killed Jenn, took her keys, and left his shoes in Ben's closet in the gatehouse.

No sooner had I made the connection than Brutus started barking his head off. Nothing like having an eleventh hour epiphany.

I peeked through the window curtains over the sink and caught a pair of taillights heading up the driveway to the castle.

Good gravy! I forgot to shut the gate!

My main purpose for being here, and I blew it.

Dialing 911 as fast as possible—because this was definitely a matter of life and death—I was put through to Sheriff Reins. "Dennis Stoddard killed Jenn Berg and Cory Bantum! He's here at the castle! Send help!"

"Hold on one minute," he said. "We've already arrested Ben. I know it's hard to take, having your husband behind bars, but—"

"He's going to kill Carl Finch next! Get over here!"

I hung up and dashed out the door to Brutus's pen. "We have a job to do, McNasty. Don't get any ideas about turning on me now." With a quick flick of the latch, I let him loose. "Go!" I pointed up the hill to the castle. "Get 'em, boy!"

Brutus ran. Unfortunately, he ran in the wrong direction and headed for the road. "No! Brutus! Here! Come! Heel! Fetch!"

No command I yelled got him to come back. He'd slipped into the night to harass—and probably eat—unsuspecting ducks.

With no time to spare, I turned and ran through the gate. My knee protested loudly. Of all the times to be left without a car. But there was no way I was calling Monica and dragging her into this, and Reins thought I was making up nonsense. It was up to me to stop Stoddard.

The slam of a car door echoed, followed by a peal of thunder. I had to move and move fast. I told my knee to be a man, and I huffed and puffed my way to the top of the driveway, vowing to throw away every cookie in my pantry if I made it home.

Panting for breath with a throbbing knee and a cramp in my side, I rounded Stoddard's Mercedes Benz. The front door was closed. Did I think it would be open? This was a civilized murderer after all. I took a moment to consider if I should knock or barge right in before deciding time was of the essence. I pushed the door open. It didn't strike me as odd that it wasn't locked until I got inside. I left the door wide open to aid in a hasty retreat.

The house was silent. Not even a creak from one of the five suits of armor standing at attention in the entry hall. Woven tapestries of coats of arms hung from the stone walls. If I didn't know I was living in the twenty-first century, I would've sworn I'd walked into King Arthur's court.

I padded along the thick fleur-de-lis rug until I came to an archway on my right. A peek inside revealed a kitchen I thought only existed in heaven. A brick oven in one wall, an eight-burner stove, and a copper sink. It made me wish I knew how to cook. Almost.

Moving on, I took the hallway to the left and found myself in a library sporting floor to ceiling book cases with glass doors, a rolling ladder, and a dark mahogany desk the size of a tank. Libraries always held secrets, either on the pages of books or in secret passageways behind the shelves. Did Finch have a hidden chamber where he kept the Templar Cross safe?

There was no time to investigate, even though my fingers were itching to hold some of the first editions that were, undoubtedly, tucked away behind the glass. I had to get to Finch before Stoddard made him victim number three. Maybe he'd let me peruse his shelves as a reward for saving his life.

Just as I was passing the mammoth desk, something sleek and black darted out from under it, making me jump. I banged into a medieval dagger on a stand and knocked it over. Thunder boomed, shaking the house and masking the crash of the dagger. Then Spook sat in front of me, licking his paw and looking up at me with his rotten green glowing eyes. "Bad cat!" I whispered. "So you come to my house when you're slumming it, do you?" He turned his back and flicked his tail at me.

I followed Spook out of the library into the back hallway. I pictured Finch entertaining guests in a den with leather furniture, studded with brass nails, a roaring fireplace with ancient shields mounted over the mantel, sipping brandy poured into cut crystal glasses from an antique decanter.

Although it was drafty in the castle, it was still hot and humid outside. The roaring fire was probably out of the equation, but my mind quickly replaced it with billowing curtains leading to a vast balcony on a stormy night.

Tip-toeing farther along the hall, past closed doors and another tapestry, this one of a knight on horseback, I paused at a register vent, hoping to catch a sound or even voices from somewhere in the house. But there was only the lingering silence.

Finch and Stoddard were somewhere in this castle, and nothing short of being whacked over the head was going to stop me from finding them.

AFTER FINDING only Spook on the first floor, I ended up outside the only closed door on the second floor. If I was correct, it led to the turret. Would Stoddard be threatening Finch's life at the top of the tower? How very gothic.

I took a deep breath and blew it out, soundlessly, before turning the doorknob. Locked. How to get it open? Once again, I turned to my trusty handbag, hoping to find a paperclip, or maybe a metal nail file. Something to try to pick the lock. Of course, I had no lock -picking knowledge, but how hard could it be?

I plowed through the contents of my bag, past my wallet and checkbook, down to the deep, dark bottom. Superglue, magnet, a pair of earrings I thought I lost.

Lightning flashed through a window behind me, illuminating the second floor like daylight. Thunder came on its heels, a loud, sharp crack that rattled the roof. Then sweet, blessed rain pattered against the windowpane. I could almost hear my knee sigh in relief.

Somewhere behind the locked door, a man shouted. It was muffled, but urgent.

I dug faster. A lighter—why did I have a lighter?—a spoon, of all things, and a pair of tweezers. That could work! I yanked the tweezers out and dropped my bag. I could really use another flash of lightning to find the little holes in the lock. I felt around with the ends of the tweezers, making what seemed like an obnoxious amount of noise, until one end found its way in the lock. My hands were sweating and shook, making it difficult to hold on to the tweezers. I jabbed and turned them, knowing with absolute certainty that I was never going to open the lock. But what was the alternative? Trying to battle ram my way through the door?

Frustrated, I tugged the tweezers out of the lock and tossed them across the floor. There had to be a better way. A way to get Finch and Stoddard out of the turret and downstairs without getting myself caught in the process.

I began pacing. My brain cycling through possible options.

A) I had a lighter. I could set fire to something, let the smoke drift under the door and up to the turret. How much fire would I need to produce enough smoke for them to take notice? The last thing I wanted to do was set the whole castle ablaze. Bad plan.

2) I could knock and run. Simple. Effective. What if they didn't hear the first knock, or even answer? Stoddard could have a gun to Finch's head, have him gagged and tied up. He could ignore it and do nothing. No, I needed something that would ensure action.

Or I could ... Yes. I had it. I knew exactly what I needed to do.

I took off, jogging downstairs and around to the entry hall. The front door was still open. Rain came down in sheets, glinting in the security lights. I needed something heavy that I could swing like a bat. Looking around, my eyes landed on a medieval mace one of the suits of armor held. I snatched it out of his gauntleted hand and bolted out the front door.

Stoddard's Mercedes was an expensive target, one that a man who collected fine and rare objects wouldn't ignore. I held the heavy mace with both hands, high over my head, and swung it as hard as I could at the driver's side window. It bashed the window in, crackling the glass into a spiderweb. The car alarm blared into the night, resounding over the thunder and pounding rain.

I struck the windshield, emboldened by the hefty, iron weapon. "That's for Jenn Berg!" I yelled. I rounded the front and whacked the passenger window. "That's for Cory Bantum!" I'd just let loose on the rear window when Stoddard came charging out of the house. "That's for Ben!"

"What on earth are you doing, banshee?" he shouted, waving his arms and running toward me.

I brandished the mace. *"Where's Finch?"*

"He's inside, of course. Now, put that down." He eased toward me, gesturing for me to lower the mace. Not a chance.

"Get Finch and bring him out," I said. "Now!" I lunged for him to scare him.

"Fine! Okay. Give me a moment to fetch him."

He turned back to the house and took a step, then another. Behind me, a deep, guttural growl broke through the rumble of thunder. I spun in time to see Brutus pounce.

A gun fired.

I screamed and dropped to my knees, closing my eyes.

When I opened them again, Stoddard was on his back, pinned under Brutus, who had all of his sharp canine teeth around the man's arm. A gun lay beside him.

"You were going to shoot me!" I said. "Good boy, Brutus!"

I hurried over and grabbed the gun, tossing it inside the broken window of the Mercedes. Stoddard tried to move, but Brutus growled and tightened his grip on the killer's arm, making him cry out. "If I were you," I said, "I wouldn't budge an inch."

God bless Jenn Berg for having such a mean, loyal, amazing dog.

I CALLED Reins and gave him the lowdown. He told me to stay put until a squad car arrived. I told him I wasn't taking one eye off of Stoddard until they had him in cuffs.

Since a police siren in Metamora was either A) the start of a parade, or 2) an emergency, both served as a signal to everyone in town to be nosy and find out what was going on. Reins was the first on the scene, Monica and Mia were second. Ben was right behind them, free of all charges.

"Thank God you're okay," Monica said, hugging me so tight I could barely breathe. "I can't believe you caught a murderer on your own, with a ... what is this thing?" She held up the mace.

"Cam!" Ben yelled, sprinting for me. Monica let go just in time to avoid being tackled. "I could kill you myself," he said, squeezing the life out of me, "but only after my heart starts pumping again. You scared the crap out of me." He held me at arm's length by my shoulders. "I'm proud of you. Don't ever go after a murderer again."

"Lecture me later," I said, giving him another hug. Mia joined us, and we held her in the middle of both of us. "I told you I'd be fine," I said to her, gathering her hair behind her shoulders. She, of course, rolled her eyes.

"And I said it would all work out," Ben said, kissing the top of her head. "I better go find Finch."

"I think he's up in the tower," I said. "The door is locked."

Ben kissed my forehead before taking off inside the house while Reins cuffed Stoddard and read him his rights.

Since the gate was open, a crowd was accumulating in the castle's driveway. "We did it, Cameron Cripps-Hayman," Roy said, ambling up to me.

"We did it, Roy." He held up his hand for an awkward high five.

Anna and Logan ran up to us, hand in hand, which was curious, but I didn't have time to dwell on that now. "The first case of the Metamora Action Agency has been solved!" Anna said, smiling ear to ear.

"Good thing, too," Logan said. "I couldn't find a thing on Nick."

"Here comes Johnna," I said, and we all watched her rolling up the driveway in an electric scooter, the knitting in the basket on the front getting soaked.

"Do you think he'll need handcuff cozies?" she asked, holding up a loop of yarn. "I'm thinking of making them for all the prisoners. Those cuffs must chafe."

Andy and Cass were next to join our group, Andy giving me a bear hug from behind. He gestured to the mace still in Monica's hand. "Did you do that to Stoddard's car?" he asked me, raising his camera to get it all on film. "Remind me never to mess with you when you're armed with a medieval club."

"I can do some damage with my handbag, too," I said. Which reminded me that I'd left my bag outside the door to the turret. "I'll be right back."

I rushed inside and upstairs. My bag was right where I left it. The door to the turret room was open, so I made my way up. At the top, I froze in amazement.

The round room was gilded from floor to—well, even the ceiling was gold. In the very center of the room, raised on a round dais, stood the Templar Cross. I had to admit, it was a relic worth committing a crime for. Although probably not murder. More like Johnna's brand of crime, if one had to be committed.

Ben stood over Finch, who was lying on a velvet sofa holding a damp cloth to his head. Ropes were tangled on the floor. "Is he okay?" I asked Ben, but it was Finch who answered.

"I'm not dead, thanks to you." He held out a hand for me to come sit beside him. "I'm in your debt. If there's ever anything I can do for you, you let me know."

His heavenly kitchen popped into my head. "Actually, there is something."

Ben let out his trademark annoyed sigh and then laughed.

24

Solving murders didn't leave much time for preparing and packaging dog treats, but in the hours before opening night, Monica, Mia, Brenda, Cass, the Metamora Action Agency, and I were getting the job done thanks to Finch letting us use his restaurant-sized kitchen.

Ben and Andy were busy building a booth for Dog Diggity in the back of the renovated barn where the Metamora Performing Arts housed their plays.

"I talked to Elaina this morning," Monica said, whipping up another batch of Cornmeal Dog Bark. "She was so excited at my proposal to partner in her shop, she said I could have the whole space as long as she could help out. I got it in writing, just in case she forgets all about our conversation."

I held back my giddy excitement. I didn't want to scare her off. With Monica you never knew what made her whims shift from one day to the next. "So you're staying then?"

"Someone has to run Dog Diggity. You're too busy promoting the town and busting bad guys to do it."

"I'll help. I promise. Plus, with my five dogs and Brutus, I'll be your best customer."

Brutus was officially a crime dog and Ben's sidekick. He even pinned a badge on his collar.

"I'll be staying with you for a while," she said, "until I can find a place of my own. When I do though, I'd like to take Isobel with me, if that's okay."

"Absolutely. The crabby old lady dog is yours."

"Where are the wrappers for these things?" Roy asked, holding up a sweetie chip.

"I've got them right here," Anna said, hefting a box up onto the butcher-block center island. "I ordered them when we set up the website and had them rush delivered."

"Sneaky," I said. "How did you know we'd need them?"

"Just a hunch," she said, grinning.

"No way," Mia said, holding up a paper bag with a cellophane window on one side. "They're polka dotted."

"And stripes," Logan said. "I picked the stripes."

The bags were aqua blue, light red, and yellow with dots in random patterns between the vertical stripes. Dog Diggity was printed in a fun script font along the top of the bag in a darker red. "They're adorable," I said. "What do you think, Monica?"

She didn't answer, and when I turned to look at her, she was crying. "I have a business," she said. "With pretty bags and a shop in a nice little town. I never thought this would happen."

"Aww, Monica!" I hugged her and was pummeled by everyone else piling into a huge group hug. All except Roy and Johnna, of course.

"Time's a tickin', Cameron Cripps-Hayman!"

I pulled back from the cluster of arms. "Good point, Roy. Let's get these treats packed up."

While everyone got back to work, Mia slid in beside me. "Can I talk to you for a minute?"

"Of course you can."

She waved me out into the hall. "I was wondering—if it's okay with my dad—if you would mind if I stayed."

"Sure you can. There's a lot of summer left."

"No. Not for the summer. I mean, what if I stayed and didn't go back to live with my mom?"

"Oh! Well, I—"

"I know it's strange with whatever's going on between you and my dad. And I'd have to stay with you since he doesn't have any room for me at the gatehouse. I understand if you don't want me here after I wrecked your car and everything. It's just that, my mom isn't home a lot. She likes to go out with her friends, and I miss my dad."

"Mia," I said, taking her hands, "you're always welcome with me, whether I'm at Ellsworth House or somewhere else. I'd like to spend time with you and get to know you. We haven't had much of a chance in the past four years. But I have one condition."

She dropped her gaze to her feet. "What?"

"Please try to stop rolling your eyes." I laughed, and she did too, looking up at me.

"I'll try."

"Liam will be happy you're staying. Are you going to keep working at the Soda Pop Shop?"

"Yeah. I really like it, and Steph needs the help."

I gave her a hug. "You're a true Daughter of Metamora, pitching in to lend a hand to your friend in need."

"Ugh," she groaned. "Those old ladies and their rules have got to go. They think they run the town."

"Well, they kind of do."

"Want to know a secret?" she said. "I like the colors you painted the house."

"Yes!" I pumped my fist in the air in victory.

Now if I could just get my weathervane back.

FINALLY, after much work and anxiety, it was opening night for *A Dog's Life!*

The Dog Diggity booth was painted the same color scheme as the treat bags—aqua blue, light red and yellow stripes, and dots—and adorned with a sign in the same cute script. The barn was packed. Every seat was filled, and people even stood along the walls. Roy mingled with the guests, introducing himself to the ones he'd reserved tickets for. Johnna sat in the front row with Betty and Judy, ready to cheer on Cass. Logan and Anna sat beside them, holding hands again. Andy had his tripod set up in the middle aisle. Whether the performance ended up immortalized in his documentary or not, it was going to be an unforgettable night.

Soapy stepped up to the microphone center stage and announced five minutes until curtain. Fiona and Jim Stein passed by the Dog Diggity booth, where Monica and I were setting up. Jim patted my hand and said, "I hear you're the town hero!" in his boisterous voice.

"Hero might be an exaggeration," I said. "I got lucky."

Fiona smiled and gave me a stiff nod. "Congratulations on your capture," she said, which was strange and a bit awkward.

"Thank you."

They shuffled to the middle of the center row and sat with Irene and Stewart, and Mia and Ben. Ben was ecstatic about Mia staying. He set up an appointment with Mr. Stein, the principal, to go over a class schedule and extracurriculars, like cheerleading or maybe volleyball. Come fall, Mia would officially be a Metamora High School Indian.

Out of the corner of my eye, I caught Roger Tillerman making his way through the crowd. He met my eyes and waved. Our disastrous date would serve as a warning to all women: wearing hoop skirts was a liability to a female's dignity. You could end up on the floor wearing your meal.

Old Dan hobbled in, escorted by his son, Frank. They took a seat in the last row beside Reverend Stroup and Sheriff Reins. Just about everyone in town was in attendance for opening night. Even Will had returned early from his antiquing after hearing the case was solved. It turned out he'd gone to his parents' house in Cincinnati. Brenda forgave him the fib, knowing he didn't have the constitution to live in the shop next door to me, a suspected murderess.

The lights flashed off and on, signaling the start of the play.

Monica and I pulled a pair of stools to the front of our booth, sat down and got comfy. Even if I had nothing to do with the play directly in terms of putting on the show, I still felt like a proud mama. Cass's Fiddle Dee Doo Inn was full and so was Judy's Briar Bird. Betty had customers all afternoon buying cookies and Mia came home from the Soda Pop Shop exhausted. The town was busier than it had been since Canal Days last fall, and heading into Independence Day, most of our visitors were staying for the fireworks in a few days.

Something wrapped around my ankle. I looked down, and a pair of glowing emerald eyes peered up at me. "Aren't you the man about town," I said, leaning down to pet Spook.

The spotlight came on, and Carl Finch stood center stage. "Welcome, friends and neighbors. Tonight's performance of *A Dog's Life!* is dedicated, in memoriam, to Jennifer L. Berg, a lovely young woman taken from us too soon. Jenn loved dogs, as do I. One helped save my life recently, as a matter of fact. Tonight, all proceeds from your purchases of homemade Dog Diggity dog treats at the booth in the back will be donated to the Brookville Animal Shelter in Jenn Berg's name. In addition, I'll be matching the donation in honor of a woman whose courage knows no bounds, Cameron Cripps-Hayman."

Hot tears burst from my eyes at the smattering of applause and turned heads, craning to find me in the back. Monica paused in her clapping to pat my leg. "That's my big sister."

I didn't know what tomorrow would bring, but right then, I was a full-fledged Metamoran basking in the warmth of my neighbors' approval and friendship.

25

The play was an uncontested success despite having such a short time to pull it together. The next morning, the front page of the Metamora Mirror's Sunday edition displayed a full color photo of the cast with a caption reading, *Dog Gone Great!*

Cass showed the unique ability to perform on all fours without speaking as the lead dog. Not to mention her howling and barking abilities during the musical numbers. Soapy proved he wasn't only an excellent mayor, but a superb actor as well, and Theresa could really sing!

"I want to be in the next musical," Mia said, pouring maple syrup on her pancakes. Lucky for us, Monica could make more than dog treats.

"You'll have to try out then," I said. "You think you'd like being on stage in front of an audience?"

"Please. I'd love it," she said then pointed at me with her fork. "You just rolled your eyes at me."

I laughed. "You're rubbing off on me."

The front door opened, and Andy stuck his head inside. "Cam? Sue's here to see you."

Talking with Sue Nelson was something I'd planned to do once the town quieted down from the hustle and bustle of the play and the aftermath of Stoddard's arrest. I hurried to the door and stepped out to a shouted warning from Andy. "Look out! The bees are back!" Even on Sunday, he was there, relentlessly battling the boring bees.

I darted around a buzzing brigade to the edge of the porch, where Sue stood. Her eyes were sunken into the deep, dark bags underneath them, but through her grief, there was a sense of relief and finality. "I'm so sorry, Sue."

"No," she said, "I'm the one who's sorry. I got so caught up in the gossip that I believed ... And you were the one who caught him."

"You don't need to say another word," I said, taking her hands in mine. "There are no hard feelings on my part, and no need for apologizing on yours."

She let out a long breath. Her eyes glistened with tears. "I hope we can put this behind us."

"You and I? Of course. Already forgotten." I pulled her in for a hug. "I wish I knew what to say or do to make this easier for you."

"You're a good friend, Cam. That's all I need."

She stepped back and smiled, then descended the porch steps. I watched her make her way down the sidewalk to the street, past Will's antique shop and Betty's bakery. Nobody should have to suffer the loss of a child, but with time and the help of her friends and neighbors, the hurt in Sue's heart would abate.

Back inside, Gus dashed through the kitchen and into the dining room with the wild twins chasing after him, and Liam chasing after them, yapping his little brains out. "That's my tough guy," Mia said. "Get 'em!"

Isobel bared her teeth and growled her crabby, old, gravelly growl. "We'd better get leashes on them," I said. "Your dad will be here any minute."

I grabbed Gus and the two furry cyclones, Mia got Liam decked out in his rhinestone collar, and Monica sweet -talked cranky Isobel out from beside the fridge.

We wrangled the dogs out the front door, down the porch stairs and out into the yard at top speed, avoiding the bees. Mia sheltered Liam by wrapping her whole body around him, and Monica practically dragged Isobel behind her.

"I played back the film of Stoddard's arrest," Andy said, joining us. "It's good stuff. I'm thinking of maybe going with a Crime in Small Town America angle. I'm going to need more footage, though, so I guess I'll be sticking around a while."

"As long as I have bees and peeling paint," I said, "you'll have a couple bucks in your pocket."

Speaking of a few bucks, Dog Diggity raised almost $250 for the Brookville Animal Shelter the previous night, and Finch more than matched it. He more than doubled it. He was very generous and promised to match our sales for tonight's show as well.

Ben's truck pulled into the driveway, and Mia jogged over to greet him. Brutus jumped out of the bed of the pickup. Sometimes I was convinced that dog was made of steel.

"Ready for a walk?" Ben asked Mia, slipping a training collar over Brutus's head.

The two of them and their dogs came up alongside Monica and Isobel, and me and my three unruly beasties. "Before we set off," I told my pack—very sternly, I might add—"there will be no chasing ducks today. Got it?"

Thing One lurched forward and bit Thing Two's jaw, starting a snarling, biting war that Gus jumped in on. Clearly, they were not paying attention to a word I had to say.

"Alright, let's go." I tugged the leashes and got them moving. Brutus padded along with Gus as Ben strolled beside me. Monica lagged behind with Isobel stopping to sniff every inch of the road, and Mia stayed with her, cuddling Liam to her chest.

"The Indianapolis PD found the murder weapon," Ben said, with an unmistakable quirk to his lips.

"Why are you smiling like that?" I said. "There should be nothing funny about a murder weapon."

"What if it's an antique owl andiron that Stoddard bought from my mother?"

"*What?* She took those and sold them? Now she's just messing with me, Ben. She knew I loved those."

"I wondered why she wanted them. She always said they were an eyesore, but that they had to stay with the house."

"That woman. I swear, she's going to—"

"Cam!" Soapy called to me as we crossed over the bridge. "A minute?" He was hustling toward us.

"Sure, Soap!" Suspicion and curiosity zinged through me, making me forget about my evil mother-in-law. I hope I hadn't done anything wrong. More fines weren't really in my budget.

Beside me, Ben chuckled. "It's nothing bad, don't worry."

"How do you know?"

"He was looking for you after the play last night. You'd already gone."

I told Monica and Mia to go on ahead when Soapy met up with us in front of the canal.

"Last night was amazing," Soapy said. "I can't thank you enough for the work you did with your Action Agency. But the packed house made it pretty clear that we need someone promoting the town full -time."

"Full -time?"

"Yes. I'm going to set aside a portion of the town's budget and use the Daughter's of Metamora fine collections to pay someone to keep planning events and bringing in visitors. I'd love that person to be you, Cam, if you'll continue on in the role."

"Planning events like last night full -time? I would love to! Yes! Count me in!" My head was spinning. I didn't even notice the impatient trio of dogs tugging on their leashes. I never imagined my volunteer work becoming a full -time paid position with the town.

Soapy gave my hand a vigorous shake. "Welcome aboard, officially! I'll have to get you a few of our town council polo shirts to wear to board meetings."

"Board meetings?" My excitement level went a notch even higher. At board meetings, I'd be privy to all the inside town info. Plus their polo shirts had the town logo on them—the town name with a little Metamora Mike embroidered underneath.

"All town employees are on the board. You'll need to have a presentation ready two weeks from tomorrow showing how you'll make Canal Days bigger than ever this year. Think you're up for the challenge?"

"More than up for it."

"Good. I didn't want to have to deal with Roy pestering me for the position, and after last night and the way he was bragging about bringing in a party of ten to the performance, he would've been on my doorstep first thing."

I laughed, but Roy was a people person. He had a natural gift of gab. I wasn't sure what my Action Agency would look like without him and Johnna now that their service hours were fulfilled.

"Come by the Soapy Savant tomorrow morning at eight sharp," Soapy said. "We'll get your new hire paperwork started and figure out where to set you up."

I promised to be on time, and Ben and I parted ways with Soapy. As we resumed walking—me being dragged along, more like—my mind zoomed in a million directions at once. I had so many ideas, I couldn't wait to get home and write them all down.

"You're deliriously happy," Ben said, giving my hand a squeeze. "I haven't seen that look on your face since we moved here."

"I think your mother is going to go through the roof when she finds out I'll be paying myself when I pay her fines." I couldn't help but laugh. Irene would be irate! "I would do it for free, Ben. You know that. But getting paid and working for the town is more than I ever dreamed of. It's perfect. You're right, I am deliriously happy."

He smiled a smile that I hadn't seen for a very long time. It was a smile that put a shine in his eyes and took away the worry lines between his brows. "In that case, Mrs. Cripps -Hayman," he said, "would you do me the favor of going to a movie with me before the fireworks Tuesday?"

"Only if you throw popcorn and Peanut M&M's into the deal."

"Have we ever gone to a movie without getting popcorn and M&M's?"

"Not that I can remember. I guess I'll go then." I stopped and threw my arms around him, dragging the dogs in against our legs, where they got their leashes tangled around each other and us.

"I do appreciate the hug," he said, "but now we're in a big, furry, slobbery knot."

We spent the next ten minutes playing the dog version of Twister to get four human legs and sixteen canine ones apart.

The sun was warm, the flowers were blooming, and the canal was sparkling. Ben was beside me, my sister was officially a Metamoran and a dog biscuit baker, and the town was basking in the wake of a successful play. All was right with the world.

Until the quacking started up, that is, and Metamora Mike flew by with his harem, landing on the bank and waddling into the water. Brutus, Gus, and the twins went ballistic. Ben held Brutus back by his training collar, but I was no match for my three monsters. They darted for the ducks and I was helpless to do anything but scream my head off at them and be dragged behind.

As they lunged in, I prepared myself for the inevitable. Once again, I found myself up to my neck in muddy water. Mike squawked and batted his wings, splashing me in the face. Just another typical day in Metamora.

Good gravy.

CONTINUE READING! CANAL DAYS CALAMITY

BOOK #2 IN THE DOG DAYS MYSTERY SERIES

Cameron Cripps-Hayman has stepped in it again.

With the town of Metamora buzzing and hustling to get ready for Canal Days, the fall festival ends up on the brink of being cancelled when a dog food supplier turns up dead.

Cam's sister, the owner of Dog Diggity Pet Boutique, is accused of the murder, and the whole town seems to think Cam had something to do with it. Probably because Dog Diggity snatched up the prime booth location for the festival and the dog food supplier was denied a spot. Was it nepotism? Maybe. But certainly not murder.

Now Cameron must sharpen her newly acquired sleuthing skills to uncover the real killer before the town's big money-making weekend gets snuffed out.

ALSO BY JAMIE BLAIR

The Deadly Dog Days Series

Deadly Dog Days

Canal Days Calamity

Fatal Festival Days

Trash Day Tragedy

Woeful Wedding Day

A Dog Day's Night

Hearing Day Homicide

Young Adult and New Adult Novels

Leap of Faith

Lost To Me

Burning Georgia

Kiss Kill Love Him Still - Series Box Set

ABOUT THE AUTHOR

New York Times and USA Today Bestselling Author, Jamie Blair, lives in Northeast Ohio with her husband, their two kids, a five pound Morkie, a cat that broke into their house and refused to leave, and a hand-me-down black cat that's been passed around the family and might just be the inspiration for Spook. She won a young author's contest in third grade, but it probably shouldn't count since her mom wrote most of her entry. She promises her mom doesn't write one word of her books anymore! Visit Jamie at www.jamieblairmysteries.com.

To be the first to hear about new releases, get early cover reveals, exclusive excerpts and giveaways, sign up for Jamie's newsletter on her website, jamieblairmysteries.com.